MURDER SO WRONG

MUCKRAKER MYSTERY #1

CLIFTON · NELSON

Murder So Wrong (Muckraker Mystery #1)
Ted Clifton & Stanley Nelson
ISBN 978-1-77342-027-1

Produced by IndieBookLauncher.com
www.IndieBookLauncher.com
Editing: Nassau Hedron
Cover Design: Saul Bottcher
Interior Design and Typesetting: Saul Bottcher

The body text of this book is set in Adobe Caslon.

Also Available
E-book edition, ISBN 978-1-77342-028-8

CONTENTS

PART I
NEWSPAPER WARS

The year 1968 saw big changes in the way Americans felt about their country and their leaders. Two street wars raged inside the country—one about race and the other about war itself. Newspapers were still king of news, but they could see dramatic change on the horizon with national news broadcasts capturing attention like never before. Journalism majors were packing universities, eager to learn a craft of skill and courage. They would change the future with facts and secrets, often about politicians.

1

JOURNALISM 101

"You can't go in there without a pass." The hand in Tommy's face was as big as the guy holding it there.

"I'm with the press." Tommy replied, trying not to sound like a wimp.

"I don't give a shit who you're with—I told you, you can't go in there without a pass."

"Okay— I'm, uh, I'm sort of working for the *OK Journal.* How do I get a pass?"

"'Sort of working?' Pal, I don't care what you're 'sort of' doing. My job is to stop anyone who doesn't have a pass. *Capisci?*"

Tommy doubted seriously this big, dumb sonofabitch was Italian, but he got the message. He needed a pass—whatever the hell that was.

"Where do I get one?"

"You know what? You're starting to annoy me. I'm not information, okay?"

His first day as the new state capitol correspondent for the *OK Journal,* and he runs into the official door monitor. He saw a few other reporters walk into the Senate press gallery with no indication that any had a pass, or that the door troll cared whether they did. Great way to start his reporting career.

"Some days he's a bigger asshole than others."

Tommy looked up and found himself staring at the most beautiful woman he'd ever seen. Her face was framed by dark, flowing hair, and a glow seemed to come from the deep blue of her eyes. He kept staring long after he should have given a response. Then he became acutely aware of the silence, and of the fact he had no idea what to say.

"His name's Bart, and he's actually a good guy," she went on, unbothered. "This is the best job he's ever had, and they told him that if he ever let anyone into the press gallery that he didn't know, he'd be fired. So he's very diligent."

Tommy managed to regain a little composure. "Well, thanks for the information. I thought he just hated me. Hi. My name's Tommy—Tommy Jacks." He stuck out his hand.

She looked at him closely. "My god—you're Ray Jacks's son, aren't you?"

Uh-oh. "Yeah, th-that's me."

Without warning, she gave him an affectionate hug. Being squeezed—enthusiastically—by a gorgeous woman was no bad thing, although in the middle of the busy hallway in the heart of the state capitol, it did feel a tad embarrassing. It also appeared to be a crowd-pleaser. He saw people smiling, and a small round of applause arose from them like a vote of approval.

She let him go, but kept his hand in hers. "Sorry, Tommy," she gushed. "It's just so great to see you. I guess you might not remember me, but we used to play right here in these halls when we were little. My father's Carl Jackson. He was your dad's assistant for a few years. I'm Judy Jackson." She smiled, still holding his hand.

He kinda remembered her, but the recollection was fuzzy.

When Tommy was a kid, his dad often left him to his own devices while taking care of party business. It was hard to believe he could forget a face like hers, but little boys tended to be fairly oblivious to little girls, at least up to a certain age. It was a testament to their slow-developing brains.

"Judy, it's—well, it's so good to see you again. Do you work here now?" Tommy tried to smooth over the fact that he really didn't remember her. But he didn't want her to leave. Or to stop holding his hand.

"You don't remember me, do you?" Beautiful *and* smart.

"Well, maybe just a little." He was grasping at straws, and could tell she knew it.

"It's okay. We were pretty young." She laughed, and Tommy was smitten. "And yes, I work here. I'm on the staff of the Senate pro tem, Bud Evans. I can get you into the gallery, if you want. They really aren't that restrictive. Bart knows pretty much everybody. If he doesn't, he starts acting all official. But if you're with me, it won't be a problem. I'm pretty sure nobody has to actually use a pass. Did you say you were working for the *Journal?*"

"Well, what I said was, 'sort of.'"

He remembered hearing Fred Simpson, city editor of the *OK Journal,* giving him an option for "sort of" employment. *Maybe we can help each other. We need a good, aggressive reporter to cover the state capitol, and you need experience and exposure. How about we try each other out? You bring us stories, and we pay you by the inch. You know—a stringer.*

He explained to Judy his stringer connection to the paper. He didn't mention he had also applied to the *Oklahoma Sun,* but was unceremoniously shown the door.

She shrugged. "If you have a pen and pad, that's enough for most people to treat you as an official member of the press, and you can go most places. If you want, though, you can go by the administrative office and ask about a pass. They may actually have them. But I'm not sure." She smiled.

They chatted a few more minutes and she gave him her card. Tommy didn't have a card of his own yet, so he borrowed an extra from her and wrote his phone number on the back. She said goodbye and walked away. Tommy watched, admired, and smiled.

After some low-level humiliation at the administrative office, Tommy knew he'd been had. He approached the door troll clutching his pad and pen, head held high.

"Judy Jackson said you're okay," Bart grumbled. "You can go in." A new lesson in adult life; beautiful women are more powerful than door trolls. Or nonexistent press passes.

Tommy spent his first day at the capitol introducing himself to as many people as would talk to him, and reactions were mixed. Some seemed to remember his dad fondly and wished him the best. Others remembered him far less warmly and turned away with dismissive grunts. Quite a few didn't remember his dad at all and showed no interest in talking to the *Journal,* on the record or off. *How soon we're forgotten,* he thought, *powerful or not. You disappear, and a new crowd takes over.*

Raymond Jacks, Tommy's father, was once head of the state Democratic Party, and had a street-fighting man's reputation for pushing back the forces of evil in state government. He was Tommy's hero. But he was also a flawed person with two great burdens—guilt and a son—and he soothed the pain of carrying them around every day with alcohol. He'd been a reluctant, usually absent, parent. His ultimate downfall wasn't booze, but the hatred of one man—Jonathon H. "J.H." Gilmore, owner of the state's largest newspaper, *The Oklahoma Sun*. Gilmore's control over state politics and the Sun's frankly biased reporting led to the election of the current Republican governor, if by only a small margin. And because Oklahoma's state government operated a lot like a banana republic's, that was bad news for Raymond Jacks.

One day in 1963, Oklahoma State troopers showed up at his office to arrest him on an amazing list of allegations. His trial and sentencing were a blur to Tommy, who lost his hero and was left alone. After a short stay with a reluctant aunt who nurtured a bitter, mysterious grudge against him and his dad, he entered probably the most formative time of his life. With the aid of a partial scholarship, he attended Oklahoma University and supported himself with various lousy jobs, mostly in restaurants, while working toward his journalism degree.

Late in the day, Tommy left the capitol and headed down Lincoln Boulevard to his apartment. It wasn't in the best part of town, but the rent was cheap. He owned very little, his top-dollar possession being a twice-wrecked 1955 Ford Fairlane in desperate need of a paint job and probably a new engine. But it was pretty much crime-proof, even in this part of town. His unspoken fantasy car was a new Pontiac GTO, although its three-grand sticker price was way out of his league. Still, a guy could dream.

On the way, he spotted Risso's, a locally famous Italian restaurant with an infamous bar in the back. It had been one of his father's favorite hangouts. He pulled into the parking lot, not sure what to expect after all these years. At least he could get a pizza to go—the kind of late dinner his dad would bring home back in the day, just before he'd pass out.

Oklahoma was a dry state with more bars and clubs than Las Vegas. You just had to know where they were and how to get in. As long as they laid low, law enforcement ignored them. It helped that policemen at all levels were among their most frequent customers.

The joint had seen better days. It seemed in need of paint and a general cleaning. To Tommy, though, it felt nostalgic—a part of his lost youth.

"Welcome to Risso's, sir. Table for one?" The waiter hefted a menu, looking pleased to see a customer.

"Can I go into the bar, maybe get a drink?" Tommy was old enough, but figured he didn't look it. He started digging for his wallet.

"Sorry, sir. We do have a private club, but you have to be a member."

"How do I become one?"

"An existing member must recommend you, sir."

"How about my dad? Would that count?"

"Your dad being who, sir?"

Tommy told him. The waiter surprised him by acting impressed. "Well, I'll be. Ray Jacks's son. I heard him talk about you. Is he still in prison?"

Being sort of famous can be good or bad, Tommy thought. "Well, yeah. He has a few more years left." So much for family secrets.

The waiter grinned. "Show me some ID. Prove you're old enough, and you're in. No fees. And your first round's on the house."

While Tommy fished out his driver's license, he mentioned that he'd just started work with the *Journal* but didn't have a press card yet.

"My goodness! Why didn't you tell me you were a reporter? Reporters get free memberships—they're some of our best customers, even if they're cheap. Come on, I'll buy you your first *two* drinks."

Tommy wasn't a big drinker, but it was nice to feel welcome somewhere. He followed the waiter to the "Private" club, and he was surprised again. The club was top-notch. It wasn't posh by New York City standards—not that he'd ever been to New York City—but it was impressive, and it was crowded.

"Wow. I didn't see that many cars in the parking lot."

"Oh, most of the club guests park out back. The back entrance is less public."

Illicit and private, Tommy thought. *Should be no mischief going on here.*

He seated himself at the massive bar and ordered a gin and tonic from the linebacker-size bartender, who looked like he might also be the bouncer. He noticed the waiter talking to some men in one of the back booths and pointing at Tommy. One of them got up to stagger, as best he could, toward him.

"Hey, Jacks," he slurred, "I'm Tony Walters. I'm the capitol beat reporter for the *Sun*. Heard about you from one of my asshole editors. They acted real proud o' themselves that they told Ray Jacks's son to get lost. Let me tell you something—those guys don't know shit about reporting. They're only good at one thing—sucking up to Gilmore. You're either a suck-up asshole, or you're fired from that fraud of a newspaper. Yeah, yeah—I know what you're thinkin'. I work there, so I must be a suck-up too. Well, you're fuckin' right. I'm the biggest suck-up of 'em all." He stumbled a bit, almost falling onto Tommy. Judging by appearances at least, Mister Walters must have spent most of his afternoon practicing his craft at Risso's, and not at the capitol.

One of the others from the booth, much taller and trimmer, came over to lead him back to his pals, all of whom seemed similarly sloshed. The tall one came back.

"Sorry about that," he said. "Tony's a wee bit drunk. He got fired just a little while ago, so he's angry—probably scared, too. Seemed the thing to do was get drunk, which, as you can see, he's successfully accomplished. I'm Steve Marsh. Worked with Tony at the *Sun*. He has this independent streak, which has gotten him in trouble before. He made a whole big speech telling old man Gilmore how he didn't know shit about good government. Might as well have resigned on the spot. He thought he was too important to fire, but turns out he was wrong. Anyway, we heard about you and your deal with the *Journal*. Truth is, a lot of us would like to see that paper survive. At least with another one in town, there's a little pressure on that old bastard Gilmore." He shook his head. "But our official position is the *Journal* doesn't exist. Our leader doesn't like competition. If you somehow beat us on a story, heads will roll. So, best of luck, even though that has to stay between us. Ever need anything, give me a call—just make sure nobody knows who you are when you do." Marsh chuckled at his own joke, handed Tommy his card, and headed back to the booth.

Tommy sipped his drink and thought about what just happened, feeling a vague chill of dread. He couldn't think why he should, but he wanted to leave. He ordered a medium sausage pizza to go. Soon the bartender brought it to him, telling him it had been paid for by the group in the corner. Tommy gave them a wave and went home.

Time alone wasn't unusual for him, but that night he felt the loneliness. Maybe it was the pizza, which reminded him of his dad. Maybe it was the drunken Walters, who also reminded him of his dad. He'd only slept a few hours when the phone jarred him awake. He was pretty sure there were only a couple of people who knew his number. He entertained an instant fantasy involving Judy Jackson and answered quickly.

"Hello."

"Tommy, this is Chuck at the *Journal*. I handle the police beat. Got something that might be of interest to you. One of my detective contacts just called me and said they were at a murder scene near the capitol building. They identified the victim as Tony Walters. Not sure if you know him. He's the top political reporter at the *Sun*."

Tommy sat, stunned. "How-how was he killed?"

"My guy didn't want to give me any details, but he said there was no question it was murder. That probably means a gunshot, and not to be confused with suicide."

"Who told you all this?"

"Sorry, Tommy. Can't risk giving that out. Just thought you might want to know about Walters." Chuck hung up.

2

DEADLY ENCOUNTER

Dead? Tony Walters, a reporter a lot like Tommy—murdered? That was not something he expected in his world. Competitive, academic-style feuds, sure. Nasty-behind-your-back-but-civil-to-your-face co-workers—you bet. But murder? He knew his dad's world was full of rumors about questionable acts, and threats of violence weren't rare. But Tommy was only aware of one actual killing. Some poor TV station guy back when he was a kid, and he wasn't even clear on that story. Dead bodies weren't supposed to be part of life at the state capitol.

His first instinct was to step back and watch things play out. He was a capitol correspondent, a new one, and just a stringer at that—not some gumshoe wearing a snap-brim fedora, with a tough-sounding name like Butch or Leonard. But the victim was someone he'd met, who was more like him than not, and the murder happened right where they worked. It raised questions—lots of them. Could he really keep his distance? The only answer was no.

Dawn approached as he drove toward the capitol. Very few cars were out this early, so the trip was quick. He walked past a pumping jack rocking out an ode to Okie wealth, slurping up the massive oil reserve from under the capitol grounds. In the back of the parking lot, he spotted a cop.

"Hey. What's going on?"

The cop gave him a dirty look. "Nothing that involves you. Just move along."

Tommy stood by the barricade trying not to feel like a dismissed child. "I'm a reporter with the *Journal.* Got a report that a body's been found here. Can you give me any information?"

"Nope."

Tommy considered his next move. He'd learned nothing at the scene, and he thought he heard the rude cop snickering at him while he walked away—not an ego booster. It suddenly hit him what to do. Marsh said Walters had been fired from the *Sun,* and he had been out drinking with some of his former co-workers last night. So the place to go was downtown to *Sun* headquarters to see if anyone there would talk to him. The illogic of the move appealed to him. *Hello, I'm Tommy Jacks with the* Journal. *I'm here to interview everyone in the building who knew Tony Walters—and I won't take no for an answer. And I want to start with J.H. Gilmore, right now!* The imagined scene was perfect in Tommy's head.

Full of his own righteousness, he entered the ornate lobby, but a gun-carrying security guard, who demanded his driver's license, was blocking his intended entrance—*Why,* he wondered, *does a newspaper need armed protection?* After the guard made a call he handed Tommy's license back. "Sorry," he said with a shrug, "there's no one available. Most of the reporters don't come in till mid-morning. Mister Gilmore's secretary said you should make an appointment with his assistant to discuss the reason you want to see him—but she's on vacation this week." He looked around and lowered his voice. "Listen, kid—I give you credit for the nerve to come here, especially as a *Journal* reporter, to ask about one of their people. That takes guts. But you're just wasting your time. I liked Walters, and I sure as hell want to know what happened. But you won't get anything here."

Tommy shrugged. "Thanks, anyway. Sir." *Need to be polite to people who carry guns.*

"Look," the guard continued, taking Tommy by the elbow and walking him through the door, "I probably shouldn't even be talking to you, but if you want to know about Walters, you should stop by Denny's on Classen Boulevard. Look for a guy wearing an old, rumpled-up suit. He'll be sitting in one of the booths with a stack of newspapers. His name's Taylor Albright. He's the biggest gossip in town, puts out a rag called the *Banner*. He knew Walters. Used to work at the *Journal*; he knows everybody there, too. If anybody knows what's going on, it'll be him. Just don't let anyone know I told you anything, Okay?"

"Sure, thanks." Tommy knew that name—Taylor Albright. There was a connection between Albright and his father. And he recalled some things about Albright's less-than-stellar career at the *Journal.*

Denny's was packed. The late-night drunks had given way to the very-early-breakfast- before-work crowd, a mixture of blue-collar and low-level office workers. Tommy sensed an easy camaraderie between people who shared demanding, exhausting life cycles—plumbers, mechanics, office clerks, and waitresses all living the ugly grind of reality.

Taylor Albright stuck out like a blinking neon sign. He wore a suit with a limp bow tie, just like the guard said. The suit looked like it had never been pressed, and likely spent its off hours bunched up. Spread on the table were at least six newspapers—*The New York Times, Washington Post,* the *L.A. Times,* the *Dallas Morning News,* and of course, the two locals. Quite a mess. Albright looked absorbed in them.

Also with him were two young men who looked out of place for their amazing neatness, like they'd dressed for a spread in a men's fashion magazine. The picture presented several contrasts. The world seemed to buzz around this calm in a sea of social and political turmoil. Albright read the latest news from across the country among ordinary people going about their mundane lives. Tommy felt almost reluctant to approach the table, lest he disturb the natural order of things. But—

"Good morning, Mister Albright? My name's Tommy Jacks. I wonder if you have a couple of minutes to talk to me?" All three men looked up at Tommy as if he'd politely declared the place on fire. Apparently they hadn't expected anyone to address them.

"Tommy Jacks?" Albright seemed to be remembering something. "Are you related to Ray Jacks?"

"I'm his son."

"Well, I'll be. An all-grown-up Tommy Jacks. Have a seat!" Albright scooted over. "Can you guys believe that? Hell's bells, your father was one great S.O.B. Nobody screwed with that guy—well, until they did, and he went to jail." Albright chuckled. It wasn't a pleasant sound.

"Sorry to interrupt." Tommy tried to get to his subject. "I was wondering if you could talk to me about Tony Walters. I understand you knew him . . . ?"

"What the hell do you mean, 'knew him?' Is he dead or something?"

"Well, yes. Sorry, I thought you knew. He was shot to death.

Either late last night or very early this morning."

Albright turned pale. "Fuck!" Everyone waited for him to say something more, which turned out to be, "I've got a meeting downtown in about an hour. Could you give me a ride?"

He'd asked that of Tommy, who was still puzzling at his mixture of reactions, but answered, "I guess so."

"Boys, you're off the hook. Tommy here'll give me a lift. I'll talk to you later." The boys said their goodbyes, eyeing Tommy like a new lifelong enemy, and left.

Albright turned somber. Tommy felt badly for dropping such news on him. It seemed he'd been good friends with Walters. Maybe.

"I don't drive," Albright muttered, as if needing to explain. "Never learned. Lived in New York City and never saw a reason to risk my life or spend big bucks on a car just to go a few blocks. Then I end up in this cowtown. The bus service is for shit. Not only does almost everyone own a car, a lot of them own two. What the hell do you do with two cars? Crazy place, but—it is what it is, right?"

Tommy decided that was a rhetorical question, so he waited, sensing Albright was unhappy about something more than public transit. He still figured the news about Walters disturbed him. He appeared to be thinking deeply, maybe about what it all meant.

"Mister Albright, I'm sorry I blindsided you. I didn't think about what I was doing."

"It's all right." Albright said with a shrug. "Walters and I weren't exactly pals. But I knew him. I admired his courage and his skill. But in this town, I guess I shouldn't be that surprised to hear something bad happened to him. So, tell me what you know."

Tommy told him, although it didn't amount to much. He also briefed Albright about himself and his relationship with the *Journal.*

"Well," Albright remarked, "looks like you managed to get yourself in the middle of a big-city mess, and in only a couple of days," He smiled, but not happily. "Congratulations. Also, don't call me 'Mister Albright.' Taylor's fine. The 'mister' implies too much respect. We need to talk, at length. I have this appointment downtown, and then I go to the printers and work on my tabloid, the *Banner.* Most people treat it like a joke, but I have a warm place in my heart for gossip. Maybe I'm just an old woman in disguise. Anyway, after that I go home. I don't go out at night. I'm a morning person. Usually, unless I have to ride the damn bus, I'm at this place by five-thirty every morning. So come back tomorrow, and we'll talk some more."

Tommy helped him stuff his papers into a tattered grocery sack, and they left. Albright said almost nothing aside from providing directions, seeming deep in thought. Tommy dropped him off in front of an office building. Albright gave no hint about whom he would see; just said he would see him tomorrow. Tommy made a note of the address, just in case.

It was still early, and Tommy considered his options. One was to go back to his apartment and go back to bed. Sounded tempting. Not only did he feel tired, he wasn't sure he wanted to be in the world right now.

3
PAST TRAVELS

Some time ago...

Three interests held the most influence over the state of Oklahoma: oil and gas tycoons, the media, and a select group of right-thinking religious leaders. The media was really just J.H. Gilmore. He kept an iron grip on what was reported and who was elected. He even had the power to shape cultural and social norms to allow him—and the rich and powerful folks who played along with him—to control state government, including deciding who won elections and who lost.

The government often bent over backward to accommodate the oil industry. After all, oil was a major employer, made huge contributions to select political leaders, and was an important supporter of religious organizations. There was little concern about the environmental damage oil's myopic moguls would bequeath to future generations. What was important was more money, more drilling, more industry-friendly laws, and less interference.

The industry had a reputation for stubborn independence. The public generally believed its businesses were owned by roughnecks who'd struck it rich. In truth, a few huge, multinational oil companies controlled the industry throughout

Oklahoma, guided by lawyers, accountants, MBAs, and geologists. The heroic wildcat cowboy who hit it big was only in the movies. The real roughnecks were often worked to death in well-paid but unsteady, high-risk jobs with few benefits. Quietly, and usually through surrogates, Gilmore and his family gathered significant shares in the massive companies.

Money and power flowed to a small handful of men of almost regal status. In truth, politicians didn't matter. They were hand-picked and told what to do, which relieved them of the need to think much.

For much of its history, Oklahoma had been a one-party state because, either out of habit or laziness, most voters registered as Democrats. There were a few Republicans, but they generally had no desire to actually govern, and left the dirty work of politics to the opposition. But the Democratic Party was divided. Most of its leadership was, by the standards of any other state, Republican. So while Oklahoma was a Democratic state, it had favored Republican presidential candidates since the end of the Second World War.

For years, Gilmore held the levers of power from his position in the conservative wing of the Democratic Party where liberal members feared to tread. That odd mix confused most people, but to insiders, the rules were clear: you were either important or you were unwelcome. Know your place; do what you're told.

Raymond Jacks was the exception. He actually believed the democratic system—of the people, by the people, and for the people—meant government should work for the benefit of everyone. To the anointed heads of state, he was a pain in the butt.

Then along came one of those strange state conventions in which an unruly, defiant mob mentality arose. Fueled by righteous inner purpose (or maybe an overabundance of whiskey) the rebels defeated Gilmore's choice for party chairman and installed Jacks, a glad-handing man of the people. Because the chairman's job had been to serve as a lackey for Gilmore, its term had been set at eight years. But now a liberal, freedom-loving, hard-drinking, union-advocate, friend-of-the-people Democrat was in control.

Gilmore dealt with the problem by changing his affiliation to Republican, joined by about half the Democratic legislators. He and Jacks instantly became the worst of enemies. The differences between them could not have been more acute if they had been different species. Neither understood nor could stand to negotiate with the other.

Jacks at once began recruiting farmers and businessmen to run against what he called "the regime." He could be persuasive, and his optimism was contagious. After only a few election cycles, he established the renewed Democratic Party as a political force even though it meant messing with the guy who owned the largest paper in the state—*not* a good move. Stories about his drinking and minor brushes with the law, and exaggerations about his perceived failures as party chairman, began to appear regularly in the *Sun.* Some contained an element of truth—no question, Jacks enjoyed his whiskey—but many were complete lies.

He consulted a series of lawyers whose advice was always the same: don't pick fights with people who own newspapers because it's all but impossible to sue them. Even if what they printed could be proven as lies, Jacks also had to prove malicious intent. Libel laws protected the free press and, in the process, shielded any powerful newspaper owner who wished to engage in character assassination. One lawyer told Jacks that if he had the money and the time, he'd be happy to represent him, but he should expect it to be a lot of money and a lot of time. His better advice was to move to another state.

By 1961, Jacks decided his next best option was to ignore the *Sun* and fight Gilmore in the political arena instead. It would still be an uphill battle, but at least he wouldn't be doomed to failure before he began. And as chance would have it, he found a powerful ally. He'd been aware of William Anderson for some time because of his generous contributions to the Democratic Party. The man never asked for anything in return, and only seemed interested in supporting good government. He was just the one who could help Ray fight his thankless battle.

"Mister Anderson, I really appreciate you taking the time to meet with me. I know you're a busy man."

"Just Bill. When you called to set up this meeting, I debated with myself about whether to talk to you. I figured it was either going to be about donations, or you were looking for someone to run against one of Gilmore's hand-picked candidates. So, which is it?"

"You got me there, Bill. As chairman of the party, that's what I do—either raise money or look for someone to stick their hand in the fire. Let me tell you, it's a lot easier to raise money than find good candidates. And you, sir, are on both my lists—candidate *and* money." Jacks laughed heartily, hoping his candor wouldn't offend Anderson.

"Yeah," Anderson chuckled, "it's got to be tough. It'd take a fool to run for governor against Gilmore's anointed candidate, what with the power he has. I wish you luck. But I think I can see my way clear to contributing a bit more."

Jacks resorted to earnestness. "I've talked to a lot of people all over the state, and there's just one name that keeps coming up for governor: yours. I know you probably think I'm just blowing smoke, but I'm not. There's no one as well-liked and respected as you are, Bill."

"Look, I know there are only a few people who'd consider running. And more than likely I'm your first or second choice, probably because I've been fortunate and made some money. The problem with me is, I'm a novice. Never ran for anything—never wanted to run for anything. I have no desire to get my brains bashed in by Oklahoma's power boys. You need someone who's fought these wars before—not me."

Shit. Of course, he was right. He was actually number four on the list, but the other three had said *hell no,* and ran Ray off. He hadn't felt entirely comfortable about asking Anderson in the first place. He really was a nice man—a family man, a church-going do-gooder. The last thing he needed was to take on the Gilmore machine. But Ray needed a candidate, and he was at the end of his short list.

"You're right, Bill," he admitted. "It's gonna be a tough fight, and whoever's running against Gilmore's man will probably lose. Nobody's ever beaten the candidate endorsed by the *Sun.* But if someone doesn't try, we might as well just turn everything over to Gilmore and crawl into a hole—let him decide what's good for the people, how government should operate, how the schools will be run. Just hand him the keys to the state and leave. Today, and maybe only today, you and I have a choice. We can join forces and try to win. Take this state back for the people, operate the government for the people, actually listen to the people. If we don't take that chance today, we may not have a choice tomorrow."

Ray's speech seemed to have had an effect on Bill. He paced, frowning. "I have to talk to my wife and kids," he said at last. "What we're talking about will have a big impact on them. If I lose, it'll be over in a year or so. But if for some strange reason I should win, then it's four years. Four years of fighting ugly battles with powerful people. And then another campaign. You're asking a lot, Ray. I'll have to give it some thought."

Ray walked to his car, looking around at Anderson's magnificent, serene horse ranch with its stables and its plantation-style mansion. *This man has achieved everything he'd ever dreamed of,* Ray thought, and yet he was considering turning his life, and the lives of his loved ones, into hell. And for what? Maybe because it was the right thing to do, and a man of character can't easily say no to a good fight against bad people. Ray felt sorry for him. The situation called for some self-medication to ease his own pain. Next stop: Risso's.

A few weeks later, after hearing no word, Ray figured Bill had made the wise decision to have nothing to do with politics. Then he got a call to meet Anderson at his home.

"Ray," he announced, "I'll run. I'm sure I'm going to regret this, but I've decided, and my family's agreed. I'll need your help. But I also want you to stay on the sidelines as much as possible. You're a red flag to Gilmore, and I'll have enough to worry about without waving you in front of him. So I want your help and advice, but I don't want you visible. Okay?"

Ray kept his answers short. "Sure. Whatever you want. I'll

help any way I can." He didn't want to sound as elated as he felt.

"You may not know this," Anderson went on, "but I went to Dartmouth a few years before I decided the academic life wasn't for me. While I was there, I ran into someone about as politically astute as anyone I've ever met. I'm going to ask him to be my campaign manager. Name's Taylor Albright. He may have a little trouble adjusting to Oklahoma, but I trust him. And I think he might know some ways to score points against Gilmore."

"Sure—whatever you say, Bill. I can help get him up to speed. This is great. The party just has a small staff, but it's completely available to you. And if you or anyone in your campaign needs office space, we have lots."

"Thanks. I sure hope I'm doing the right thing."

Yep, Ray thought. *Me, too.*

4

REPORTER'S DEAD END

Tommy reconsidered the hide-under-the-covers option. It seemed a little early in his career to abandon all hope. He felt a slight thrill after deciding to head back to the capitol to see if he could track down Judy—a happy thought. Besides, she might have some inside information on what the police found out about Walters's death. Since the crime occurred on the capitol grounds, people in high places would want to be in the know, he figured, and maybe she'd share what they'd learned. Or he could just gawk at her. After all, they had been play-mates once, or so she told him.

"Look, we haven't got any news on that, and if we did, we wouldn't be handing it out. That's up to the cops. And, no, I haven't seen Judy this morning. Excuse me, I have work to do."

That brush-off was delivered, with visible delight, by a very well-dressed junior staff member and the only person Tommy found who he'd dare approach. The first items of legislative business for the day were scheduled for the afternoon. Most members were in committee meetings and not available for comment. He had Judy's card, but it didn't say what office she worked in. He found a dime and called from a pay phone in the lobby, but no one answered. He was unsure what to do next—then he spotted his new best friend.

"Hey, Bart. How you doin'? Keepin' everybody safe?"

"You know; you really sound like a wise-ass. Why are you trying to annoy me?"

"Sorry. I wasn't trying to annoy you. Forget it. Could you tell me which office Judy works in?"

"Nope, I can't. If she wanted you to know, she'd have told you. Now, scram, and leave me alone."

Bart may have been damn near twice Tommy's size, but enough was enough. "Listen, jackass, you have no right to talk to me that way. I'm a reporter for the *Journal*; I have a right to be here, and a constitutional right to ask questions of anyone I want. She's a friend of mine, which you know, and she forgot to tell me which office she works in. Is that some kind of state secret? If you can't answer my question, you can sure as hell be polite about it. I don't have any power here, and no one listens to me. But think about this, Mister Bart—I write columns in one of the two biggest papers in this town. And I can say just about anything I want. You ought to think about that before picking a fight with me." Tommy puffed up his chest and set his hands on his hips. Much of what he'd said wasn't quite true, but he felt better for saying it. Besides, you can't sound righteously angry while detailing the nuances.

"Okay. Okay." Bart actually seemed a little cowed. "You're right. Maybe I shouldn't be such an ass. I don't even remember your name, but I'm sorry. I don't want you writing about me."

"Tommy Jacks." Tommy stuck out his hand with a smile. They shook hands, and Bart smiled back, although not really happily, he noticed.

"Look," Bart explained, "I'm just having a bad morning. You might not know the capitol reporter for the *Sun,* but he was a friend of mine. They found him dead last night. Right here, just outside in the parking lot. Guess I'm a little on edge."

Now Tommy felt bad. "Hey, look—there's no one here yet. Let me buy you a cup of coffee." They headed down the marble stairs to the main lobby.

"Thanks." Bart's voice softened. "By the way, Judy works for Bud Evans. He's president pro tem of the Senate. His office is right there by the Senate chamber."

"Oh, yeah, I remember now. She told me that. Thanks." Tommy wasn't sure what else to ask Bart, or whether to ask him anything at all. He didn't want to harass the guy if he was upset about Walters, but if he knew something, it might be useful. "I didn't know Walters very well," he ventured, trying to be careful. "I just met him yesterday. He was at Risso's when I dropped by to get a pizza. He seemed pretty upset. Guess he'd been fired. Did you know anything about that?"

"Fired?" Bart looked skeptical. "They wouldn't fire Tony. He was the best they had. He was probably just messin' with you. He was always kidding around."

Kidding around? Tommy thought. Sure didn't sound like fun and games—especially not Steve Marsh's story. Then again, maybe Bart knew differently. "Have the police said anything about it?"

"Not to me. You know, I'm just a flunky here. Nobody hardly talks to me. I came on to you like I was important, but I'm not anything. Tony always treated me really good. He'd stop and talk, tell jokes. He was my friend. I can't believe someone killed him. He was great friends with Judy, too—he was always talking to her. You should ask her about him; she'll tell you. He was the best."

"Well, thanks, Bart. Think I'll go see if I can't find Judy. I'm sorry about all this. If I hear anything, I'll let you know. See you later."

He headed back up to the fourth floor, using the stairs so he could take time to think. He felt badly for Bart, but it didn't last long—he was going to see Judy. Then again, although it probably wasn't strange that Judy and Walters would know each other—the capitol was its own little community—for some reason, it bugged him. He found his way to Bud Evans's office.

"Hi, I'm Tommy Jacks. I'm a friend of Judy Jackson's, and I'm wondering if she's in this morning."

The secretary said she thought Judy was with Senator Evans at a meeting with the Chamber of Commerce downtown. She said she'd leave a note to let Judy know he'd stopped by.

Now what? He decided on another visit to Risso's. They served lunch, so maybe someone would be there getting ready. There were some other guys at the booth with Walters and Marsh. Tommy wanted to talk to them, too. Maybe someone at Risso's could tell him who they were.

Risso's looked particularly ugly in the mid-morning sun. A few cars sat in the lot, so he figured someone had to be inside, but the front door was locked. He ventured around back and found an outside door to the kitchen that was open. He entered to a blast of mariachi music from a big radio. *Italian food prepared by Mexicans?* The kitchen staff consisted of two guys, both with backs turned, caught up in food prep. Tommy called out, but the music was too loud. He left the kitchen unnoticed, heading for the main dining room where things would be quieter. He saw what looked like an office, and headed toward it.

"Hey, can I help you with something?"

He jumped. He hadn't noticed the man at the table drinking coffee and reading the paper. It was the waiter from the night before—the one who'd let him into the bar. "Maybe. You might not remember me, but I was here last night. You showed me to the bar in the back."

"Sure. You're Ray Jacks's kid. Coffee?"

His name was Larry Lopez, and it turned out he owned Risso's. He'd bought the place after the original Risso died about twenty years back and decided to keep everything as it was, aside from hiring his family to cook and wait tables. He said a lot of the regulars called him Larry Risso. He never corrected them.

Tommy told him about Walters.

"I can't believe that," he said, looking shocked. "My god, that's horrible. He'd get a little loud sometimes, but everybody liked Tony. Why would anyone kill him?"

Tommy shrugged. "Was he a regular?"

"Oh, sure. When the legislature was in session, he was in the bar most nights. There's always a lot of people from the capitol in here for drinks while the session's going. Usually we don't see them any other time, and that was Tony, too. I think he bought drinks for people and got information he could use that way. But everybody seemed to like him."

"Last night he was with four other guys. Did you know any of them?"

"One, for sure. Steve Marsh. He's the big-time sportswriter at the *Sun*; used to be the star quarterback for the Sooners. He's the one who came and got Tony and apologized to you." He thought a moment. "Three of them left just after you did— Marsh and two others. I didn't know the other ones, but it seemed they worked at the paper. I'd never seen them before. The guy who stayed is a lawyer. I'm not sure of his name, but I've seen his picture in the paper with a story about some big case. Steve might tell you who the other guys were. But they all seemed like they were Tony's friends."

"You know what they say," Tommy said. "Most murders are committed by friends and family."

Tommy headed east into the flat, broad suburbs, toward the *Journal* building where, he'd been told, he could always find a desk, a free phone, and a typewriter. He had a feeling Marsh wouldn't talk to him, but he had to make the call and try. He also wanted to talk to Chuck, the police reporter.

Tommy had to be cleared through the front desk by one of the editors. That made him wonder again why newspapers seemed to think security was so important—something odd about that. Maybe it was all those threatening letters to the editor. Free speech in action, with tight security.

As he suspected, he couldn't get hold of Marsh. He left a message with the woman answering the phone who, in a completely unnecessarily snooty tone, informed Tommy that Steve did not normally return phone calls from people like him. The high status accorded to sportswriters, especially sports columnists, and particularly ones who used to be star athletes, was a fact of life in newspapers and absolutely in football-crazy Oklahoma. If there were stars in journalism in the middle states, they were more likely to be sportswriters than political writers.

Chuck the police reporter, on the other hand, lived at the bottom of the heap. His job was mostly as a fact collector, writing quick and dirty pieces about auto accidents, robberies, drug raids, and other dreary news about the underbelly of society. He usually practiced his craft at night, prowling some of the seamier sections of town, including police substations. He looked like he hadn't been in the sun for a long time. He sat at a desk in a darkened corner, chain-smoking and drinking coffee from the largest cup Tommy had ever seen.

"Appreciate you giving me the heads-up call about Walters. Know any more about that?"

"Not really. As soon as the cops found out he actually was not one of the lowlifes they usually deal with, they clammed up. Said anything new would come from the chief himself. Which is like saying that's the last we'll hear until they arrest somebody."

"Well, if you hear anything, I'd really appreciate it if you'd let me know."

"Sure, no problem."

One more dead end. Tommy felt useless.

After a little typewriter time, he headed back to the capitol, stopping along the way at Del Rancho, his favorite sandwich place. If he had to order a last meal, this would be it: a steak sandwich with onion rings, everything fried. Of course, he figured that last meal might come a lot quicker if he kept eating such stuff.

The secretary told him Judy was in a meeting with the senator and other important folks, and wasn't expected to be available for the rest of the day. She seemed evasive, though, which led him to think maybe she wasn't supposed to tell him something. It was apparently a common strategy. He left Judy a note and wandered the halls a while, stopping a few people and trying to engage them in conversation. Most brushed him off and went about their business.

A day of frustration and rejection. He thought maybe he should become a truck driver, schoolteacher, cook—anything other than an annoying reporter. He went home to the covers, and to dream about Judy.

5
NEW DAY

Tommy was up early, headed for Denny's and Taylor Albright. He felt almost over his blues, ready to get some answers from somebody about something. For no particular reason, he felt energized, like he was making progress. In fact, nothing had changed. The optimism of youth is unbounded by logic.

And maybe it was anticipation of talking with Albright. Tommy thought there was a lot more to the guy than met the eye. He'd reacted to news about Walters's murder like it was a personal blow. But he never said how he knew Walters, or why he wasn't too surprised that "something bad happened." Tommy cringed a bit after realizing Albright had been very effective at extracting everything he knew while giving very little in return. It seemed he had a lot to learn about being a journalist.

Denny's looked packed. Tommy squeezed his old Ford into the last spot with no concern about parking lot dings—another advantage of driving a well-abused vehicle. The crowd inside intrigued him. His experience was skewed toward night, and he was happiest waking at mid-morning. Seeing all this bustle a little before six in the morning was like discovering a world he hadn't known existed.

Finding Albright was easy—same booth. He sat alone, his

pile of papers covering most of the table.

"Good morning, Mister Albright."

"Taylor."

"Right. Morning, Taylor."

"In most cases, the cheerfulness of youth is an affront to people of my mature years. Take a seat and order."

Tommy did as directed, even if his upbeat mood took a downward shift. He smiled, anyway, if just to annoy Albright. He found the front page of *The New York Times* and began to scan. There was the latest from Vietnam. He was, like most journalists, against the war, and had little respect for Lyndon Johnson. Still, he tended to lean Democratic, if only because that was what his father was. He just hoped someone would run who could beat Johnson. He glanced at an article about Richard Nixon's campaign. He vaguely recalled Nixon as Eisenhower's vice president. Hadn't he retired or something? Not someone he would pick. Back to Nam—all the news looked bad. The generals kept saying everything was going great, but the reporting—especially the photos—told another story. The war made no sense.

"Taylor," he asked, "what do you think about Vietnam?"

"It sucks," Albright said. "The U.S. has gone from a hero nation that helped defeat Hitler and save the world from evil to a war-mongering bully. Killing thousands and thousands of people in the vilest way, in Korea and Vietnam. My God, in Vietnam we're using chemicals, which we said we would never do—we signed international agreements saying we wouldn't. It's supposedly to kill vegetation. Of course, people live where the vegetation is—who the hell decided that was the right thing to do? All to keep people we don't give a shit about from living in a communist society, even if it's of their own choosing. And we rationalize this soul-crushing genocide because these heathen people do not worship our God. Johnson should resign, and his generals should be court-martialed and locked up. The whole world has gone nuts!"

Okay, wrong question. Talking about Vietnam was not going to get him to the subject he had in mind. Tommy knew and agreed with everything he said. And besides, the whole mess could have a serious impact on him—he was subject to the draft, especially now that he'd graduated. Even so, he didn't feel the same fiery indignation he'd just seen from Albright. Might be best to stay away from hot-button issues until he had a better idea who this guy was. "How did you know Walters?" Tommy thought his voice squeaked when he asked. He needed to work on that.

"Well, aren't we being inquisitive this morning? Is this going to be in your column, or are you just being nosy?"

Okay, here goes. He tried a slightly lower tone. "I'm a reporter. Being nosy is part of my routine. So I guess it could be in my next column, unless you want this to be off the record."

Albright seemed amused. He took a gulp of coffee and eyed him. "First lesson: Tommy, nobody gives a shit about your job or your lofty role as a reporter. You're a pain in the butt, and, given the opportunity, everyone will avoid you and not tell you a thing. On the record or off, you'll be ignored, or yelled at to leave the high and mighty alone. The people's right to know is crap. The elites don't want the people to know a damn thing, and as the people's representative, you're considered scum."

Journalism 101 hadn't been that candid. Tommy knew the job would be tough, but no one told him it was impossible. "So, what does that mean—I just give up?"

"Lesson two: Most journalists *aren't* very nosy. They go to news conferences, they collect news releases, they repeat what they hear from the people in power, and publish all that garbage like it was the truth. You could be like that, but the *Journal* won't pay you for it. They get that already, for free, more or less. If you're going to survive, you have to find the truth. To do that, you have to talk to people who want to talk to you. Those people will always have an agenda. They're always looking to fuck somebody. They have dirt on someone they hate, and they want you to show the world so they can get an edge. The problem is, what they have for you might be a lie. Maybe they just made it up, or they got it from a questionable source who wants them to use it to destroy an enemy, or maybe to destroy the poor asshole journalist who used it in the paper, or maybe it's all just a joke. People might talk to you if you have a voice in a paper like the *Journal,* but your challenge will be to find out what's real and what isn't, what can be printed and what can't, who to trust and who not to trust."

Tommy had an uneasy feeling that lesson three was that he was an idiot to get into the newspaper business in the first place and that he should go back to school, become a park ranger, and go monitor bears. Then it occurred to him that Albright didn't have a voice in the *Journal* anymore. He'd been fired. But it seemed clear he wanted to talk to him, even if Tommy didn't know why. This discussion wasn't as much about journalism as it was about establishing whether Tommy could trust Albright—and whether Albright could trust him.

"I'm new at this," Tommy admitted tightly, "but I'm not stupid. My bullshit meter's been working pretty good for a while.

You want to help me, and you want me to help you. I'm agreeable up to a point. I do believe in truth."

"You need to go talk to your father."

"Where the hell did *that* come from?"

"You need to go see your father and ask him about me and Walters. You need to establish who you can trust."

"First off, Mister Albright, I don't trust my father. So why in hell would I go see him?"

"You want to be a reporter? Or just some whiny little kid?"

Tommy's impulse was to shove his oatmeal into Albright's face and storm out. He felt angry at himself, Albright, and his father especially.

"Look, I get it. You want something, and you need me to help you. But why the hell should I trust you? What do you know?"

"I know a lot. I was Anderson's campaign manager. I was down in the muck and mire. I worked very closely with your father—we became friends. I know for a fact he was framed. And possibly, with a little luck, I can prove it. Walters was part of our little circle of conspirators. He hated Gilmore more than anyone. And now he's dead. Maybe I'm dead too, soon. That's how much I know—maybe I'm next. So you hate your dad. Fine. That's none of my business. But he's the one who needs to tell you some things—not me. Go see him, and then we can talk again. Good-bye." Albright got up, tossed some bills on the table, and left. He didn't take his papers.

Albright seemed angry, but why? Tommy was the one being told what to do. He was the one with a right to be angry. He looked up, and couldn't see Albright anywhere. Where the hell had he gone? If he didn't have a car, how could he leave?

Tommy went outside. No Albright. Jeez, what a mess.

"McAlester," the sign at the city limit read, "home of Oklahoma State Penitentiary." It had an odd ring of a touristy attraction. Big Mac, as it was called, was not considered a prime vacation destination if you didn't count the bizarre practice of transporting impressionable pre-teen Boy Scouts for tours that included visits to the electric chair. That middle-of-the-Bible-belt outing was meant to instill a wrath-of-God appreciation for what happened to sinners. A lot of good, upstanding folks believed it had a meaningful impact on the boys.

Tommy still felt upset about what happened with Albright. He knew he could just ignore the old guy and do whatever he wanted about Walters's death, which included nothing. But he had a nagging feeling Albright might be an important part of how the mystery could be solved.

The drive to McAlester was uneventful, but getting in to see his father was an exercise in monkish patience. It would have gone more smoothly if he had known the various requirements for family visits before getting there, and especially if he'd filled out the paperwork in advance. Of course, up until then, he'd had no plans to see his dad. One more hitch or delay in the tedious process and he would bolt for home, he swore to himself. Getting into Big Mac was proving to be just about as tough as getting out had to be. Just before his patience ran out, he was told everything had been approved and his father was headed to the visiting room.

The room surprised him. It was full of groupings of small tables and chairs—no glass barriers and phone receivers like in the movies. It made him feel uncomfortable, less safe; even if the signs on the wall assured him all prisoners and visitors were searched just like he'd been before he came in, and even if a guard stood on duty. He asked the guard about the open setup and was told they were in a "contact" room, as opposed to "no-contact," meaning it was for non-violent offenders who didn't make trouble. Tommy took a seat and waited nervously.

His father walked in. This was the man he had admired and loved his whole young life. He knew his father's weaknesses, but he'd idolized him anyway. His dad once seemed able to do anything. When he was accused of a laundry list of crimes, Tommy hadn't believed they were true—at first. But as the trial went on, it became hard to not lose faith. When his dad pleaded guilty, it all came down on him. He'd lost his hero. How could his dad allow it to happen? Tommy moved to Tulsa to live with an aunt, his deceased mother's sister, who made it clear she didn't care for him. Next came abandonment and bitterness. Before long, he started hating his dad.

Raymond Jacks looked frail, older than the years he'd been gone could possibly account for. "My goodness, Tommy. It's so great to see you. I've written you so many letters, but you never answered. Tommy, I'm so sorry about how things turned out for you—it's all my fault, and I'm so sorry."

Tommy felt his own tears, and couldn't resist reaching out to hug him. Why in hell had he not come to see him before? What a fool. His anger was still real, and the hurt wasn't going away, but his need to have his dad in his life was powerful, too. For now, he held onto his dad as if he was afraid he might run away if he let go. Building trust was not going to be easy. But Tommy knew he would eventually forgive because his father was his family, and he needed a family.

They talked for a long time. Mostly about Tommy. About going to school in Norman. About graduating early. About prison. Mostly it meant they just wanted to be close again, and to remember how much they meant to each other. Years crumbled. Anger withered. Tommy told him about his new job and how he was just starting to learn about being a journalist. It was not until the guard announced their time was almost up that Tommy even remembered why he had come in the first place—Albright.

He rushed over how he met Albright, and how he was the one who told him to talk to his dad about the two of them, and about Walters.

"Tommy—stay away from Albright. He's dangerous, stay away!" It was all Raymond had time to say before he was ushered out.

Tommy yelled, "I'll be back as soon as I can!" The next time he could see his dad would be in two weeks. Because of overcrowding, the Department of Corrections was limiting visits to every other week.

On the drive back to the city, he kept hearing his dad's warning about Albright. "He's dangerous"—what did that mean? Did Albright know his dad was going to warn him away? Or did he mistakenly think that his dad would say something good about him? If so, what? He had a head full of questions.

6

INSIDE SUN

The headquarters of the *Oklahoma Sun* stood in downtown Oklahoma City on Broadway, just a few blocks off Main Street. The multi-story building appeared regal, with classic columns and an air of superiority. Some people described it as a fortress. Critics said it looked more like a high-class prison. Either was appropriate, considering its occupants. It was a fortress with generals and an army, or it was a prison with guards. The top floors were reserved for management, with the highest floor reserved for J.H. Gilmore, his son Robbie, and their staff, most of whom were security people.

The *Sun* was founded in the 1880s by people whom history had forgotten. In the early 1900s it was taken over by a young and ambitious J.H. Gilmore who became the *Sun's* driving force, a machine of influence and political control. It grew into the voice of Oklahoma, whether to do with politics, industry, social norms, or moral authority. The *Sun* spoke its mind and set the tone for day-to-day life in the growing state—all under the watchful guidance of Gilmore.

It may have seemed a paternalistic approach, viewed from a distance. Up close, all decisions were based on building political power and the acquisition of immense wealth. The paper was the way for J.H. to have his say in everything. And it was his expectation that everyone—everyone who mattered, anyway—would agree with him. Opposition was neither welcome nor tolerated.

"You've got to rein in these assholes," J.H. roared. "I've told you this before, and I'm getting sick and tired of your failures." He was not in a good mood.

His son, Robbie, stood at attention in front of his desk, suffering another dressing-down for something he hadn't done right, or at all. "Listen, J.H.," he answered, "we're working every angle we can. Walters's murder was a complete surprise. We thought we were getting somewhere, figuring out who was helping him."

"Well, I'm not sorry the bastard's dead," J.H. pouted. "But we've got to find out where he was getting his libelous information and what the people who were giving it to him planned on doing with it. You've already spent a fortune on your goon squad, and all we get for it is a dead end. We're about to have our seventy-fifth anniversary bash, and I want this mess cleaned up before that, understand?"

"Sure, I understand, J.H. We'll push harder, and we'll get some answers—soon." Robbie had not called his dad anything other than "J.H." since he was about fourteen years old.

"Soon? It'd better be goddamn soon!" That was his dismissal.

Robert J. "Robbie" Gilmore had worked in almost every job at the *Sun* while growing up, and he was good at all of them, even if he was the owner's son. He loved the business, and dreamed of the day he would take over and run the paper the way he wanted. But so far there seemed a good chance his father would live to be a hundred or older without ever giving up control. In the meantime, Robbie seemed to do more private detective work than anything else. J.H. was turning more paranoid by the day. At one time he had a battalion of loyal friends whom he enjoyed being with. Now he saw only enemies. Everyone was out to get him, one way or another.

Robbie strode quickly down the wide hallway to his office at the other end of the top floor. He told his secretary he wanted to see "the guys" in his office immediately. She began making calls.

First to arrive was Rod Baker, head of the *Sun's* security department and an ex-Oklahoma City cop. He still had deep connections inside the police force, all the way to the top. There were lots of rumors about Rod, mostly involving drinking and women. He'd been on the job at the *Sun* for years, and his loyalty to J.H. was well known.

Next came Larry "Pudge" Peters, a massive former linebacker from the Sooners' national championship team some years back. The job description that suited him best was "muscle." His loyalty was to Robbie.

Last came a real, functioning staff member—Steve Marsh. His loyalty was very much to himself. He'd been recruited by Robbie because he had a working after-hours relationship with Walters. Why Marsh agreed was harder to figure. But there he was.

"Just had my ass reamed once again by J.H.," Robbie said with a sigh. "In case you can't guess, I'm tired of taking the heat for your failures. You all had your assignments, monitoring and tracking Walters. Now he's dead. And by your own admission, you knew nothing about it. How in the hell can that be? You were either with him or following him—what the hell happened?" Ass-reaming, like most things, flowed downhill.

Marsh spoke first. "I took him home, put him in bed. He was so shitfaced, I thought he'd sleep till noon the next day. How was I to know he'd get up and drive to the capitol? It makes no sense—he was dead to the world when I left him. If he'd been found dead in bed, I'd get it. But not dead in the capitol parking lot."

Robbie grunted and turned his glower toward Baker.

"Don't give me the evil eye, Robbie," he growled. "Had a man tailing him, and it was just like Steve said—the guy was tucked in bed and out like a light. He wasn't going anywhere. So my guy went home and was going to pick him up again in the morning. You never said twenty-four-hour surveillance. Besides, we had to keep costs down."

Pudge had nothing to say. He looked the most pained of any of them. When Robbie was mad, Pudge always seemed to think it was at him.

"Okay," Robbie said. "It's over. He's dead. What do we do now?" Robbie focused on Rod, the ex-cop. If anyone would know how to identify Walters's contacts now, it was him.

"I think we know where this has to go," Baker said. "We were watching Walters because we thought he'd lead us to proof that Albright and Jacks were involved in his blackmail scheme. Well, he didn't. All that means is we don't have proof. We still believe it's Albright and somehow, even from jail, Jacks is involved, too. I told you we can reach into prison and make Jacks very uncomfortable, but you said no. Not sure I agree, but I understand the risks. And it's your call. If we're not going at Jacks directly, we can put surveillance on Albright and on Ray's kid, Tommy."

Robbie wasn't completely sure about that, either. "It's one

thing to tail our own employee. We could have made a case that we thought he was misusing company assets. But where's the justification for watching Albright, and especially the kid?"

"Robbie, there's no choice unless you want to back off completely and go tell J.H. we've decided to give up." Rod knew how to get Robbie to do what he wanted—just bring up J.H.

Robbie paced a few minutes. He knew he had no choice, but it felt out of bounds to him. Following a kid working for the rival paper sounded like trouble. Where J.H. would instinctively charge toward trouble, Robbie tried to avoid it.

"Okay," he said, "that's the plan. We use our resources to get close to Albright and Tommy Jacks, and add surveillance on both. Rod, I think you ought to hassle Albright any way you can. Ask some of your police buddies to see if they can pick him up for something—anything—to send a message. Marsh, you should try and make friends with the Jacks kid. You said you met him the other night. Approach him, talk about Walters, see what he knows. Okay, let's get to work."

Robbie could at least report to J.H. that a new plan was in motion. But there was an ache in his gut because it might not be the right thing. He hoped it would work out so he could go back to just working for a newspaper and stop all this clandestine crap.

The whole thing started when Walters approached J.H. for a raise. It was unheard-of for anyone from the newsroom to go directly to J.H. about pretty much anything, particularly a raise. He might as well have asked J.H. for his right arm. J.H. advised him, icily, that the personnel department was the appropriate channel to go through for that, and started to walk away.

"I'm not going to the goddamn personnel department," Walters shouted. "Aren't you the boss here? Why can't I talk to you? I'm not dirt, you know. You think you know everything—you don't know shit, even about how government works. You just bully people into doing what you want, like the way you're getting your puppet governor to hand over the vo-tech schools to your pal Reeder so he can line his pockets."

It was like there was an alarm button in J.H.'s pocket. Within seconds, two security guards appeared and escorted Walters off the executive floor. J.H. swore he would get the name of the loudmouth offender and have him fired. But he got busy and forgot.

Walters's direct approach had not worked, so he went to Plan B. He had the goods on Gilmore and his son. If they fired him, they'd regret it. He had to have money, and they were going to give it to him. If not, he'd tell the world what he knew.

He would go home and write out his demands: one letter to J.H. and a second to Robbie. In one way, Walters hated the Gilmores for their power and untouchable wealth, and in another, he admired J.H. The elder Gilmore was exactly what Walters wanted to be—a ruthless, conniving, money-grubbing business owner. The son was more irritating because he was a fraud. Robbie pretended to be good while doing the same things as his father, and worse. The letter to him dripped with disgust.

After finishing them, he celebrated with a prodigious amount of alcohol, resulting in a coma-like night's sleep. He awoke midmorning the next day, groggy and with a pounding headache. After coffee and aspirin, he felt well enough to deal with typing copies of his letters to keep. He secured the originals in envelopes and addressed them to the Gilmores. He thought about hand-delivering them, but wasn't sure he could get into the building. Dropping them in a mailbox was his best option.

He stopped at a diner on his way home for a huge breakfast and, feeling somewhat worse, headed home and to bed to await his fate.

That fate was mysteriously delayed for weeks. Walters hadn't heard anything about the letters, and he hadn't been fired, which seemed unthinkable after his outburst at Gilmore. So far, all was strangely quiet. He started to feel invincible.

Then Gilmore suddenly remembered he'd meant to fire that asshole who'd accosted him in the hallway. He called security. They identified the man as Tony Walters. That shocked him. He'd read a lot of his copy, and thought he was good at what he did. Still, he couldn't talk that way to J.H. Gilmore. Before he could act, Walters's letters arrived. One to his office and another to Robbie. Now both knew Walters had to be fired—but they also needed to know who else he'd told about what the letters said.

Word came that, during a drunken oratory at Risso's backroom bar, Walters declared to everyone within earshot that he had the famous J.H. Gilmore by the balls and was ready to squeeze. J.H. immediately made it clear that, strategy be damned, he wouldn't pay a man's salary while the bastard humiliated him in public. He called the personnel department and shouted instructions to can Walters and to have the notice hand-delivered to his house, with copies sent to the capitol press room.

7
JUDY JUDY JUDY

It seemed all Tommy could think about was Judy. He realized he was smitten, or even madly in love. At his age, it was hard to tell the difference. Seeing his dad in prison had made the kind of life that involved relationships with other people more important to him. For years, Tommy had one goal—to graduate. When he wasn't studying, he was working to pay for college. He had never allowed time for or interest in personal relationships. He noticed shapely coeds with all-American masculine appreciation, but from afar. He'd lost his mother and been abandoned by his father. Relationships meant pain.

Today, though, his goal was to find Judy and ask her to lunch or dinner. He wanted to be with her. Driving down Lincoln in his old junker, he smiled. He felt a little silly. He blushed at his own thoughts all the way to the capitol parking lot.

"Tommy, right?" Bud Evans's secretary asked.

"Yes, ma'am." She was a different woman from the one he'd asked about Judy before. She seemed much friendlier.

"Looking for Judy, aren't you? She was just talking about you the other day, but she's not here. We're actually worried about her. We didn't see or hear from her yesterday, and no word today, either. We even called the police this morning. Do you know where she might be?"

Tommy was stunned. Walters dead, and now Judy missing. He felt lightheaded. *Fainting—that'd be a real he-man reaction, you schmuck.* He felt his way over to a chair, head in hands.

"Are you all right?" She brought him some water.

"Yeah, yeah, fine. Sorry about that. Probably should've had breakfast. Did the police go to her place? Have they said anything?"

"They went to her apartment. As best they could tell, it looked empty. They didn't go inside—something about it only being a day since we'd seen her. Told us if we hadn't heard from her by tomorrow, they might go in and look. Senator Evans got real mad. He called the police chief about it, so they might do something sooner. Maybe you ought to go lie down until you feel better."

Tommy mumbled thanks, asked if it was okay to call later, and left without knowing where to go. Why would Judy be missing? How on Earth could he find her? He didn't even know where she lived. He started to feel sick, and sure as hell didn't want to puke on the marble floor, so he headed outside. The fresh air helped clear his head. He sat on the steps, trying to think. The facts didn't add up too much. If Judy was really missing, and not just staying in bed with a boyfriend or playing hooky, he figured it had to have something to do with Walters. Bart had said they were always talking. So, what had they been talking about? Bart probably didn't know, and Tommy didn't feel like dealing with him, anyway. His next step had to be to find Albright. If Judy was somehow involved with Walters, then his only path to her, as far as he could see, went through Albright. He forced himself to make the rounds for his next column, listening to some senators cry crocodile tears over taxing cigarettes to pay for schools, then headed to his car.

It struck him on the way how little he knew about Albright—no address, no phone number. Nothing but Denny's. He headed there. The morning crowd was long gone, and there was no Albright camped in the corner booth. No one in Denny's would know where he lived; he went there specifically to be anonymous. Tommy sat in his car and worried—about Judy, and about what to do.

He remembered the address he'd jotted down where he dropped off Albright the day he met him. That might be something. He headed to Second Street, just off the main area of downtown—an infamous part of the city, and one he knew something about. It was called Deep Deuce, and back in the day it had been alive with nightclubs jumping to some of the best jazz bands to be found. People who lived and worked in Deep Deuce were mostly black, but everyone went there for the music. Tommy had once written an article for the OU *Daily* about the clubs and the bands.

He parked down the street from the building where Albright had gotten out. The first thing he saw when he stepped out was enough men for a football team standing here and there along the sidewalk, talking in voices too low for him to hear and watching him in a way that posed no obvious threat but still felt like one. Or maybe he just felt out of place, and that made him feel vulnerable. He walked steadily, nodding to a couple of them, getting nothing in return. Yet again he felt grateful he drove a heap of a vehicle. Nobody was going to mess with a car that looked like it had already been messed with.

The building looked surprisingly uptown by any standard,

but in this neighborhood it seemed downright palatial. He read the directory. Most listings were lawyers or dentists. Some didn't say what they did. He wrote down the lawyers' names, skipping the dentists. What nagged Tommy was that the guy at Risso's had said that one of the men who stayed and talked to Walters after their encounter was an attorney, but he couldn't remember the guy's name. It was a long shot, but worth a try.

Outside, all the street loiterers were gone. Their sudden absence somehow made the scene more ominous. He hurried to his car and left, letting out a sigh of relief once he was clear of Deep Deuce. He figured Risso's would be busy, and his best bet was to try to get a minute or two with Larry Lopez to see if he knew any of the names.

Joe Louongo, Lopez told him. It took him only a glance to pick it out. The guy was a transplant from New Jersey, or maybe New York. Whenever business slowed down long enough for him to talk, he filled Tommy in on what he could remember, like the rumor that Louongo had some connection with organized crime. Almost every major crime figure in the city—Italians, Mexicans, Native Americans, everybody—had hired Louongo. He was always in the paper, smiling, claiming innocence for his clients whether the case was theft, murder, robbery, or general mayhem. Louongo had a lot to smile about.

It was a twist Tommy hadn't expected. Organized crime? When he asked Lopez if he was sure, he shrugged. It wasn't the kind of thing anyone knew for sure. Then Lopez circled back and delivered another shocker. "Look, Tommy, if you really want to know about Louongo, you should ask your dad. I think he worked for him somehow."

He had to keep from screaming. *My dad?* The room seemed

to spin a little. After a gulp of a milkshake to steady his nerves, he thanked Lopez and went outside. He wanted to hide. He climbed into the back seat of his ratty Ford and stretched out as best he could manage given his six-foot-two frame. Whenever his mind got too fogged up to function, sleep was the answer—the only thing that helped.

He woke up about an hour later, feeling worse. His instincts told him to get something to eat and go home. Probably sound advice, but he wasn't taking it. Instead, he headed back to Deep Deuce. He had no idea what he would say if Louongo was there. He'd think of something.

Everything seemed quiet. Louongo's office was on the second floor. And it was locked. He knocked—no answer. All the other offices on that floor were lawyers, too, and they sure as hell wouldn't tell him anything. Dejected, he headed home.

Partly on impulse, partly out of the urge for self-preservation, he pulled into Denny's to grab a bite and maybe call the senator's office to see if the nice lady had any news. He was shocked to find Albright in his regular booth with his two natty companions.

"Where the hell have you been? I need your phone number, right now!" He said it louder than he'd meant to, but he was angry.

The two fashion models went on alert, hands inside their coats. It occurred to Tommy in a flash that he might be in danger. Were these guys Albright's bodyguards?

"Tommy," Albright answered, just as angrily, "you should shut the fuck up and sit down." He signaled to his companions and they relaxed. "Now, what the hell's the matter?"

"Judy Jackson's missing. Did you know that?"

"What do you mean, missing?"

"Missing is what I mean—you know, missing!"

Albright frowned. He leaned over and whispered something to the closest suit, who got up with the other and left. "How do you know that?" he asked Tommy.

"I went to her office this morning. The secretary told me they'd called the police because she hadn't been in yesterday or this morning, and nobody'd heard from her. I wanted to talk to you because I'd been told Judy was a friend of Walters. It all seemed like too much of a coincidence to me—Walters dead, and now Judy missing. Are these things connected?"

"I don't know. Maybe. Who told you she was a friend of Walters?"

"Some guy at the capitol. I think he's some type of security guard. He told me Judy and Walters used to talk all the time. And who's this lawyer, Joe Louongo? Is that where you went when I gave you a ride downtown?"

Albright's eyes flashed. "What do you know about Louongo?"

"Nothing. I was looking for you and went to his building. The owner of Risso's told me he was a criminal lawyer, and he was with Walters the night he was killed. He also said he thinks Louongo used to work for my father. Why aren't you telling me what's going on?"

"Because I don't want to get you killed."

"Killed!" Tommy said that a little too loud—heads turned.

Albright kept his voice low. "You're the son of a good friend. I wanted Ray to talk to you and tell you to back off. You have no idea what you're getting into. It's not something for a kid who still needs training wheels to get involved in."

"Fuck you!" Tommy hissed. "Where's Judy?"

"I don't know. I didn't know she was missing. If she's left, there was a reason—she can take care of herself." Albright grabbed a napkin and scribbled two phone numbers. "You need to go home now. Let me look into this. Give me a call tomorrow at one of these numbers. And stop playing detective before you get yourself into real trouble."

Tommy grabbed the napkin, giving him a dirty look. "I'll do whatever I want. You can be guaranteed I'll find out what's going on, whether you like it or not." He got up and left.

Tommy headed down Classen Boulevard toward his apartment. He needed time to figure things out, or at the very least to sort out what he'd learned. *Killed!* What the hell was going on here? Once he got to the Northwest Highway, he remembered he was starving. He settled for McDonald's and went home. He locked his door that night.

8
MY VIEW

"Thanks for coming in this morning, Tommy. You know, I think we've been a little remiss in our communications. It's a problem we sometimes have around here. Have a seat." After coming in from an interview with a Republican legislator blowing a gasket over anti-war demonstrations, the greeting from Fred Simpson seemed warm to Tommy.

"I was sort of wondering when someone would tell me if I was doing what I was supposed to, or if not, what I should be doing," he replied.

"Yep, someone should. What happens with us is we get going in ten directions at once and sometimes we forget some stuff—not that you're 'stuff.'" Fred chuckled, although he seemed to realize it wasn't funny. "We'll get you set up on a schedule for regular meetings to talk about your progress and get you paid. Our assistant city editor is June Newton. She'll be the one you'll coordinate with, and I'll introduce you once we're done. She'll give you guidance on your articles and handle administrative matters for you. Of course, you can come in and see me any time about any concerns you have. But before we talk about your columns, and what we'd like to see you focus on from here, I wanted to go over some of the paper's history. I know we discussed a bit of this in your interview, and you probably already know a bit about the founder of our paper because of your dad, but I wanted to make sure you had a good sense of what drives us around here."

Tommy was getting a completely different vibe from when he'd interviewed for the job. Something had clearly changed. Fred was treating him like someone important. That was fine, but why? And why now?

"This paper's founding was a direct result of Bill Anderson running for governor. I'm sure that, with your dad's involvement in the Democratic Party, you must know something about how bitter things got between the candidates. Driving much of the hostilities was, of course, the support Mister Anderson's opponent received from *The Sun*. In a lot of ways, it was an election between J.H. Gilmore's and Mister Anderson's views about the future of Oklahoma. It was about as nasty as any race in the state's entire history. After dealing with the *Sun* and its biased viewpoint, Mister Anderson vowed to bring a new voice to Oklahoma—an honest voice that represented everybody, not just a few. That attracted some committed newspaper people who believed in a free and unbiased press. One of those was Taylor Albright." Simpson paused, eyeing Tommy directly.

Tommy said nothing, but realized, *So there's more to this meeting than professional guidance and a paycheck.*

"Again, as I'm sure you're aware, Albright was Mister Anderson's campaign manager. He was also a friend. After Anderson started the paper, he asked Albright to come aboard and write a column with an emphasis on the capitol and politics. It sounded like a natural fit. Albright's column was called 'My View,' and, as far as he was concerned, it was exactly that.

He was opinionated and aggressive. It started off weekly, and pretty soon we were running it three times a week. It was a big hit with our readers, and there was a lot of controversy. To put it simply, he pissed off almost everyone at the capitol, and bludgeoned the *Sun*—and of course, Gilmore—to the point they threatened to sue. It was great fun while it lasted." Simpson sighed. "But he got sloppy. He made a mistake by quoting an anonymous source on some changes Gilmore was promoting for state oil lease laws—accused old J.H. of lining his own pockets. Well, the anonymous source was most likely a plant, and what he gave Albright was a lie. The shit hit the fan. Long story short, Albright resigned as a condition of a settlement with Gilmore. And the *Journal* lost a lot of steam.

"Albright was a beloved member of this organization, and his downfall was ours too. And the changes to the state oil lease law *did* become an absolute boon for the industry. The specific information Albright had from the source was wrong—but Gilmore did make millions."

Tommy knew this wasn't a cautionary tale about anonymous sources. It was about courage and commitment not always being enough to win the good fight. You could be right and still lose.

"Your background at the OU paper is impressive. Some of those stories you did were first-rate, the kind of stuff that wins Pulitzer Prizes. When we hired you, we thought contacts you had through your dad would be your greatest strength, but now we think you'd be the perfect person to restart the 'My View' column. We'd run them anywhere from one to three times a week, depending on what you can generate. What do you think?"

Wow, was his first—unstated—reaction. This was way too fast. Someone was pulling strings. Was it Albright, or maybe Anderson? And why? "Well, Mister Simpson, I'm not sure what to think. It seems fast. Are you sure I can do this? I'm sort of, well—sort of new."

"No one's questioning your writing skills. You'll just need to find new and different ways to approach politics and its undersides. That's what you did at OU. All the stories you covered had been there for years—all somebody had to do was dig a bit. We're not asking you to be Albright. We're asking you to do your best at pushing your way in and asking hard questions. And the answer to your question is that I believe in you, and Bill Anderson has taken a personal interest in your future. He believes in you, too."

An alarm bell went off in Tommy's head. "Let me ask you something. Does this have anything to do with some kind of payback to my dad? I don't want any handouts."

"Not as far as I know. And even if you are getting the opportunity because of your dad's past connections, so what? I'll guarantee you'll be measured on what you do with it. If you stink, we'll say so, and if you get fired, it'll be for what *you* do— not because of what someone else does or thinks."

"Fair enough. Then my answer is, that sounds fantastic. I'll get started."

Fred took Tommy to meet June Newton, a plain, middle-aged woman and the nicest person he'd met at the *Journal.* She was a mother hen, in fact, asking Tommy where he lived and whether he ate wholesome meals. She also gave him his first paycheck, which was incredibly small but much appreciated. They would meet on Friday afternoons, when possible.

"You need to be careful," she told him. "This is not like covering a humanities department scandal at OU. It's real-world ugly. What you've done so far is good work, but you need to remember—Tony Walters was a political reporter just like you. Take that to heart. The paper wants you to push and dig up inside information when you can. But no one here wants you to get hurt. You have to be extra careful right now until the police find out what happened to Walters. If you need help at any time, you give me a call, understand?" She opened her lap drawer to show him a deadly-looking Colt automatic.

He was impressed, and maybe a little intimidated, by a new appreciation of her. He assured her that she would be the first person he called if he needed armed assistance. Having a mother hen, especially one that's armed, is a good thing.

He thanked everyone he saw on his way out, feeling on top of the world until he remembered Judy's disappearance. He needed to call Albright. His mood began to slip, and by the time he got to the capitol press room, it had hit bottom.

He called both numbers he had for Albright; no one answered. *That's just like him,* Tommy stewed, trying to figure out his next move. The phone rang.

"Jacks, press room."

"Tommy, meet me at Louongo's office immediately." Albright hung up. Everything about him was abrupt and grating.

He parked a few doors down from the office building, glad to see no one hanging around on the sidewalk. He was nervous enough. Louongo's office door was unlocked, so he went in. No one sat at the receptionist's desk. "Hello, anyone here?"

One of the office doors opened, and Albright leaned out to give Tommy a nod.

"You know," Tommy started in, "you have no right to order me around. You could have told me what you wanted before you hung up. I'm sure I don't know what's going on, and maybe there's some reason to be secretive, but do you have to be so rude?"

"Sorry," Albright said in a way that broadcast he really wasn't. "We've found Judy. Walters's murder spooked her. She went to a friend's house somewhere in Kansas. She's okay."

"Well, that's great." Tommy exhaled, flustered with relief. "Why didn't you just tell me that over the phone?"

"Tommy," Albright sighed, "I know I can be annoying. I'm sorry, and I'll try to do better. I should have told you that part over the phone because I knew you were worried about her, but I was more focused on why I needed to see you. Let's just call it one of my many faults, and I'll issue a blanket apology for all of them, okay?"

One of Tommy's pet peeves was people who, when in the wrong, managed to twist things around to seem they were wronged, and tried to make you feel badly for them instead. He scowled.

"Look, she's okay," Albright continued. "She told me to say 'Hi' to you, and to tell you she'll be back in a few days. Now, let's move on."

"Did you know the *Journal* asked me to resurrect the 'My View' column?"

Albright sputtered. "You're kidding. No way can you write a column with that name. That'll just stir up a bunch of shit for you, all for nothing. Why would they do that? I'll talk to Bill— that isn't right. Simpson must be out of his mind. You know, he almost lost his job over letting me use some questionable material about Gilmore. The *Journal's* reputation got dragged through the mud because of what I did. Somebody's not thinking straight over there."

"So, you're saying you didn't know?"

"I didn't."

"Why would they do that, then? It only makes sense if you'd asked them to." Tommy was aware of Albright's big stink—he'd studied about it in one of his journalism classes. At the time, he couldn't believe a good journalist could be as sloppy as Albright was said to have been.

"Maybe they hate your ass because you're such a whiny pain in the butt. So you start that column again, and suddenly you're an enemy of the *Sun* and Gilmore, which puts you at risk."

"Okay, why'd you ask me here?" Tommy snarled "Just to insult me?"

"Yeah, that was it." Suddenly, Albright had a bright smile on his face. It broke the tension. They laughed. It had been a while since Tommy had laughed so hard—a long while.

"Okay, so why, really?"

"I wanted to give you a few answers. Not everything yet, but a few. I want to help you expose some bad people. It has to be done the right way, or it could turn deadly, especially for you. I need your help, and you need mine."

Tommy nodded, even if that didn't put all his reservations to rest. *You can trust me,* he thought, *but you can't keep me in the dark and expect me to understand what's going on.* "I don't really get," he said, "why the *Journal* wants me to revive your old column, but that's what I'm going to do. You give me what I need to make it work, make it powerful, and it can do what we both want. I'll protect you from anyone ever knowing, if you like.

You may not think so, but I'm pretty good at what I do."

"I know you are. That was never my concern. It's always been about you putting yourself at risk. Your father doesn't want you involved in any of this, and I tried to stop you because I knew that. But you're in it anyway, so you need help and protection. You still need to discuss these things with your dad, though. He's not going to like it, but to really make this work, we need him involved."

"Okay, but—what is it we're trying to do?"

"Trying to make the world a better place."

Louongo entered, a burst of energy. He was short; sort of a smarmy leprechaun energized by some vital, if suspicious, inner force. He looked at Albright and Tommy.

"Well, sonofabitch. You just have to be Tommy Jacks. Has anyone ever said you look just like your old man? What a great sonofabitch he is. You know, if he would've let me defend him, he'd have never gone to jail. I don't give a good goddamn about Gilmore—I'd have found a judge to bribe, and this whole mess would've gone away. You know what your dad told me? I couldn't believe it, but he said he wouldn't bribe a judge. *Can you believe that?* How would these poor judges survive without bribes? It's like a community service. But, oh no, not Jacks— he's got ethics. I asked him right there, how could he have ethics and have anything to do with me? He just laughed and said, yeah, I got him on that one. I mean, my god, someone with my talents, and your father just ignores me."

Tommy didn't say a word.

9

NOSY WORK

Albright's companions showed up to whisk him away—where and why, he didn't say. He seemed more reticent around Louongo, only advising Tommy to spice up the column with legislative gossip, adding that when he wrote "My View," he'd always included the latest dope on romance, pregnancy, and weddings, especially if it embarrassed the powerful. He pulled Tommy aside before he left.

"I'll see you later today. Or rather, come by Denny's in the morning. Don't listen to Louongo. He's full of crap, and if you talk to him too much, it starts to rub off on you." He left.

Tommy ignored Albright's advice. "What did you do for my dad?" he asked Louongo.

Louongo changed the subject. "You know, those two companions of Albright's seem a little light in the loafers, if you know what I mean?"

"I guess it's none of my business."

"*Everything's* my business, and I think it's damn weird. Your dad was Albright's pal. I sure as hell wasn't—we don't get along at all." He returned to his chosen subject. "He calls 'em bodyguards—you think maybe that's some kind of joke? Sure wouldn't be back in Jersey, I'll tell you that. That Albright's a wise-ass. Thinks he knows everything—well, maybe so in New

York, but not in Jersey, I'll tell you that. I don't give a damn if they carry guns or not—no way can they be bodyguards. That's just crazy."

"Why does he come here?"

"Albright? Legal advice."

"What kind?"

"Sorry, Tommy boy—attorney-client privilege. I always follow the rules." Wink.

"What about what you did for my father?"

"Oh, that. He'd call me his counselor sometimes, but mostly he was just kidding. I was what you'd call a 'forced volunteer.' Generally, that meant I worked for almost nothing. He said it had to be that way so I could stay invisible. Your dad was one smart S.O.B."

"I'm not sure I understand. Why would you volunteer?"

Louongo leaned back. "Your dad helped me out big-time, once. I got crossways with some asshole state senator from Roger Mills County. That bastard was about to have me lynched, or at the very least have my license revoked, all because I did the best damn job I could do to get a guy released from the county jail—and what does the guy do but disappear. Well, hell, it wasn't my fault he ran. Turned out he'd been arrested for finagling with the teenage daughter of a senator *who went nuts.* Had the state police pick me up right here in the city and hauled my ass all the way out to Cheyenne. I'm not kiddin', I thought I was a goner. Threw me in jail with some of the evilest people on this planet. I was lucky to survive the night. They messed me up pretty damn bad. Your dad was in town visiting some of the moron Democrats who happened to be elected officials out there when he heard about me. He knew the senator. Told him he'd probably committed a crime, throwing me in jail like that, but if he'd let your dad handle it, maybe he could get it worked out where the dumbass wouldn't face charges. Long story short, he got me released. I agreed to not press charges, and the senator agreed to leave me alone on the condition I never stepped foot in Roger Mills County again—*not* exactly a hardship. I wanted out of there so bad. I could've fought it, but there was always some chance he'd send his thugs after me. I got the hell out of Dodge."

He still hadn't really answered the question, though. Tommy asked again, "So, what did you do as a 'forced volunteer'?"

"Well, legal stuff, so I think that's also privileged information. You ought to ask your dad. He can tell you."

Tommy pulled out the big question; the one he had to ask. "Is it true you were with Walters the night he was murdered?"

"You're kind of a nosy guy, aren't you?"

"Yeah, a little. The owner of Risso's told me you were in the booth with Walters. Marsh, the sportswriter at the *Sun,* was there, too—he came over to talk to me. You were there. Do you know what happened to Walters that night?"

"No. And if I did, Tommy Reporter, I wouldn't tell you." The tone in the room changed. Louongo seemed to turn dangerous.

"I don't understand. Why wouldn't you want me to find out the truth?"

Louongo sighed, sounding impatient. "I liked your father. He was a good guy who always treated me well. You and that Albright guy are snoopy reporters, always trying to screw somebody. So I don't tell you anything."

"Come on, Louongo. My dad helped you. All I'm asking is that you tell me what happened that night when you were with

Walters."

"Look," Louongo seemed to soften, if only a bit. "Maybe you're okay, I don't know. But nothing happened that night that I know anything about. I talked to him about some legal stuff—he was trying to get free advice, so I wasn't about to tell him much he could use. Told him to come see me in my office, bring money for a retainer, and then we'd talk. He got nasty with me, and I went home. End of story. I know nothing about the murder. Now, I've got work to do. So, please—show yourself out."

No way did Tommy believe that story. Louongo had been at Risso's that night for a reason. It might not have been because of Walters, but he wasn't attending a causal gathering with quiet drinks, either. He decided to go to the capitol and get nosy.

After an irritating hour of checking up on the latest in the war between the teachers' union and state government, and another of suffering the Baptist-influenced madness of a whole committee of senators' intent on letting Oklahomans carry guns wherever and however they liked, he went to Evans's office. He told the nice secretary he'd gotten news about Judy and that she was fine, which she already knew because Judy had called her to explain and apologize for giving the office a scare. Tommy resisted an impulse to leave, and was rewarded by learning her name—Gail Collins—and leads on two upcoming shotgun weddings, both linked to childbirths of suspicious heredity, with dirt on a divorce as a bonus. She also mentioned her busy week with a bill the senator was working on to establish a new method of allocating highway funds, over which the whole legislature was up in arms. It would send more money to cities and less to rural areas, so she predicted it would be the most contentious bill of the session. Just as he'd learned at OU, the most valuable sources were almost never the leaders, but rather the people who worked for them.

He went to the press room to type up a column based on these revelations, called it in, and headed home. He stopped by Risso's. A pizza to go sounded comforting.

"Evening, Larry. Looks like business is good tonight."

"Well, hello, Tommy. Yep, we're busy. And that always makes me happy." Lopez was smiling like he'd been doing it all day.

Tommy went to the bar for a drink while he waited. He spotted Bart, who looked out of place.

"Hey, Bart."

"Hey, Tommy. Let me buy you a drink." He seemed a little too happy. Tommy suspected he'd been there a while.

"I wouldn't have guessed I'd find you in a place like this."

"I'm old enough."

"I just meant you don't seem the type. Although, here I am, and I'm not the type either."

"Well, I had a bad day. Besides, I used to work for Larry as a bus boy. He's still a friend."

"Sorry about your day. Hope it's nothing serious."

"Just one of our great leaders treating people like crap. Happens all the time. He's the asshole, and I'm the one who gets sent home." With the Senate idle that day, Bart was sent to the House side. He didn't care for that because he didn't know the representatives as well, so it made him uneasy. His was assigned to a conference room where a meeting was to take place, discussing, of all things, the highway money bill Tommy had just written a column about.

He'd nodded to each representative who entered, grateful that he knew at least some of them. But once the meeting started, he heard yelling inside, even through the big doors. It meant nothing to him, so he didn't pay much attention until some representatives came stalking out, leaving a door open. He heard one representative call another a "bag of shit," heatedly adding that anyone who thought the bill would pass was completely out of step with the rest of the state and that the House, being dominated by rural members, would stop this nonsense in its tracks. He finished his tirade with a remark about "big-city Nazis," but not before warning another stunned representative that he should be careful should he ever find himself in Perkins, where they shot criminals like him. Bart heard chairs knocked around, more shouts, and suddenly the representative who he believed was doing all the talking burst through the door.

He saw Bart standing there, and asked him what the hell he was doing. Without waiting for an answer, and at an unnecessarily high volume, he accused Bart of being a spy.

By this time several other official types had come running up, all of whom outranked Bart. They immediately sided with the representative, telling Bart he shouldn't have been listening at the door, and ordering him to report to the capitol police office.

His boss was far more understanding, but thought it best if he left for the day. He assured Bart that everything would settle down by the following Monday.

"So, I left. They made me feel like I'd done something wrong, but I didn't. I was just doing my job. If that guy hadn't been yelling at the top of his lungs, I wouldn't have heard a thing.

But, no—I'm accused of being a spy. For who? I don't even know what I was supposed to be spying on. I would've liked to punch that little jerk from Perkins right in his fat nose."

More dirt. Tommy was starting to feel like a real reporter. He made a mental note to find out more about this highway bill. "I'm sure your boss is right. This'll all be forgotten by Monday."

"Yeah, I hope so. That job's all I have. Not sure what would happen to me if I lost it."

Tommy felt a twinge of sadness and connection. He bought another round, and told Bart if he needed a ride home, he was available. As it turned out, Lopez had already offered because they lived in the same neighborhood. Tommy collected his pizza and headed home, where he jotted down pages of notes. It was becoming a habit: *always make notes for future reference.*

It was six a.m. Saturday, and business at Denny's was slow. Plus, no Albright. Tommy sat at the counter with a coffee. Just as he was about to give up, Albright walked in, his arms full of newspapers. He headed for one of the back booths and slid in, safe at home away from home. He moved with an arrogance Tommy wasn't sure he was aware of, ignoring the world around him while he dealt with vital matters. Tommy still had very mixed feelings about him. "Good morning, Taylor."

"Well, Tommy. You're up bright and early. Have a seat and tell me what you know." He seemed in a good mood.

"Not sure. I was a lot smarter a couple months ago before I left school. Now it's like I get dumber every day."

Albright laughed, an honest and friendly laugh. "Welcome

to my world."

An uncomfortable camaraderie seemed to be developing between them. No one would call it friendship yet—more like a cordial, mutual need. They turned to the papers and their own thoughts over breakfast.

"Where can I get a copy of *The Banner?*

"Going to steal my stuff, are you?"

"Might, if it's any good."

Smiles exchanged.

"Everyone needs inspiration. I put out maybe a couple hundred copies at a time depending on how my printer benefactor is feeling. That's usually a couple of times a month. No set schedule. I think I have some old ones. I'll toss a few in my bag just for you. I'm about halfway done with the latest, but that could be another day or two. Maybe weeks."

Tommy changed the subject. "Louongo said you saw him for legal advice. What's that mean?"

"Louongo," Albright sighed. "Louongo is an old gossip who lies from the time he wakes up in the morning until he goes to bed at night."

"Is that an answer?"

"Yes," he said, his tone stern. "I'm not going to tell you why I occasionally visit with my attorney. It doesn't seem to be any of your business."

"What do you know about Bud Evans's highway bill?"

"My god, it's the third degree right here in Denny's. Why do you want to know?"

Tommy related some of what Bart told him.

"That might be something you want to dig into. That rep from Perkins is Mitch Douglas. He's a little banty rooster who's hated by everyone except his beholden up in Payne County, by Stillwater. It's been estimated," he said, "that Mitch may have half the permanent residents of said county on some kind of government payroll. That bill would be a big deal to him and his brother who owns a highway construction company right there in Perkins. Some people think there's enough money going to Payne County for highway construction to build a four-lane freeway from Stillwater to Tulsa *every year.* I'm sure Bud knows that and wants it to stop. But rather than attack Mitch directly, he's going to change the way money is allocated. That's going to be a monumental fight. This is where careers in journalism are made. Graft and corruption in politics is not exactly new, but it's always something people want to read."

Something inside Tommy was heating up.

10
SUNDAY DRIVE

A front-page editorial in Sunday's *Oklahoma Sun* strongly opposed the highway funding bill and the manner in which it was being steamrolled through the legislative process, claiming its support came from "greedy big-city construction companies." Evans was named as sponsor of the "misguided legislation." The editorial asked his constituents to call him to stop the bill for the good of the state.

Many government observers scratched their heads, puzzled over why the *Sun,* particularly Gilmore, would care. There had to be some connection that involved money. No one suspected Gilmore's reason would be what the *Sun* editorial implied, being support for the interests of the farmers and ranchers of rural Oklahoma, whom the editorial held up as the vital economic and moral backbone of the state and the country.

The Sunday *OK Journal* made no mention of the highway bill. Tommy's column, his second under the "My View" banner, discussed the upcoming presidential race from the state politicians' rather reactionary perspective, partly because that was a topic of the day, but mostly because it was the only topic he was ready to go to print with. Anderson wasn't pleased. It looked like a major breaking story was being ignored by his paper while the *Sun* was on a righteous crusade about it. He called the managing editor. After the ME got an earful, he in turn called Fred Simpson. After Simpson got his earful, he called his assistant city editor.

"Listen, June, I just had my butt chewed by the ME. What do we know about the highway bill?"

"I saw the editorial. Figured there'd be some blowback. I'm not sure what we have on it. The only one who's even mentioned it is Tommy. He called and updated me on things he's working on, and that was one of them. He mentioned some representative from Payne County who apparently threw a fit over it, even threatened some of our city reps. I'll get hold of him and find out what he knows."

Meanwhile, Tommy had decided to take a drive on his day off rather than sit around his apartment feeling alone. It was a beautiful day to enjoy the peculiar freedom of being on his own, headed nowhere. That nowhere was Perkins.

He took the two-lane back-roads route through the small town of Jones where kids played outside rundown houses, some stopping to watch him drive past. Theirs was a life he didn't understand—not bad, just unknown. They were small-town people who probably worked in low-paid government jobs or the little stores in town. Many lived on farms, growing crops or raising chickens or something, in a world bound up in its own memories, uninterested in the evil ways of city people.

He passed miles of small farms, and often spotted a house or a barn, but on the bigger farms he couldn't see the houses from the road. He saw a sign telling him he was entering Perkins, home to "Pistol Pete." He crossed a river into a downtown that looked like places he'd seen in old movies. Its main street was lined with little businesses. He saw a couple of churches and blocks of houses stretching away. Its population had to be small, probably fewer than a thousand, even counting the farms immediately around. He pulled in front of a drugstore. Its window advertised fountain service inside.

Walking into Johnson's Drug was like entering a time machine. It wasn't a replica of a turn-of-the-century drug store—it *was* one. Tommy sat at the counter, greeted by an eager teenage boy wearing a white apron and a paper cap. He thought they actually called them soda jerk hats, but in case that might be offensive, didn't ask.

He ordered a milkshake and was surprised by how richly satisfying it was. "Must be great to live in a small town."

The fountain boy was busy cleaning his equipment, no longer seeming interested in his customer. "Yeah. I guess."

"What kind of jobs are there around here?"

"Farm work, oil field, government." He sounded annoyed.

"If I was going to move up here, who would I see about a government job?"

"Dunno. Somebody in government, I guess."

Well, that made sense, even if it was perhaps intentionally unhelpful. Time to move on. He meandered out, and noticed racks of papers for the *Sun,* the *Journal,* and the Perkins *Gazette,* a free weekly. He grabbed a *Gazette* to read later.

He took a quick walking tour of town to find nothing open on a Sunday afternoon except Johnson's Drug—and therefore, no one to talk to. He drove on toward Stillwater. Oil rigs and pumps dominated the scenery. Numerous side roads seemed only to go into the oilfields. He turned off on one and drove up to a drilling operation. He stepped out to get a better look. The crew on the rig was busy and mostly ignored him. The equipment was old and filthy, and most of the men looked young and filthy. Drilling for oil was dirty work.

One of them, an older man, walked toward Tommy. "You want something, buddy?" It wasn't an especially friendly greeting.

"Just driving by and thought I'd watch a while."

"Well, this is private property. You should leave now." Not a polite request.

Tommy gave the man a little wave. While he turned the car around, he watched the roustabout, who watched him back.

Entering Stillwater felt familiar—a small town with a big university, a lot like Norman. Among its little stores and government offices were businesses geared toward college students—restaurants, bars, small apartment buildings, bookstores, and more bars. Stillwater wasn't Perkins.

On one side of the road stood the campus, an amazing number of grand buildings set in vast spreads of trimmed grass and tended flower beds. They looked out of place. In what most people would describe as a poor, somewhat backward part of the United States of America, rose this statement to the value of higher education for all—or at least for anyone who could afford the tuition. Tommy suspected the financial commitment might be more about the structures, the physical presence of the institution, and civic pride than about dedication to the abstract ideal of quality education.

Sensing a need for nourishment beyond a milkshake, he noticed Smokin' Joe's had more cars in its lot than anyplace else, and decided barbecue sounded perfect. It smelled even better. The crowd looked mostly like visiting parents with their college sons and daughters. It was loud and smoky, a place for

Oklahoma comfort food on a beautiful Sunday afternoon. He enjoyed the atmosphere and the brisket.

To work it off, he walked across the street and onto campus. It felt like home. The OU campus in Norman was where he'd been his happiest. There was something safe and comforting about the familiar dynamic of young people learning and interacting, imperfect as it might be. It gave him the feeling there was a better world being planned and built before his eyes. The potential of the future was a powerful stimulant.

He found the campus bookstore—not much activity there. He picked up a copy of the school paper, feeling an almost overwhelming nostalgia. Still, his most pressing need was for a late afternoon nap. He got back on the road home.

By the time he reached his apartment, the nap idea was morphing into something more like an early bedtime. He hadn't done all that much, but was definitely tired. His phone rang, unusual for a Sunday.

"Hello."

"Tommy, where've you been? I've been calling you all day." He didn't recognize the female voice at first, but the list of possibilities wasn't long.

"June? Is there something wrong?"

"Yes and no. Did you see the editorial in today's *Sun?*"

"Nope, kind of took the day off and drove up to Stillwater. What was it about?"

"The highway bill. The *Sun*'s very opposed to it. The brass is upset because we had nothing on it. I told Fred that you were working on it. So anyway, Vince Young, one of our top reporters, was assigned to have something ready for Monday's early edition. He'd like to talk to you."

"Not sure I can tell him much—at least, not factually. I had a lead on Representative Douglas out of Perkins kind of going nuts about it in a meeting, but most of what I have is just speculation. Nothing you could print."

"Just give him a call. Let him decide if it's news or not. Okay?"

No, it wasn't okay. By a long shot, it wasn't okay. Tommy didn't know what he had, if anything, but if he shared it with this Young guy and he used it in a piece, Tommy was screwed. "Okay. But you do know what you're asking, right?"

"I know. This is your story, and to have you divulge your information to another reporter before it's ready can't feel right. But the brass wants something in the paper about this bill tomorrow, and Vince needs a hand. Maybe another time, he can help you. You decide what you can do, whether you give him a call or not." She sounded very much like management.

"What's his number?" Tommy decided he'd take one for the team. Still, he sure wasn't going to give Young everything he had. He was developing the distinct impression that the news business was mostly about everyone looking out for themselves.

First thing Monday, he stopped at a 7-Eleven for a donut, coffee, and a copy of the *Journal*. Young was a good reporter. His story laid out the facts, as far as they were known, and avoided the juicier stuff Tommy shared, especially the part based on a source he'd warned was fairly unreliable. Young did mention the exchange between Mitch Douglas and a security guard because he had corroboration from capitol security. He also had a quote from Douglas. "The economy of Oklahoma is dependent on agriculture and oil and gas, and those industries rely on good roads throughout the state. If some of the city politicians think they can rob rural Oklahomans of their right to good roads just to score political points, they'll soon find out that it doesn't work that way." Pretty strong statement to give to a newspaper, but it was becoming increasingly apparent Douglas was a loose cannon. When he felt attacked, he'd counterattack twice as hard.

Elsewhere in the paper, he found a short, uncredited piece in the city section, likely by Chuck the police reporter.

"Two men, Max Jones and Nathan Oliver, both legal residents of New York, were arrested on misdemeanor assault charges brought by Rod Baker, a security officer for the *Oklahoma Sun*. No other details were provided by Oklahoma City police. Their attorney, Joe Louongo, a well-known local criminal lawyer, issued a statement saying, 'The police have once again arrested the wrong people on the false testimony of an ex-cop.' Louongo said he expected his clients to be released early Monday, and they would pursue a lawsuit against the police department for false arrest."

Tommy didn't recognize the names, but it was clear who they were—Albright's bodyguards. Time for a trip to Denny's.

PART II
THE CAMPAIGN

1962. The cold war heats up as the Cuban missile crises takes the world to the brink of conflict. The Vietnam war proceeds with no end in sight, although America isn't involved—yet. Racial tensions continue to be front page news, with riots erupting on the University of Mississippi campus following James Meredith's attempt to enroll. James Bond's *Dr. No* is an instant success. Marilyn Monroe is found dead at her home in Los Angeles; her death is ruled a suicide.

11

VISIONS OF GRANDEUR

"Today, I announce my candidacy for governor of the state of Oklahoma. Some of you may know me, and if you don't, then we have a handout with some biographical information. In many ways, my approach to government is simple. I'm a Democrat who believes in a small, responsive government that conducts itself in the best interests of the people. I believe that public schools are the foundation of our future. I believe in a system of higher education open to as many people as possible. I believe in fair and unbiased laws and the enforcement of those laws based on facts, not on the agenda of the powerful. I believe in good roads. I believe in a tax system that only takes what's needed and asks the more fortunate to pay a little more. I believe that, if at all possible, everyone who wants a job should be able to find one and earn a living wage. And I believe in open government. My goal is to make Oklahoma a great place to work, and to live, and to bring up a family. While we all may have different backgrounds, faiths, and goals, I think we can find common ground, and in doing that we can make the lives of our citizens better, more productive, and happier. Thank you. Thank you very much."

Bill Anderson's official campaign kickoff on the capitol steps was attended by about twenty of his supporters, a few members of his new staff, and a handful of reporters. It seemed like an inauspicious beginning for a difficult journey. Anderson believed everything he said. It would have been easier if he'd just been another political bullshitter.

"Sounds like he believes in a government we could never have. What kind of chance do you give him?" The *Sun's* top political reporter tossed that question to a local television reporter named Tracy Clark.

"How would I know? You're the brains around here. I just show up, look good, and smile." Tracy had an edge about her. It suggested she knew more than she'd share.

"Well, you handle that lookin' good part just great." Walters grinned, likely because he meant it. "Think I'll go ask Anderson's campaign manager. Bound to be quotes I can use out of that. Can you imagine hiring some knucklehead from back East to run a campaign in Oklahoma? How is some wise-ass New Yorker going to do any good out here in the sticks?"

"Be nice, Tony. I think this Anderson guy is a real person. Not one of your usual politicians."

"I'm always nice, sweetheart."

She rolled her eyes and walked away. He watched, long enough, before turning away to attend to business.

"Going to be kind of tough running a campaign in a state you know nothin' about, won't it?"

"Might be. I'm Taylor Albright, and you are—?"

"Tony Walters. *Oklahoma Sun.*"

"Mister Walters." Albright nodded. "You a real journalist, or do you just write what Gilmore tells you?"

Walters smiled, surprised by how Albright handled himself, New Yorker or not. "I write in a town with only one newspaper.

Most of it, I think, is in the ballpark of 'fair.' But I gotta keep my job. And if I'm ordered, then I'll go after your Mister Anderson. I wouldn't like it, but I'd do it."

"I guess we'll have to live with that. On occasion, just try sneaking in a little truth."

"You never know when that might happen. Back to my question. What could possibly motivate this man to take on such a lost cause?"

"He's my friend, and I believe with everything in me that he's the best man for the job." Albright looked Walters in the eye to make sure the reporter understood he was serious.

"Well, it's still a lost cause, even if it's a noble one. Wish you luck." They shook hands, looked at each other a little longer than necessary, and Walters walked away.

Albright had second-guessed his decision to be his friend's campaign manager from the moment he agreed. He didn't belong in Oklahoma, and knew little about it, surely not enough to run a statewide political race. Only Bill's persuasion had brought him in. So here he was in the middle of nowhere, ready to conduct an honest, no-mud-slinging campaign against Rick Butler, the Republican candidate backed by the largest newspaper in the state and almost everyone else with the power to control politics. Even the current governor, who was term-limited, quietly supported Butler—and he was a Democrat.

At Albright's disposal was the chairman of the Democratic Party, who seemed to know everyone if only because of the amazing amount of time he spent in bars. Raymond Jacks was likeable, for sure. Whether he was competent was an open question.

At least Anderson had money. It wouldn't win the election

by itself, but would make it easier to run against such long odds. The people who'd support him would be loyal and honest, not money people like the ones who gravitated to Butler. For the most part, it would be a self-funded adventure. That made Albright admire his friend even more.

"Saw you talking to Walters from the *Sun*," Raymond Jacks walked up. "Don't let him fool you. He'll seem reasonable until he isn't. You handle him a lot like a rattlesnake. Don't give him a chance to bite." He smiled.

"Thanks, I'll keep that in mind. I reviewed the campaign strategy report you put together. I liked the emphasis on television and small-town newspapers. I also think we need a big push toward minorities in Tulsa and Oklahoma City. What do you think about the Tulsa paper? Could it give us an endorsement?"

Jacks shrugged. "It's possible. They've always been conservative, but they don't strictly follow one party or the other. They tend to focus on candidates. Definitely not a Gilmore tagalong; they make up their own minds. You'll want to get in front of their editorial board as soon as possible."

Albright found the candidate surrounded by followers and pulled him aside. "We'll have our first week's agenda meeting tomorrow morning. Let's meet up at campaign headquarters to go over it, say about nine?"

"Sure. Do we need Ray there?"

"No. I'll keep him posted. I have other ideas for him. We'll talk about it tomorrow."

Albright rented an apartment downtown because it seemed more urban there than elsewhere, and thus better suited to him—plus, it was on one of the main bus routes. Not driving had never been a concern in New York City, but it had already become an annoyance here where driving was the norm and buses were for the poor and unlicensed. It meant uneven service, dirty buses, and surly drivers. Albright adapted. He picked a spot on Classen Boulevard for the campaign headquarters because he could walk there from his apartment.

He used cabs when he had to, but his new hometown wasn't as densely inhabited as New York, so cab service wasn't always a sure thing. That called for a lot of patience. Unless the weather interfered, he walked the several blocks to the newsstand to get his papers, and took the bus to Denny's on Classen Boulevard for his favorite part of the day. The newsstand sold most of the morning papers and opened early.

He headed for the nearest bus stop, but Walters came up behind him.

"Hey, Albright. Need a lift?"

"Sure, thanks." God did work in mysterious ways. They headed out. "So," Albright asked, "how did you end up at the *Sun?*"

"Just lucky, I guess. I was working in Dallas for the *Morning News*. I was about the third guy on the totem pole on the politics beat. Good job, great paper. I learned a lot there. My editor was one of the best. At the time, I had a wife and two kids—upstanding and normal. One of the risks in this business, though, is that you cover these guys and get to know them, and before long you're going out drinking and raising hell with them. That helped my career with some good inside stories. Didn't help my home life, though. Spent lots of money we didn't have, came home late at night or early morning a little bit drunk. My wife left me. Took the kids and went to

Florida to live with her horrible parents. Marriage over. The alimony and child support payments started. My drinking got worse because I started doing it alone. My writing went to hell. My editor suggested it might be time to dry out—maybe even find another place to work, a 'fresh start,' he said. Long story short, I applied at the *Sun,* and they hired me, sight unseen. I showed up and right away started working long hours. Even cleaned up my act. For now, anyway."

"Why the *Sun?*"

"It was close by. It ain't the *News* when it comes to quality, but it felt comfortable. I knew some people there, so I made some calls, and right away I heard back that they were interested. Later I found out their turnover for political reporters was pretty high. I got in good with my new editor, wrote a lot of stories, stuck to the facts, and before long, I was in like Flynn. I don't deal much with Gilmore and, as they say, the rest is history."

"Why is it so important to Gilmore to have Butler win?"

"You'd make a decent reporter," Walters chuckled. "Nosy and irritating. I'm not going to tell you why. I don't want my fingerprints on anything you're doing. Anyway, you'll figure it out soon enough. Gilmore and his friends won't try to hide anything. It's part of their arrogance, which could make them vulnerable. Looks like your stop up ahead."

Just before he got out, Albright said, "I'd never divulge any information you happen to toss my way. I understand the fine line you'd be walking."

"That won't be a problem, because you won't get anything from me that I can't put in the paper. If Butler's way ahead of Anderson, this'll be a friendly match. If the race gets tight, it'll get ugly. And I mean ugly. If there are any skeletons in your buddy's closet, they'll come out. Be careful."

Albright watched Walters drive off. He liked him in kind of an odd, uncomfortable way. But he didn't trust him.

Albright had been up for hours, reading papers and planning the meeting, and was at campaign headquarters early to greet Bill Anderson. "I had an interesting chat yesterday with Tony Walters, political reporter for the *Sun*. He says if the race gets tight, it'll get nasty." He looked up. "Bill, is there anything in your past that could spring up and surprise us?"

"You mean like women, criminal activity, or buried treasure from my pirating days?"

Albright barely smiled. "Yeah, although I would have said mostly women."

"I think the most dangerous thing I ever did was to join the Dartmouth debate team with you," Anderson chuckled, before adding, with a sigh, "Taylor, I'm no saint. I've been drunk and enjoyed it, I smoked those awful cigars you used to pass out, and I have ogled many a woman in tight jeans. But I guess my faith and my commitment to my wife, even before we were married, kept me from going too far astray. So there is nothing in my past that would hurt me politically or sell too many newspapers."

Albright pursed his lips. "There won't be any ethical barriers to keep Gilmore's people from just plain lying. Bald-faced, flat-out lies. If we get close—if we look like we could win— they'll pull every dirty trick in the book."

Anderson nodded. "I expect that. We'll run a clean race,

and hopefully the people won't be fooled by anything they try. Ray Jacks gave me the same warning. It almost felt like he was sorry I was running, because he knew what it'd be like. But I can stand the heat. We'll fight back with the truth and keep talking about what we'll do for the people. I believe we can win, even against the odds."

Albright was proud to know a man like Bill Anderson, even if he was too idealistic to be in politics. They might not win, but they would go down doing their best. And if a few dirty tricks fell out of Ray Jacks's bag, so be it. Bill didn't have to know.

At the end of the day, Albright locked up the headquarters and headed for his apartment. The evening seemed nice, with a cool breeze, and he felt good about their plans. Maybe it would all work out some way, and not be a royal disaster.

A man walked up, a bit too quickly, into his path.

Albright hesitated. "Help you with something?"

"Yeah. Go back to New York."

Sounded like trouble. The man looked serious, and like he'd practiced getting into other people's spaces.

"I'll be on my way." Albright began to step around, and the man hit him square in the face. He'd never been hit like that—hard—on purpose. His back slammed hard into a tree. He slid to the ground.

The man bent close. "We don't want no foreigners messin' around. Just get on the bus and go back where you came from."

"Fuck you!" He could have said something else—he could have explained that he wasn't actually a foreigner, and if he decided to leave, he'd most likely fly—but Albright wasn't afraid, even if he should have been. The man seemed to sense that, and backed up.

Another voice came in. "Hey! What the hell's goin' on?" Jacks came running toward them with his hand in his coat pocket. "I just called the cops. You, stay put!"

Albright figured from New York experience that Jacks was faking like he had a gun. But the guy bought it. He ran to a car, made a U-turn, and sped off.

Jacks helped Albright up. "Welcome to Oklahoma, cowboy." He clearly thought he was funny. And actually, he was.

12
STRATEGY

Anderson had never told Albright what he did after he left school and returned to Ada. The subject had never come up. Once he'd decided Ivy League academic life wasn't for him and he went home, he was unsure what to do with himself. He had enjoyed some things about Dartmouth, and felt a strong sense of obligation to complete school on his generous scholarship. He'd wanted that scholarship more than anything, and felt badly after realizing he gravitated to things that were more hands-on than studying and academia. He had learned so much in a short time and met so many interesting people, but he never found his dream. He never felt like he belonged.

Back home, he took on the job of running his uncle's newspaper, the *Ada Weekly,* and found he loved it. Dealing with people, many of whom he'd known most of his life, was much more fulfilling for him than spending time alone, buried in textbooks. The work was boring and predictable, but just what he needed. It was a very small paper, so he was responsible for everything—on occasion, he even helped print it. He wrote all the stories, conducted all the interviews, and took all the photos. He felt connected to the world around him. If events had allowed, he might have stayed in that dead-end, comfortable job forever.

Because his uncle was battling cancer, he took over the position of running the *Weekly*. Then a company that owned several small-town papers made a bid to buy his uncle out. He didn't want to sell, but he needed the money. The new owners offered Anderson a job, but it wouldn't have been the same. He didn't want to be an employee.

His uncle gave him a small bonus off the sale money, and his parents staked him to a little cash they'd meant to give to him after he graduated. It felt like a fortune. This was his opportunity to make a future for himself.

One of the stories he'd written for the *Weekly* was about plans to build a huge Air Force base near Oklahoma City. The Defense Department wanted a central supply depot, although rumor was that it might be for bombers, or even have something to do with nuclear bombs. It sounded exciting, if not a little foreboding.

He could see a demand for affordable housing for returning veterans, which was a big deal everywhere, and nowhere more so than near a new monster base outside Oklahoma City—if it actually came to be. He'd developed a vision of the perfect place to live, a whole new community of middle-class families. *That* was what he was going to build.

But becoming a developer was different. He'd worked quite a few construction jobs, mainly with relatives in and around Ada, and he was good at it, but it wasn't the same experience. And the eventuality of an air base somewhere near Oklahoma City was a fact, but its exact location wasn't. Most speculation centered around the eastern reaches of the city, but there were other possible spots—one near Ada, ironically.

He spent months talking to people and considering options,

then he took his gamble. He had a cousin who'd built houses in the city for years and was a great homebuilder, but he was losing money. Anderson teamed up with him and a few other interested businessmen, developed a plan, and approached a bank. In part because of the amazing optimism of the time, the banker was sold on the idea. The loan had a lot of strings attached, and Anderson would have to invest most of his nest egg. But he was in business.

Then there was the matter of where the base would be built. He gambled on a spot just to the south and east of Oklahoma City, assuming it would need a lot of undeveloped land that was reachable by car. He bought up parcels through straight-out purchases or options. Soon he had control over a huge territory. He was in deep. If the Air Force picked a different site, he would lose everything with no way to pay it back. That caused many a sleepless night.

When the announcement finally came, he learned his gamble had paid off—big. The Air Force put it right in his lap.

His cousin turned out to know a lot, not just about home-building, but also about the process of development. That meant business plans that helped Bill borrow more and begin developing neighborhoods because the demand was immediate and overwhelming. Quicker than he could have imagined, he was a success.

That would turn out to be a good thing some years later when he spent like a drunken sailor on a campaign for governor he wasn't even sure he wanted to win. His strategy was to meet with small-town officials, and especially local newspapers, which played to his strengths. He knew these people; he was one of them. He knew their problems, their worries, and their dreams, and he knew his opponent's political objectives connected with none of them. Most Oklahomans were focused on what directly affected them—how can you make my life better?

"This race is not about my priorities, but yours. Tell me what is important to you. I will listen," he told a small but attentive crowd in Tecumseh. "What I think matters in our state are our schools, our road system, and a fair and honest legal system. Rural Oklahoma in particular is impacted by our abundant oil and gas. I'm a supporter of oil and gas, but I don't believe the rules should be written by and for the industry. For too long we've allowed the oil and gas industry to dictate terms to farmers and ranchers, with little input on how those rules impact your lives—that needs to stop."

As is often the case with such speeches, it raised soft applause. Rural people tended not to be very demonstrative. But many would come up to him, shake his hand, and promise to support him.

They had six stops scheduled for the day, two of them interviews with local newspaper editors. Albright seemed ill at ease and grumpy, while Anderson was in his element. Trying to build momentum for the campaign with rural voters, then transferring that to major population centers certainly wasn't a strategy used by most state candidates. But it seemed right to launch the campaign in the friendlier atmosphere of small rural towns.

"I like what we're doing here," Albright told him. "It'll build some momentum, and we'll get endorsements from the local papers that we can use in advertising. Plus, in case you haven't noticed, you're getting better at giving speeches. This can go on for another few weeks, but then we have to hit the two major cities—hard. I know we can't expect support from the *Sun,* but we need the Tulsa paper's endorsement. With that, I think we have a fifty-fifty chance. Without it, we'll have to rely on television to get our message out, and that'll be expensive."

Anderson grinned. "I agree, although I'm probably more optimistic."

"I know. I'm grumpy. I've heard that from the staff. Maybe I need to stay at headquarters."

Anderson could tell Albright was pouting and laughed. "Maybe so. Shouldn't take the big-city guy out into the real world without some kind of preparation. Fine. How about you go to Tulsa and do some interviews, maybe meet with the paper? You can lay some groundwork."

Albright looked like he'd been offered an ice-cream cone on a hot day. He tried to suppress a smile. "I think that's smart. I'm not much use to you out here—this is your world."

Anderson figured Albright for one of the smartest people he'd ever met. His knowledge on almost any subject was legendary. At Dartmouth he'd been considered a potential future leader of the country—a politician, maybe an adviser to the president. Everyone had seen great things for Taylor, but so far they hadn't panned out. Anderson suspected it was his abrasive personality. He cussed at the wrong times and in front of the wrong people. And diplomacy was not his strength by a long shot. But there was no one he would rather have by his side.

"You need to talk to Ray, too," he told Albright. "At the last newspaper, the editor pulled me aside and said he was spreading rumors about Gilmore's son—some kind of sex scandal. He needs to understand I want a clean campaign. Any mud-slinging will only come back to hurt us."

Albright nodded. "I'll take care of it. There's some kind of feud going on between Gilmore and Jacks, and it doesn't have anything to do with us. But I'll tell him he needs to pull in his horns until this is over."

Anderson didn't want a fight with the state party. He knew nasty gossip went on all the time, but he wanted a campaign about the issues. Ray Jacks had done some good work for the state's Democrats, but he also represented everything Anderson thought was wrong with politics and politicians. "I want to be clear. Tell Jacks that if I find out he's engaged in dirty tricks or mud-slinging on my behalf, there'll be hell to pay. He may not think I'll go after him, but he's wrong. Make sure he gets it."

13
DIRTY TRICKS

"Sonofabitch!"

Ray Jacks threw a book across the room. He fumed, looking for something else to throw. He'd just talked to Taylor Albright, who'd made it clear what Anderson said: if Ray broke the rule, his life would be hell. Jacks had gone through this—cajoling some know-nothing into running for councilman or some other office, only to find that two months later, the know-nothing is telling him how to run a campaign *and the Democratic Party*. And of course, hearing the message from Albright, in his highfalutin' tone, only made things worse.

He needed a drink. Risso's was his unofficial auxiliary office. All right, he'd done some things, and he knew they could come back to bite him. But they had nothing to do with Mister High and Mighty Anderson. They were personal. And he didn't plan to stop. At Risso's, he thought about Tommy, who was staying the night with a friend after a pool party. So no need to worry there. He knew he was a lousy father, so preoccupied with his own nonsense he couldn't recall ever going to any of Tommy's school activities or sports events. He rationalized it by telling himself he'd never wanted kids anyway. Of course, the moment he thought that, he felt guilty. Self-medication seemed like the only answer.

After more than a few rounds he was feeling mellow, exchanging opinions with the bartender about national politics.

"Jacks, do you live in this place?" The question from Tony Walters, who'd just come to sit next to him, sounded judgmental—and way too loud.

"Screw you."

"You know, I'm the one getting screwed, all right? I'm having a fine morning, and guess what—Robbie Gilmore wants to see me. I've managed to see that man maybe twice in my life, and it's never been good news. So guess what he wants. He wants to know if I know what you're up to. Before I could tell him you're the biggest asshole on the planet, he goes on and tells me you're spreading rumors about him. I don't know, Jacks, but my guess is you've crossed a line. I'd be worried if I was you."

"Are they paying you to deliver this message?"

"Nope. This one's from me, on the house. You know I'm no fan of Gilmore's, but if you think you can make up shit about Robbie and use it in the campaign to help Anderson, you've opened the biggest can of worms ever. And you know I don't like you, but I don't hate you either. If you've got any sense, you'll stop whatever it is you're doing."

"From one asshole to another, let me buy you a drink."

Walters hesitated. This was dangerous ground. He knew Risso's was more or less safe, but having drinks with the enemy was risky behavior. "Sure, why the hell not?"

"None of it has anything to do with Anderson. I know you don't care, but Anderson really is who he seems to be. This is just me poking the bear. The Gilmores have caused me all kinds of grief—did you see that story they had on their TV station about how I'd screwed up the Senate race? It was ugly, and mostly lies—why the hell did they have to run that?"

"Don't act all innocent. The Gilmores don't like you or your party. Big shock—lots of people feel that way. So they own a TV station that runs something that makes you look bad. For all you know, they had nothing to do with it personally. Maybe the station did it because, in fact, you *did* screw up."

Jacks downed his drink and ordered another. Walters was right. He'd overreached, and it could cause a lot of grief for him and Anderson. He needed to back off. He wasn't going to tell Walters what really made him angry. He'd deal with that after the election. "You're right. I screwed up. Why don't you report back to your boss that you talked to me, and I got the message? Anyway, it was just bar talk. Never intended to get out into the open."

"Just a piece of advice—you live on the edge long enough, eventually you'll fall off. When that happens, you won't be the only one hurt." Walters threw some bills on the bar and left.

Ray thought about ordering a pizza for Tommy and going home, then remembered he wasn't there. He ordered another drink and stared at himself in the mirror. He knew he was way off base with all that crap about Gilmore's son. He'd been out with some people, having a few too many, and suddenly this idea pops into his head: beat Gilmore down with gossip. Brilliant thought—if you can't beat 'em, out-bullshit 'em. He'd heard stories about Robbie's extramarital affairs for years, but they were so out of character for the guy that they never broke into the open—hardly anyone with political clout would believe them. Nevertheless, he'd started telling people in the bar he had the goods on Robbie and his affairs and that, if there were only a paper in the city that would print the truth, all of it would become known. At the time, he thought it was pretty clever. Now he just felt stupid. How could he keep doing this stuff?

The bartender came up. "Hey, Ray. Some guy over there in that back booth says he'd like to buy you a drink and have a chat."

Ray glanced over. He couldn't make out the guy's face. "Tell him, 'Thanks, but no, thanks.' Not in the mood to chat." The bartender shrugged.

The guy came up to the bar, much to Ray's annoyance. "Mister Jacks, I'm Allen Clark. I used to be the general manager at KVY. I have some information you might like to know. I hear you're not in the mood to chat, but you might want to reconsider." Clark turned and headed back to his booth.

KVY was the biggest television station in Oklahoma City, and it was owned by Gilmore. In fact, it was the very station that had run the story about Ray's alleged incompetence. That alone was enough to intrigue him, but he'd also heard Clark's firing was ugly, and no one else in the market would hire him afterward. Plus, his very beautiful daughter still worked at KVY as a reporter. He made his way to the man's booth, if unsteadily.

"Didn't mean to be rude. What information are you talking about?"

"I've heard some very unflattering things about you, Ray," Clark said. "The Gilmores seem to think you're the devil himself."

"Look, if you just want to call me names, I'll head back to the bar." Ray started to slide out.

"Sorry. Didn't mean it to sound like all that came from me. I have no idea if you're a bad guy or a good guy. I wouldn't know. I was just saying I know the Gilmores hate you. So that makes you my friend."

"So you hate the Gilmores, too. Is that because they fired you?"

"Yeah, I hate 'em. I didn't used to drink, and now I do. I sit in a dark bar, alone in the middle of the day, getting drunk. Then I look up and see Walters talking to you. It seemed strange, Walters being a *Sun* reporter, but I didn't care. I wasn't even listening, but I heard what you said about that story and how it was lies. It just seemed too coincidental. Then Walters got up and left, and I could tell you guys weren't pals. For some reason, I thought I should tell you the truth about that story."

"You had something to do with that story?"

"Yep. I was the one who forced the reporter to put it together—because of Robbie Gilmore."

"No shit! Maybe I ought to punch you in your smug face. What the hell are you bothering me for, anyway? I've had one too many people piss on me today, buddy!" Ray was drunk and angry. Clark was not as drunk, and seemed to realize he may have miscalculated the whole matter.

Larry Lopez and the bartender came over. "Ray, you've had too much," Lopez said. "Time to go home and sleep it off. I called a cab, and I want you out of here—now. Go home!" The bartender grabbed Ray and helped him out of the booth, mostly by lifting him.

Ray let himself be taken home. He went straight to bed. The best end possible for a bad day.

He woke up the next morning with a massive headache. He knew there was something he was supposed to remember, but it wouldn't come. After a lot of water, aspirin, and coffee, he went back to bed. If there was anything he had to do that day, he was going to be late for it.

There was a ringing. He knew it wasn't the phone because he'd unplugged the contraption. So it had to be the doorbell. And it wouldn't stop. He wasn't sure he cared until he thought of Tommy. Maybe he'd forgotten his key. He dragged himself out of bed. On his doorstep stood Carl Jackson, his right-hand man.

"Carl, what the hell are you doing here?"

"I guess your phone's not working. There've been some issues at work I thought you should know about. My god, Ray, you look terrible."

"However bad I look; I feel ten times worse. What's going on that's such an emergency?"

"Albright wants us to put out some press releases. He's mad because he couldn't get hold of you, and he pushed real hard to have them ready for his review by noon today. He told me what they should say and where he wanted them sent. I couldn't get hold of you, so I called my daughter and asked her to put them together. But I didn't want to send them out or give them to Albright without your approval."

"Okay. You did the right thing. How is Judy?"

"She's fine. Finished school now, with a degree in political science. She got a job in Bud Evans's office. She's good at writing—anyone's better than me." He handed Ray drafts of two press releases with a sigh. "One of them's about you."

Ray read that one.

FOR IMMEDIATE RELEASE

Effective immediately the Bill Anderson for Governor campaign has relieved Raymond Jacks, Chairman of the Oklahoma Democratic Party, of all official duties related to representing and promoting the campaign. Bill Anderson appreciates the great contributions Jacks has made, and said he will always consider him a leader of the Democratic Party. However, due to certain matters that have come to public attention, Jacks has been instructed to cease representing the Bill Anderson for Governor campaign. For more information or clarification, please contact the campaign manager, Taylor Albright.

"You're right," Jacks agreed, "Judy's a good writer. Tell her thanks for me. Release 'em—do what Albright says." He walked off in search of more aspirin. He didn't read the other release.

14

EVERY DAY IS MUCH THE SAME

Neither candidate for governor drew a primary opponent. No surprise there—with the power of the *Sun* behind him, Butler was considered a shoo-in, and no Republican wanted to antagonize Gilmore and lose. The *Sun* characterized Anderson as a certain loser, soon to be forgotten. Oddly, with only thirty days left until the election, independent polls showed the race much closer than expected, even if polling in Oklahoma could be notoriously inaccurate. Still, Albright brought that up to anyone who'd listen, and insisted it was a sign of an upset in the making.

"Mister Albright. You summoned, I'm here."

Albright looked up. He knew Jacks was not at all pleased to meet him at Denny's at the ungodly hour of seven in the morning. But he also knew Jacks would want to know what he was after. They had talked about various campaign issues over the months, but their relationship had been cool since the news release that distanced Jacks from the campaign.

"Thanks for coming, Ray. I know this isn't your favorite time of day, so I really appreciate you doing this."

"Okay, Taylor. What the hell is so important you have to drag me out of bed? Is this just your way of shovin' my nose in it?"

"I recognize you're a pain in the butt. On the other hand, you seem to understand politics and how to work the system to your advantage. Over the past few months you've been a great help, and I've appreciated what you've done. I know you think you were mistreated. You knew better than anyone that leaking that information about Robbie Gilmore was maybe the one thing that would get Anderson fired up. Well he's forgiven you, and I think it's time you forgave him, too."

Jacks chuckled. "I hope that's not the only reason you started my day this early."

"No, but before we get to that, could you explain why you started those rumors about Robbie? You must've known what was going to happen."

Jacks frowned. "It's not a very comfortable story for me to tell."

"So, you did have a reason?"

"Well, getting drunk was a factor. But really, it was me being extremely pissed at Robbie. We've known each other for years—actually went to school together. Anyway, he's not his father, and I always figured him to be embarrassed by how J.H. bullied everyone in the state."

"So, this was some kind of old grudge against him?"

"Nope. This was a new one. He was, and still is, having an affair with my slut of a third wife, Patty."

"Oh."

"Yeah— 'Oh.' I have no idea why I married her. She has the IQ of a turnip. But let me tell you, she has one gorgeous body. Guess I just figured out why I married her—plain old lust."

"This had nothing to do with politics or the campaign?"

Jacks shook his head. "Nothing. It was me trying to kick

Robbie's ass. And I was drunk, so I didn't realize how stupid it was, and I didn't think of how Bill might react. There are times when I just live in my own world, and let the chips fall where they may."

Albright started laughing and couldn't stop. He had no idea it was simply about an angry, two-timed husband. He laughed so hard he started to cry. "Sorry," he waved a hand. "I know, I shouldn't laugh. You can't imagine the schemes I'd dreamed up, trying to figure out why you did that. Never did I think of Robbie having an affair with your wife." He couldn't help himself. He started laughing again.

Jacks simmered visibly. "Okay. But that'll do. It's been hell for me."

Albright stopped, embarrassed, although he did consider excusing himself to go to the restroom and laugh some more. Who was the real asshole at this table? "Sorry. Has she left you?"

"Sort of. She's been in and out of the house. Tommy's seen her. He doesn't know anything about it. I also think she's taken some things, some of my papers. I've tried to call her, left notes at the house saying I need to talk to her. I haven't seen her in a while. It's a mess. My whole life's a mess."

Albright decided it was best to change the subject. "I know how this will sound, but I've started to believe we can win this thing. The polls are a lot closer than anyone would've guessed. Bill's building momentum. That strategy you put together, starting with the rural spots and working back into the cities, has worked. At last count, there were forty-four small-town newspapers endorsing Anderson. My calculations show we'll have to have somewhere around forty percent of the vote in

Oklahoma and Tulsa counties. If we get that, we could win."

Jacks seemed relieved to talk about something else. "They'll have the same data, and that'll mean a big push. Any idea where they might hit Bill? Where do you think he's vulnerable?"

"Most obvious, lack of experience. I'm sure they'll make a big deal about Butler's years in city councils and the legislature. My feeling is, people are tired of the same old politicians all the time, so that angle might backfire. I also think they'll start pushing on Bill's willingness to raise taxes to pay for programs. He's been too honest about that. Anytime he's asked how he'll pay for improved schools, he just gives 'em the obvious—raise taxes. It's the truth, of course. But Butler says he'll improve schools and *cut* taxes. A few people see that as the bullshit it is, but the rest just go along with the fantasy."

"Gilmore's gonna get frustrated if there's no dirt to throw," Ray reminded him. "That's his favorite strategy. Keep in mind, if they don't have anything, they'll make it up."

"Yeah. That's one of the reasons we want you to rejoin the campaign in an active way. We need your advice and knowledge."

"Okay. I was always available, even if I was in the doghouse. Not sure what I can do at this point, but whatever you need."

"What I'd like," Albright said, "is for you to reach out to all your sources and see if we can find out what they're planning for the stretch run. We know their schedule, but we don't know what ads are in the works, how much air time they've bought—anything that might give us some idea. Of course, the big one would be if we could find out what their final attack might be about."

"I can reach out. But the people who know aren't going to

talk—at least, not to me. I'll give it my best."

"Great. That's all we can ask."

Jacks's new assignment was dirty tricks espionage, right up his alley. His first target was Risso's. Want to learn secrets? Either sleep with someone (not likely, in this case) or drink with them. He sure as hell could drink.

First, he had to mend fences with Lopez. "Look, Larry, I'm sorry about what happened the last time I was in here. You know me; I'm not a fighter. Just a bad day. I promise, no loud, inappropriate conversations or threats of violence. Okay?"

"Ray, I like you, and you're one of my best customers. But this ain't no damned biker bar. I have families in the dining room. I just can't have that sort of thing."

"I know, and you're right. I'll stay on my best behavior, just for you."

"You're a bullshitter, Ray Jacks, but okay. Just play nice."

Ray took a stool at the bar and the bartender set down his favorite. "How's it going?"

"I already apologized to Larry, and I owe you one, too. Thanks for not hurting me the other night."

The bartender chuckled. "It's not my job to hurt customers. Unless they deserve it."

Jacks was sure he never wanted to deserve it. He took a couple of sips and surveyed the room, recognizing several people. He saw some he might chat with, but they seemed engaged in some kind of business. There was a one-on-one going on in one of the back booths between Steve Marsh, the *Sun* sportswriter, and Tracy Clark, the very attractive television reporter and daughter of the guy Ray had the blowout with. At that point, his addled brain kicked in, remembering what he'd been trying to remember the morning after getting kicked out of there. Allen Clark had been ready to tell him something important before he lost his mind and yelled at the poor guy. The more he remembered, the more embarrassed he felt.

He didn't know of a way to get in touch with him. He decided to take advantage of circumstances and see if Tracy would ask Allen to give him a call. Interrupting would be a little rude. He hoped Larry wouldn't throw him out again.

"Hello, Miss Clark. I'm Ray Jacks. Really sorry to interrupt. Some days ago, I talked to your father, and we had a little misunderstanding. I don't know how to get hold of him, and I was wondering if you'd mind asking him to call me so I could apologize." Ray handed her one of his cards. He felt a noticeable glare from Marsh for butting in on a private conversation.

"Sure, Mister Jacks. I'll give him your card." She was polite, lovely, and dismissive. Ray headed back to the bar.

The crowd began to file in. These were Ray's people, and he enjoyed their company. Conversations ranged from sports (mostly the Sooners football team), to politics (with a consensus that Butler would win but Anderson was making a good showing), to women (about whom it was agreed they were good, they were bad, and they were necessary). Ray didn't notice when Marsh and Tracy Clark left.

He recognized a couple of guys in the crowd as CPAs for one of the Big Eight accounting firms downtown, and thought he recalled they also were auditors for the *Sun*. He joined them for a while, but, as he expected, they *were* accountants. Attorneys will blab about anything, but accountants, even if they loved to drink, seldom spilled a bean. He went back to the bar.

It was getting late and he figured he'd better head home. Once again, he wasn't sure where Tommy was. He was confident his son could take care of himself, but he still felt like it was a good time to check in on him.

"Mister Jacks, may I join you?" The lovely voice came from the stunning Tracy Clark, who'd just showed up at his elbow. She stood almost as tall as Ray, with blonde hair and a body people could mistake for Marilyn Monroe's. Her piercing grey eyes bore hints of intelligence and an odd, intriguing sadness.

He sputtered a little. "Of course. Maybe we should take a booth." He asked her preference and fetched her a white wine. "Sorry again for interrupting you a bit ago."

"It's no problem," she said, smiling only slightly. "I wanted to tell you, I haven't seen my dad in days. I was wondering—when you last saw him, how did he seem to you?"

Now maybe he had a clue about that sadness in her eyes. "You saying he's missing?"

She nodded. "I've been worried. He's been depressed since he lost his job. The police haven't been any help. They keep telling me there's no evidence of foul play, and that a grown man can come and go as he pleases. But you said you had some kind of disagreement with him, and I was wondering if it might have anything to do with him disappearing."

Jacks hoped it didn't—a lot. "I'm not sure what happened." He shrugged. "I was a little drunk. But I don't think it would've made him do anything rash."

"What did happen?"

Ray told the story, trying to make himself sound a little less like an ass than he'd been.

"So, you have no idea what he wanted to tell you?"

"No. My big mouth got in the way, and he never got to say. But he mentioned that piece about me, so it might've had something to do with that."

She looked a little embarrassed. "He told me that was a hit piece on you, ordered by the Gilmores, and it made him sick to go along with it. He's an honorable man. Maybe it's about something even worse, and it's eating at him. Can you help me?" She began to cry and took a handkerchief out her purse.

Help? he thought. He'd do absolutely anything she wanted.

15

LOOKS LIKE RAIN

Fantasies of Tracy Clark pushed Jacks's grudge against his adulterous third wife to the back of his mind. He paid no attention to the irony.

They had talked for a while at Risso's. He even laid off the drinks and half-sobered up while they spoke. They exchanged contact information and arranged to meet again. Jacks headed home.

He checked on Tommy, and found him asleep in his room. He felt sorry for the kid with such a horrible father. For about the millionth time, he promised he'd do better, even if he wasn't sure he believed it anymore. Tommy's mother had been the love of his life. When she died, something inside him died with her. He hated how he was, but couldn't seem to change. The one good thing was that Tommy was much smarter than him and completely independent. He knew that in some uncanny way he'd helped to make Tommy a resilient, tough kid, even if he deserved plenty of blame and no credit.

He had a restless night, and woke feeling alone. He went to Tommy's room, but it was empty. On the kitchen table was a short note.

Dad,

Had some things to do this morning didn't see any reason to wake you. Patty came by again and rummaged through your stuff. Not sure what's going on, but she's difficult to be around. I tried to ask what she was doing, but she told me it was none of my business. Think I will stay with John until you guys figure out what you're going to do. If you're going to stay married, you might want to talk.

Tommy

John was a friend, and Jacks had his phone number. *Maybe that's best,* he thought. He was sure Patty carried out her raids when she knew he wasn't there. He didn't count on seeing her anytime soon.

His first wife's death had swept Ray into a dreadful, almost totally debilitating fog for over a year. His second wife filed for divorce, and he was over her in a week. Patty was already gone in his mind, and he didn't give a damn. If he ever had a fourth wife, the whole experience of marriage, divorce, and recrimination might only take a few days—unless maybe it involved Tracy Clark. He smiled at the absurdity of the thought.

She was supposed to meet him at about six to discuss her father and go over any information he might find before then. They were meeting at a coffee shop on 23rd Street by the university. She mentioned she was watching the amount of alcohol she was drinking because it contained too many calories.

Ray wasn't sure how to proceed. He needed help. He called the *Sun.* "Hey, Walters, it's Ray Jacks—don't hang up on me."

"What in hell do *you* want?"

"Thought I might share some things with you, and see if

you would help me, too."

"No. Sometimes I wonder if you have a screw loose or something. Your name's like poison around here, and I don't need any grief. So don't call me anymore, okay?"

"Just a second. Did you know Allen Clark is missing?"

"Used to be manager at the TV station?"

"Yeah."

"Look, that might have something to do with your world, but I don't see any connection to mine. Go tell the cops. I've got to go."

"Wait! Just one more second. I think it's connected to Gilmore."

"What does it have to do with him?" Walters came off like he wanted to sound skeptical.

Jacks could tell he was interested. "Before Clark disappeared, he wanted to tell me about something that involved Gilmore, but he never got the chance. I think it's connected."

"Oh, I get it. You want me to investigate my paranoid boss and see if he did something to the guy. That'd be a *real* smart move for me. I admire your guts, but I question your sanity."

"See me at Risso's this afternoon, about three. I've got some things that'll surprise you." He hung up. He had no idea if Walters would show up. Just in case, he needed to find out some surprising things—quickly.

He thought about calling Steve Marsh. He still didn't know why he was meeting with Tracy at Risso's, but the timing suggested it might have had something to do with her father. She'd brushed Ray off in front of Marsh, but came back to talk to him alone. He decided to talk to Tracy about Marsh before doing anything in that direction. What he needed was someone with absolutely no ethics who could weasel information out of people on the cheap— Joe Louongo.

He called Louongo's office; no answer, of course. How the man managed his practice without any help was beyond Jacks. Of course, it was possible he was in his office, and not answering his phone because he was dead, taking a nap, or patronizing the building prostitute who ran a modeling business one floor up. Or maybe he really wasn't there. He decided to play the odds and make a visit.

Louongo sat at his desk, looking busy. It was pointless to ask why he hadn't answered his phone.

"I need your help, now," he announced himself. "You got time?"

"For you, my friend, of course I have time. How may I help?"

He brushed aside Louongo's bullshit and got to the point. "For one, I need to know anything you can find about the disappearance of Allen Clark." He gave the background information on who Clark was, and the unfortunate incident a few nights earlier. "Second, look for anything that might give us some indication what the Butler campaign's planning for the stretch run. The real prize would be anything about attack ads they might have in the works. Also, any air time they've bought—any surprises."

"You want that today? *That's a week's worth of digging, and you want it today?*"

"I know. Just do what you can. I have a meeting today at three with Walters from the *Sun*—if he shows up. If you get anything on Clark's disappearance before then, that would be very helpful."

"What does Walters have to do with it?"

"As far as I know, nothing. My gut's telling me he's no friend of Gilmore. For reasons that aren't worth going into now, I think Gilmore has something to do with Clark's disappearance. I doubt I'll get anything out of him, but he's the closest thing I have to an inside man."

He told Louongo to call Albright if he had anything, and he would check in with Albright later. For the moment, he made a call to arrange his next visit.

While Louongo was a high-profile sleaze lawyer who'd made numerous appearances on TV and in the newspapers, the next stop was to see a much less visible lawyer named Lawrence J. Alexander III. Known as LJ3 to his elite clients, and Larry to his friends, he was the highest-priced lawyer in town that nobody'd ever heard of. He represented people who did not want publicity and could pay to keep their names out of the paper and off TV. While Louongo was a sledgehammer looking for something to smash, LJ3 was all kindness and gentility—until you got in his way. He was also a Democrat, and someone Jacks trusted.

"Ray, you do seem to live a life on the edge. Always chasing some phantom menace with your sword drawn. You do know, don't you, that the chairman of the state Democratic Party is not expected to be a knight in shining armor?" LJ3 had a way with words.

Ray found it soothing just to listen to him. "I know. I'm under the impression that I can fix everything that's wrong with the world, even while my own life's a joke. After this election's over, I'm quitting. Don't know what I'll do, but it's time to move on to something a little less stressful."

"I'll believe that when I see it. If you do decide to find a calmer way of living, let me know. Maybe I can help."

"Thanks, I will."

"Anyway, I have no inside information on the Butler campaign. I'm a major Democratic supporter, so they don't invite me to their planning sessions. What I hear is that they think they have it won, so it could be they don't have any last-minute plans. I doubt that, though. Gilmore has the reputation of not leaving things to chance. More than likely they have something in their hip pocket they can use if the race gets tight. Not sure how you'll find out anything about it until they use it.

"I know Allen Clark, though. He came to me some time ago, asked me to represent him. He never hired me—I think my fee was an issue. I cannot, of course, tell you what all that was about. But I do find it very alarming to hear he's missing. I believe I can tell you this much: that your suspicions that this is somehow tied to Gilmore are correct. You need to push the police to take a more active role in investigating what's happened. I'll reach out to a captain I know in the department and convey my concerns. I won't mention you, of course. Also, I think it might be a good thing if Tracy Clark gave me a call."

Jacks could feel comfortable in a lot of different places with a lot of different people. He wasn't a violent man, and thought most people deserved the benefit of the doubt. For his next stop, though, he thought it appropriate to pack his small pistol in his jacket pocket, just in case.

Frank Martin ran a greasy, dingy auto repair shop on the west side of town near the stockyards. He also ran most of that part of town's prostitution, drug trafficking, auto-theft rings, and loan sharking. In sort of an "I guess I'd understand that" way, he also was a major contributor to the Democratic Party.

"The party of the small businessman and crime bosses" was not a slogan Jacks endorsed for the state party, but he still took the man's money.

Big Frank was jovial, large, and scary. Ray wasn't sure whether the stories he'd heard about him were all true, but he wasn't about to annoy the guy.

"Well, sonofabitch, look who's here. Damn, Ray, I give you tons of money—you can't just drop in and ask for more, can you?" That seemed funny to Big Frank, who shook and jiggled.

"No, got to agree, that wouldn't be right. I just wanted to know if I could ask you something."

He went on to explain the incident about Albright being attacked. He was looking for some protection, but didn't want it to stand out.

"So you don't want my usual goons, is that what you're saying?" After a full minute of solo laughter, Big Frank had a suggestion. "There're two guys in town who could protect you or your friend from an armed invasion if need be, let alone some punk like that. They aren't exactly your normal Okie types, but there's no one tougher. So don't let their dandy looks fool you. Plus, no one out here really knows anything about 'em. They're on sort of an extended vacation from another part of the country, you might say."

Jacks left with advice on how to get in touch with the two non-Okies and a promise from Big Frank that he'd call them and let them know they should take the job. He liked Big Frank, but always felt a little relieved after leaving his company. He found a pay phone and made some calls. Louongo had left a message with Albright, which amounted to, "Got some news for you, but can't talk today—meet me at my office in the morning." Albright said he'd been very mysterious—and irritating, of course. Ray told him about the bodyguards. Albright said they sounded totally unnecessary, but he agreed anyway.

Ray headed to Risso's to see if Walters would show up. He had no news to spring on the man, and he was pretty sure things wouldn't go well. He'd play it by ear.

"You're a lying bastard, aren't you? I have no idea why I keep letting you fool me into believing you're a normal human being." With that, Walters got up to leave.

"I'm not lying to you. I thought I was going to have proof about Clark and Gilmore, but I don't. All I have is speculation—that's not the same as lying."

"Speculation? About what? You haven't told me a thing. You're going to get my ass fired over nothing. Jacks, I'm done with you." Walters left. Some days it was just hard to please some people.

Albright got a call from someone named Max Jones, who said he had been asked by Raymond Jacks to get in touch. The whole tone of the conversation was much different than what Albright expected from a bodyguard, but what the hell did he know? Jones agreed to meet him at Denny's around five, along with his partner, Nathan Oliver.

Albright arrived thirty minutes early, ordered pie and coffee, and opened his newspapers. He felt comfortable being alone and was an admirer of Denny's coffee and pie, so he was prepared for some pleasant solo time. It didn't last long.

"Mister Albright?"

"Yes." Taylor looked up at two men dressed for the runway

at the latest men's fashion show. The combined value of their suits would probably exceed, by a considerable factor, the sum paid for all the clothing worn by everyone else in Denny's.

"Sorry to interrupt. Would you like us to come back in a little while?"

"No, no. This is fine. Did I make a face? Sometimes I can be a little abrupt with people. Have a seat." Albright wasn't sure why he felt compelled to explain himself.

"We understand you're looking for someone to provide security for you during the remainder of the campaign."

"Well, yes. I wasn't sure it was necessary, but Ray Jacks thought it made sense. The supporters on both sides can do some dumb things. So that's why." Of course, he knew it hadn't been an avid supporter, but someone tied to Gilmore, who'd roughed him up. He figured he ought to play it close until he was sure about these guys.

"Good. It's our understanding we'll be officially working for the Democratic Party—it might create bad publicity for the candidate if the campaign hired us directly and anyone found out. Mister Jacks has already settled the issue of fees and payment, so we're ready to get started."

"Okay." Albright hesitated. Having bodyguards already felt strange. "So, what now?"

Max went over their plan, which was basically them staying around Albright as much as possible for the next several days. Once they had a routine figured out, they'd be less intrusive. They assured him they knew what they were doing, and that there was nothing they couldn't handle—all in such a matter-of-fact way, and with such confidence, Albright figured it just might be true.

Jacks decided to go by his house to freshen up a little before he met Tracy, all the while telling himself his behavior was getting a little ridiculous. As soon as he unlocked the door, the phone rang. He hurried, catching his knee on a table and cussing a little before he answered.

"Ray Jacks."

"Mister Jacks, this is Sergeant Nichols at the downtown station. Larry Alexander asked me to give you a call and let you know that we found Allen Clark." Nichols sighed. "His body was discovered in a field just south of Guthrie a few minutes ago. Looks like he was shot in the head. Probably self-inflicted."

"Jes-us," Jacks exhaled, feeling his knees weaken.

"Have to hang up, now," Nichols whispered. "Remember, I never called you, and you never heard from me." He hung up.

"Shit."

16

WHY, OH WHY

Jacks slumped into a chair and began staring at the wall. What would he tell Tracy? Maybe he could just ask her to call the police. *Oh, yeah,* he thought, mocking himself, *that makes sense: Say Tracy, there's some horrible news you need to get from the authorities—I'll be off getting drunk.* No. It was up to him to break the news. He hoped she wouldn't hate him. He left, feeling deep pain in the pit of his stomach.

She came into the coffee shop about ten minutes late, looking fantastic, quite used to turning men's heads wherever she went. "Sorry, I'm a bit late. Had a few errands to run." She noticed his pained expression. "Is there something wrong?"

"There's no easy way to say this. I heard from a source at the police department. They found your father's body. He'd been shot. Tracy, they think he—he killed himself."

She went pale. Her lovely face turned into a mask of grief. She left for the restroom without a word.

After waiting longer than he felt comfortable, he figured she had probably gone for good. He was about to leave when she came back. Her eyes were dry and hard. "I don't give a damn what the police say," she muttered, "this wasn't suicide. Sure, he was upset about his job and a lot of other things, but most of all he was mad. He was ready to fight the Gilmores, and anyone else who stood in his way. He wouldn't have killed himself. Never."

From broken and sad to angry and defiant. Jacks knew by instinct he was on dangerous ground. She was on the lookout for someone to vent her anger on, and he didn't want to be that someone. "How can I help?"

"Call me tomorrow. I'm a reporter—a damn good one. I'll find out what happened." She left.

At least her storm was headed in a different direction. He didn't know whether to feel relieved or even more worried. It was early, but he decided to head home, see if he could find Tommy, and maybe take him out for a hamburger. He needed to make sure the boy was okay. Of course, Tommy turned out not to be there. You can't ignore someone, then suddenly decide you need to see them, and expect them to be waiting around for you, he admitted. He called John, whose mother said they hadn't seen him for the last few days. If they did, they'd have him call.

He called Albright.

"Yeah." Albright lacked both personal *and* telephone manners.

"Just heard Allen Clark was found dead. Cops say it looks like suicide. His daughter—she's Tracy Clark, the reporter at KVY—says that's crap, that he wouldn't have killed himself, mostly because she thought he was spoiling for a fight with Gilmore."

"Do you think any of this is connected to the election?"

"No idea. I was the one who told Tracy, and she took it kind of odd. She got upset, went to the restroom for maybe ten minutes or so, and came out mad as hell. It was almost like she had some idea who killed him. She did tell me she was going to find out."

"You don't think Gilmore or his son would actually kill people, do you?" Albright sounded skeptical, in a queasy sort of way.

"They sure wouldn't do it themselves, but they might make a suggestion, like it might be nice if so-and-so wasn't around, and let their underlings take the hint. They have some scary people working for them."

"Maybe the guy did kill himself," Albright countered. "It happens. Life gets so miserable; he just can't take anymore. It's normal for his daughter not to believe it, but it might be the answer."

"Yeah, sometimes the simplest answer is the right one, nasty as it is. I'll call Louongo and see if he can get more on it. Maybe I'll stop by Denny's tomorrow and we can talk. How are the bodyguards working out?"

"I have a feeling I'm safe from most threats of almost any kind unless, of course, I somehow annoy Max or Nathan."

"Well, they come highly recommended by one of the lowest of the low, so that should say something."

"You're not making me feel safer."

Ray called Louongo. No answer, no big surprise. Tommy came in.

"Hey, Tommy—long time, no see."

"Hey, Dad. You know I'm here most of the time, right?" Just a whisper of sarcasm.

"Yeah, I know. You're a good kid, Tommy."

Tommy looked a little embarrassed and quite pleased, all at once. "What's going on between you and Patty? Is she just stealing stuff for some reason?"

Ray chuckled. He really liked Tommy. Why did he treat him so badly? "How about we go out and get a burger and fries? Maybe go to Johnny's. I really like that place."

All smiles. "Great with me."

Tracy was almost too angry to drive. Suicide—what a load of crap. No way her father had killed himself. He'd sunk into depression and did little but drink over the past few weeks, but she knew he'd made up his mind to fight, even if he knew it would get ugly. The absolute last thing he would do is kill himself. Someone had murdered him.

The weight of her deductions pressed upon her. She began to feel frightened. She could be at risk, and so could Judy Jackson. She had to find her, right away. She was already close to the capitol, so it made sense to drop in and see if Judy was there. If not, she could still use the press room to make some calls.

"Hi, Tracy," Gail Collins greeted her. "Judy was here earlier, but I'm not sure where she went. Maybe to get coffee or something. Want me to tell her you came by?"

"Thanks, Gail. If I could just write a little note and leave it on her desk?"

Tracy went to the press room to think. She found a desk in a corner that wasn't being used, with a working phone. She called Judy's apartment, and got no answer. It was getting a little late—had Judy heard about her father? If so, maybe she panicked. A sense of frustration and exhaustion overcame Tracy. She put her head on the desk and began to cry. Soon her sobs were uncontrollable.

❧

Judy was ready to leave for the day. Some days she felt happiest if she could stay and work late into the night, but today was tense and full of trouble. She didn't know why, but she was worried. She had talked to Allen Clark, and having him involved in her problems was making her nervous. She regretted having confided in Tracy about her trouble, and she was angry at her for telling her father about them, even if she knew Tracy was only trying to help.

She'd gone down to the main floor of the capitol to the little coffee shop to have a moment or two alone. Gail was getting on her nerves, asking if everything was okay. Of course, it wasn't okay. The last thing she needed was for Allen Clark to confront Robbie and then, to top it all off, get himself fired. She wanted to scream at him, "What the hell were you thinking?" She sipped her tea and tried to calm down. It would be time to go home soon.

"Hey, Judy," said a young voice, just coming in. "Day's almost done. I still haven't gotten used to standing all day. My feet are killing me. But this is a great job."

"Hi, Bart."

Bart was a new junior-level security guard who had kind of attached himself to her. It was his first day, and she could see he needed a friend, so she'd helped him get oriented.

"I can't believe I'm actually working at the capitol. I saw the governor today. There are important people everywhere. This is the best job I've ever had."

Bart's enthusiasm made her feel better, and a little envious.

If only her life were that simple.

"Hey, just heard something sad," he went on. "Maybe you know this guy—Allen Clark, from the TV station? One of the guys I work with just told me he killed himself. Said he heard it from one of the detectives. They haven't announced it yet, but that's what he said. I hate hearing stuff like that, don't you?"

Judy was stunned. Allen Clark, dead? She immediately thought of Tracy, then herself again. What should she do?

"Are you okay, Judy?"

"Oh, Bart. Sorry. Guess I'm not feeling too good today. Think I'll go on home. See ya later."

"Sure, take care of yourself."

Everyone had left the office, but Tracy's note was on her desk. Her sadness felt like it would explode—she couldn't imagine how Tracy must feel. The note said she'd be in the press room for a while, and to call if they missed each other. Judy knew she should rush there to console her, but she held back. She had to think first. Suicide didn't make sense—she'd just talked to Allen a few days ago, and he'd been all fired up about going after Robbie. She'd begged him not to do anything more, but he'd insisted he could take Robbie on for being a lowlife without bringing her back into it. He hadn't sounded like he was about to kill himself—if anything, he'd sounded like he wanted to kill someone else.

She snapped out of it and headed to the press room. Tracy was her friend, and she needed her. She wasn't there, nor was anyone else. She thought about going to see her own father, or maybe even Ray Jacks. She needed someone to talk to who could help her sort things out. But neither of those was a good option. She hadn't said anything to her dad up to now, because it would break his heart. Her dad was her whole world. She couldn't bear to crush him by telling him what she'd done. And talking to Jacks would be just plain stupid. He was her dad's boss, and her dad seemed to think he knew everything. She wasn't so sure about that, and certainly didn't want him involved in her personal problems.

Her only real option was to go home and try to reach Tracy.

The phone was ringing. Judy had fallen asleep on the couch and had no idea what time it was, but it had to be late.

"Hello."

"Judy, I'm so glad you're there. I've been worried sick."

"Oh, Tracy. I'm so sorry. I heard at work about your dad. It's just so terrible. Where are you?"

"I just got home. Spent four frustrating hours with the cops. They insist it's suicide, and I know that isn't right. But I can't get them to look at it any other way."

"Of course it's not suicide. Your dad was all fired up."

"I know." Tracy sounded a little fired up herself. "I don't know why the police are so eager to declare this solved, but that's what they've done. They haven't even had an autopsy, but they're already releasing information to the press saying he killed himself. I made a few enemies at the police station tonight. Also, if you can believe this, my boss was there, and he and I got into it. He's the guy who took my father's job, hand-picked by Robbie. Bottom line, he fired me."

"Fired you? What kind of S.O.B. fires someone right after her father dies? My god! What is going on?"

"Yeah, I don't know," Tracy said, sounding a bit less angry, perhaps tired. "That may have been my fault. I wanted to go on the air, but he said I was too emotional, and I called him every name in the book and a few I made up on the spot. Can't remember everything I said, but there wasn't much of his manhood left by the time I was through. My only regret is that I didn't slug the little slime ball."

"I'm so sorry," Judy apologized, beginning to cry. "Your dad's been killed, and I think it has something to do with me. I'm so sorry."

"Judy, listen," Tracy said, "we don't know how or why this happened, but it sure as hell isn't your fault. This story'll be the headline in the paper tomorrow, so you need to get a good night's rest and be ready to deal with it tomorrow. No hiding, now. We'll work through this together."

17

THE ELECTION

A few days before the election, the *Sun* ran a story insinuating Bill Anderson had fathered a child with a woman who had gone to his high school in Ada. It also ran an editorial reiterating the paper's endorsement of Rick Butler, with an emphasis on his ethics and high moral standing. The editorial acknowledged doubts regarding the woman's claims, but insisted that Anderson's judgment remained in question.

The newspaper in Ada took notice and followed up. It discovered the woman had borne five children by five different fathers, none of whom was listed on their birth certificates as Bill Anderson. They had gone to the same high school in Ada, but she was ten years younger, and the paper couldn't find anyone to say they even knew each other. She also had a fairly extensive arrest record for public drunkenness, and had been overheard in a local bar claiming she'd made a "killing" off the *Sun* story. Confronted with the facts, she told the Ada paper's reporter: "I will sue your (expletive) off if you run this story." Many of the fine people of Ada, especially those who actually knew Anderson, got a good laugh out of it.

Next, television commercials suggested Anderson, as a developer, had bribed Air Force officials to learn where the new base would be built in advance of any announcement, although they provided no evidence. The Air Force, in an unusual move, issued a statement calling the TV spots "completely false."

For the final month of the campaign, television and radio ads endorsing Butler were all negative. Anderson, usually not named, was characterized as an out-of-touch millionaire trying to buy the election. One showed him at the race track in Hot Springs, suggesting by inference that he was a big gambler and may be involved in organized crime. He raised racehorses, although he had on many occasions said that all gambling on horse racing should be outlawed. Several dark, grainy TV spots suggested he owed millions to the state for property taxes, though without a shred of evidence.

Most people believed whatever stories fit their opinions about which candidate should get their vote. Two polls were taken during the final week. One, by the *Sun,* showed Butler ahead by five percentage points. The other, by The Associated Press, showed the race as a dead heat.

Election Day broke, and so did widespread relief. Most people thought elections were important, and a major part of life in a democratic country, but they also saw campaigns as petty, childish schoolyard fights between men who should know better. The only good news came when they were over.

A confident man like Butler might sleep in on election day. He showed up at the polls with the press in tow around eleven, all smiles, guaranteed a huge victory. Anderson was at the polls around eight, no one with him but his wife. Only one TV station sent a camera crew to the polling place, expecting to catch the mayor casting his vote there. Anderson surprised them instead. He told them he thought it would be a tight race, and he was glad it was over. The crew liked him, but knew he was going to lose.

"Election day, and the damn bars are closed."

"They don't do that anymore, Ray, even in Oklahoma."

Jacks could sense Albright was already in a bad mood, and his jokes probably weren't helping. "Thank god. We can drink later."

"Why are you in such a good mood?"

"I have no idea." Jacks wasn't really in a good mood, just putting on a good face. In fact, he felt as low as he'd been in a long time. His legal problems were piling up. He was sure some were Patty's doing, with Robbie's help, using his papers she'd stolen. When things get so bleak that it feels like you can't go on, some people, like Jacks, turn to comedy. "My mood is my business, Albright, ol' boy. By the way, did you ever get your bodyguards registered so they could vote?"

"If this was the old West, I think someone would've shot you by now. And no, they wouldn't register. Something about not wanting a paper trail. But they did assure me their votes would be included—I have no idea what that meant." Albright smiled.

"We should've put those guys in charge of winning this election. I think they would've made it happen."

"Don't give up yet. The polls are open till seven. Close races can go either way."

Jacks nodded. "Optimism is the word of the day."

The journey to this point seemed longer than it had been. Campaigns lasting months can feel like they take a lifetime. Emotions, tensions, and conflicts made each day its own universe, as if the world stopped to concentrate on this one thing, here in Oklahoma.

Jacks felt responsible, but not in charge. Anderson had taken on this impossible task at his urging, and he, and especially Albright, had grown into their jobs, and with amazing skill had turned what most thought would be a rout into a close race.

Anyone who cared to look closely could see Anderson was a man of honor, and his opponent wasn't. Anderson laid out his agenda in detail while Butler talked about how great Oklahoma was and would be under his guidance, never mentioning specifics. In a genuinely free election, how could there be a doubt that Anderson would win? But the people in charge didn't want that.

Jacks thought about that, a lot. In an election like this, honest people, good people, who wouldn't tell a lie, are persuaded—ironically, with misdirection, cronyism, and fear—to do something not in their best interests.

Fear, more than anything, pushed people into bad decisions, and the *Sun* knew that. Its editorial page ran pieces insisting if Anderson won, the oil and gas industry would slow down. Thousands of people would lose jobs, the *Sun* warned, because of regulations and restrictions he would put on the business. And the paper took care to remind its readers that almost every family in Oklahoma had some financial connection to oil and gas. Of course, Anderson had never mentioned any new regulations. Rather, he talked about better spacing and pooling legislation to benefit landowners, usually farmers and ranchers. But the skillful editors at the *Sun* turned it into a threat against the industry, and therefore, the state.

The lowest blow came when the *Sun* ran a snide editorial that seemed to suggest Anderson was not the Christian he claimed to be. They quoted Anderson's answer, when asked if he was truly Christian: "That is between me and my God, and none of your business." That contrasted with Butler's answer: "I will not question my opponent's beliefs or lack of belief. All I can tell you is that my life is guided every day, in everything I do, by Christ's loving hand." Anyone who knew Butler had to laugh. He was a notorious womanizer, and hadn't been to church in years until the months before the election.

The election was a show, and everyone had a part to play. But Anderson didn't know that—he thought it was real, and that letting people know who he really was would make a difference. "Ray, I'm glad, especially today, that you're back with us. In some ways, I should be angry with you since it was your speech out at my ranch that got me into this mess. But I'm not. No matter how it turns out, I've learned a lot. Maybe I'm not so innocent anymore, but I'm wiser. For example, if you came and asked me the same question you did months ago, I'd have you kicked out of my house." Anderson smiled and chuckled.

Jacks chuckled with him, sheepishly. "I sure understand, Bill. I was a little worried about showing up today."

"Well, we're just about done. Don't let this get out, but I'm not sure whether I'll be happier winning or losing."

Jacks was pleased to hear it. "You *have* become wiser. I hope you win. You'd make a great governor." He left to find a phone. He'd been calling Tracy almost every day since her father's death, leaving messages at the television station until they told him she'd resigned, which he figured might have been a reaction to what happened. Then Albright told him that he'd heard she'd been fired the very night she found out about her father's death. That seemed so low, Jacks almost didn't believe it. For a time, he decided that if she wanted to talk to him, he'd hear from her, as sad as that made him feel. Now, he changed his mind. He'd try again.

"Hello."

"Hey, Tracy—Ray Jacks. I'm glad you answered. I've been calling, but I didn't want to intrude if you didn't want me to. Um, I'm not sure that all came out right."

He could hear her sigh. "It's not you, Ray. I got so depressed, I had to leave town for a bit. I have a friend in Dallas, and I stayed with her until I felt like I could deal with things. I just got back yesterday. I was actually going to call you today."

"Listen—all I wanted was to let you know if there's anything I can do, please ask. I heard you quit or got fired, and none of it makes any sense. Are you okay?"

"Not really. The day you told me about my dad, I was mad as hell," she said. "Ready to fight anybody and everybody, all at once. Next thing you know, I lose my job, find out nothing about what really happened to Dad, had the police tell me if I kept harassing people they'd arrest me—just more shit than I could handle. I thought I was tough, but it wasn't long before I felt beat. I need help to find answers. That's one reason I was going to call you. I'd like to tell you what I think happened, and see what you think I should do."

"Maybe we could meet this evening. I'll be at the watch party at the Skirvin, downtown. If you're up to it, why don't you meet me there?"

"It's been a few days since I've put on makeup, but I guess I can. See you there."

Jacks headed for Deep Deuce. "Louongo, where the hell have you been?" He was surprised to find him in his office.

"Shit, Ray, there's no reason to get pissy with me."

"Why the hell not? I can never get you on the phone. I ask you to do some things for me, and you disappear."

"Okay. Things didn't go as planned. I have a life, Ray, and I'm sorry if I'm not available to you every minute—at no cost to you, I might add."

"Maybe our deal has come to an end." Jacks was pissed. Louongo was a pain to put up with, and if he couldn't get what he wanted out of him, it wasn't worth the aggravation. He headed to the door.

"Okay, wait. Look, I've had some troubles. Things got messed up. But I did find out a few things."

Jacks sat down. He wasn't happy about it, but he needed Louongo. "What'd you find?"

"Some very interesting connections with your old pal, Frank Martin."

"Who with?"

"Allen Clark. The street says Frank had something to do with that guy's 'suicide.'"

"'Something to do with' it? What's that mean?"

"They say it was Frank's guys who popped him."

Jacks hadn't seen that coming. How in the hell was Big Frank connected to a TV station manager? "How sure are you about this?"

Louongo shrugged. "Hard to say. Most people I deal with are liars."

"What's your opinion of Big Frank?"

"Very, very dangerous man who I don't want to know, and even more, I don't want him to know me."

"So you think he could have people killed."

"Ray, I'm not sure how you got to know this guy, but there's no one more dangerous than him in this town. In his part of the stockyards, he's king—and ruthless. You need to be very careful around him." Louongo wasn't bullshitting. Unusual for him.

Jacks went home to pick up Tommy for the watch party. If the boy hadn't been so excited, he would have canceled on him, but he was trying to be a better dad. He thought about Frank Martin and Allen Clark, and it still didn't make sense. Big Frank dealt in the underworld of evil. How did that touch Clark?

"Dad, promise me when we get there you won't treat me like a kid, okay? I'm fifteen now."

"Okay, Mister Jacks. How about a cocktail before dinner?"

"I know you think you're funny, but you're not."

It always shocked him to realize how much he liked his son. And, yes, he thought he was funny.

"Are you going to the watch party?" Carl Jackson had a lot to do with putting it on, otherwise he'd have stayed home.

"Dad," Judy sighed, "I don't feel like going. Is that okay?"

"Sure, honey. Do you think you need to see a doctor? I can stay home if you need me to."

She'd been staying in her old room for days, telling him she was just tired of her apartment and wanted to rest someplace else. Carl knew it wasn't a good sign.

"No, it's nothing serious. I'm just a little blue. You know, the thing with Tracy's father still has me upset. But I'm okay. You go and have a good time. I hope Bill Anderson wins."

18
ELECTION RESULTS

Jacks declined several alcoholic offers. If these people only knew, he thought, he'd be getting a standing ovation. But no one knew or seemed to care. He figured the band was hired just because it was loud, and not shy about proving it. Tommy found a group of people about his age and seemed to be engaged in productive conversation about things probably unrelated to politics. Jacks kept a close eye, but he seemed perfectly capable of handling himself—one more benefit of being left to his own devices for so long. Jacks sighed.

"Hey, did you just sigh?" Tracy was gorgeous—and sneaky.

"Oh, hello. Didn't see you come in. My goodness, you look lovely. Guess you didn't forget how to put on makeup." Why did everything he say to her sound so dumb?

"That *was* a sigh, wasn't it? Worried about the outcome?"

He shook his head. "It's my son. He's right over there—kind of tall, skinny kid with dark hair." He wanted to wave at Tommy, but knew he'd hate it.

"Oh, I see him. He looks like you, Ray. Very handsome."

He smiled and decided to keep his mouth shut about that, for once. "Why don't we move away from the bad-but-loud band so we can hear one another?"

Tracy gave him the kind of look that reminded him she was

trained to ask tough questions and get answers. "Where's your wife?"

"Good question. I'm sure you know I'm married for the third time, and my current wife, Patty, has left me. By her own admission, she's having an affair with Robbie Gilmore. My second wife and I had an ugly divorce after she accused me of being a drunken asshole, which I was. My first wife, Tommy's mother, died of breast cancer. Except for Tommy, my personal life's been a disaster."

"Sorry," Tracy apologized, looking a little abashed. "My reporter personality takes over sometimes, and I get a little pushy."

He shrugged. "It's okay. Ask whatever you want." He wasn't sure what she was after—maybe just curious.

"I guess Oklahoma City really is just a small town," she sighed. "Robbie might have something to do with my father's death, and your wife's having an affair with him. I'm officially sick of the Gilmores."

"Well, he and I go back some ways. And he knew Patty before we were married, so there's history there. But, about your dad—you mean, Robbie fired him?"

"Yeah. Most people think he was fired over something to do with politics, or how he ran the station. But, no—he was fired because he threatened Robbie. He told him he was prepared to divulge damaging information about Robbie, which, I'm sad to say, started with me. If I hadn't dragged my dad into this, he'd still be alive." She bit her lip.

"So, what was it about?"

She seemed to have a hard time looking at him. "This is horrible, I know. But I can't tell you. It involves someone else.

It's private, personal. I can't tell anyone what really happened, and that's why I feel so helpless."

He realized he needed to give her more time. "Whatever happens, I'm here to help, any way I can. But I don't think things are going to get any easier for either of us. My fight with Robbie's just getting started. Thanks to Patty and the documents she stole, I'm thinking he might be cooking up some kind of case against me, though I have no idea what. Its possible he can make it sound like I was boss of a crime syndicate." He sighed. "I wish we could've met at a better time."

"I'm not going to run away. Let's see how things turn out." She smiled, but it looked a little forced.

Jacks understood. He didn't want her to go away. He could only hope she wouldn't decide he was too much trouble.

Albright whispered to Anderson, "We're getting some early results. It doesn't sound good."

"Don't panic, Taylor. It's going to be a lot later before we know anything for sure." Anderson didn't whisper. He smiled. He'd given it everything he had, and now it was up to the people. If they elected him, he'd do his best. If he lost, he'd go home without regrets.

A respectable crowd gathered in the Skirvin ballroom, but their enthusiasm hadn't shown up. Many had driven from distant parts of the state and were avid Bill Anderson supporters, but they'd been on the losing sides of elections most of their lives. The rural voters tended to be reserved teetotalers, more comfortable at small church gatherings than in big-city ballrooms lined with free booze and shrimp.

Anderson circulated, thanking everyone for their help. He remembered names, sometimes even children's—a natural with people. The evening wore on. Someone asked the band to play a little less loudly, which apparently offended the musicians' artistic sensibilities, because they left early, to polite applause.

Televisions covering the election were turned up, now that they could be heard. One station expected the vote to go down to the wire. Another said early results from Oklahoma County favored Butler. All forecast that by eleven they could call the election.

"Kind of strange," Tommy remarked to his dad. "Most of those kids I was talking to think Anderson's going to lose. You'd think if you were at his watch party, you might be a bit more optimistic."

Jacks shrugged. "My guess is they heard it from their parents: *no way Anderson'll win.*

And a lot of their parents didn't vote for him, either."

"Everybody's so cynical. I'm not going to be that way when I'm in charge."

"I hope you're right." He sighed. "This could go on a while. We should go home."

"Don't you have to be here?"

Jacks shook his head. "If he wins, they don't need me here to shout 'Hooray!', and if he loses, I'm not sure I want to be here." Tracy had already left, and he wasn't interested in waiting for a post-mortem. He thought Anderson had a slim chance, and he'd grown to respect and like Albright; he even hoped that he might stick around, at least a while. But usually, once a campaign ended, all the relationships that seemed so important just a few weeks before ended, too. And he knew he had a brutal future coming up, maybe fighting to keep himself out of jail, besides trying to hang onto his job after a tough loss. He knew Tommy wanted to go to OU, but had no idea how he'd pay for it. Tommy was tough, but could he handle being on his own? *My god, what a mess.* He felt fear for the first time in a long time.

Albright held up his hands to get everyone's attention. "They may announce this on TV in a little bit," he said, "but we just received numbers for Oklahoma County. Anderson at forty-one percent and Butler at fifty-nine. If those turn out to be right, we think we'll win."

The response was muted. Not everyone understood what he meant, and much of the crowd had gone home, leaving an uneasy mixture of supporters and vultures waiting to hear Anderson concede.

"Might as well let everyone go home," Anderson said. "We'll know in the morning."

"I think we'll know in less than an hour," Albright protested. "That's what I hear from election officials. Maybe we could hang in there just a little longer."

"Okay, Taylor. But if we don't know in forty-five minutes, I'm going to my room. I'm tired."

Everyone was tired, and nobody more than Albright. He'd started this whole thing on a lark, and now he regretted it. He'd imagined it would be fun, that he could joke about it after he got back to New York. He hadn't imagined how involved he'd become and how important the race would be to him. He was fairly certain he cared more about winning than Bill did.

He was enamored with these silly local politics. He hated the ugliness, yet he was addicted to it: this illogical process full of lies and half-truths that dominated people's discussions and lives, a system based on distortion of facts and vicious infighting among powerful people—and he loved it.

He'd never found his place in the world, and he realized it just might be in the middle of the country, fighting against evil. If he was honest with himself, he wasn't planning on leaving anytime soon, even if he knew it was absurd and that he should go home, find a job, and stop chasing illusions of glory. What he would do if Anderson lost, he wasn't sure. Maybe he could help Jacks, or find another candidate for something, and run that campaign.

An hour later, Anderson had gone to his hotel room. Jacks left long before. Albright sat at a table with some guy from Shawnee who owned a small grocery store. The guy was a little bit drunk, talking about his children and how much they meant to him, even if they were impossible to be around.

Someone turned up the TV. "Looks like we can declare a winner," the anchorman said. "With ninety-nine percent of the vote counted, Anderson has forty-nine percent and Butler fifty-one. Rick Butler, the Republican from Oklahoma City, will be the next governor." Someone turned the TV off.

The guy from Shawnee left. Albright sat, feeling shocked, and wondering why. Consciously he'd never doubted Anderson would lose. But somewhere in his gut he'd imagined they'd win, like the good guys in the movies. It was what *should* have happened. The Gilmores and their power shouldn't have been able to defeat a man who would have made a truly great governor, one who really cared about the people. It just wasn't right.

"Sorry, Taylor. We were rooting for your guy."

He knew the voice. "Thanks, Max. Thanks, Nathan. You know, Ray said we should have put you guys in charge. Maybe we would have won."

"Mister Jacks is full of shit."

Albright chuckled. "Yeah. He sure is."

"What you and Mister Anderson need to do," Max continued, sounding like he'd considered the matter, "is start your own newspaper and stomp all over the *Sun* and Gilmore. They have too much power. Someone needs to take them on at their own game." He offered the thought as if it were Nathan's, too. Nathan never said much.

Albright looked up. "Max," he said, "that is one hell of a thought. Another newspaper in this town. What an idea." He shook his head. "I'm not so sure Mister Anderson will want to gamble his millions on it. But I'm going to ask. How about a ride home?"

Maybe a new day would dawn, full of hope, Albright thought as they headed for the car.

19
BIRTH OF A NEWSPAPER

"A newspaper?" Anderson looked stunned, and even sounded a little hysterical. "You've got to be kidding, Taylor. That'd cost millions. And the anguish would be worse than the campaign—for one thing, it'd never end. I have no idea how that idea got into your head, but I won't waste my family's future in a permanent war with the Gilmores. I lost the election, and that's it. It'd be great if someone *else* would start one. Hell, I'd take out a lifetime subscription. But I can't risk any more money on the Gilmores. They won using every dirty trick in the book—and yes, that was wrong, but it's not up to me to fix it. I did what I could, I tried to beat the system. It didn't happen. I lost. I'm out!"

Apparently, it was a little soon for Albright to bring up a whole new harebrained idea. He'd known it was a bridge too far, and his friend had just responded as expected. It wasn't up to Anderson to solve the problem of too much power in the hands of too few people. He'd run for governor on the idea that people should take their state government back from the power elites and lost. Leave the poor man alone. He sighed. "You're right, Bill. Stupid idea. That's just me, trying to get you to waste your money chasing windmills. Sorry. Never should've brought it up."

"Well, good." Anderson looked thoughtful, maybe even conflicted.

Albright felt ashamed.

After that, every time they got together to finish up some lingering detail of the campaign, like paying bills, closing accounts, or doing what they could for contributors, the idea of starting a newspaper would somehow come up. Anderson was still against it—at least, at first. But one day he agreed that *OK Journal* sounded like a good name for one. He even started talking about some of the brighter newspaper people he'd met in the small towns along the campaign trail, particularly Fred Simpson of the Seminole *Producer,* whom he called the smartest and most dedicated person he had ever discussed politics with, aside from Albright. Later he remarked that if they, or somebody, ever did announce a new daily newspaper for Oklahoma City, there'd be hundreds of qualified and talented people who'd come to work for it.

But he still didn't like the idea.

Albright wrestled with a growing guilt. How could he lead his friend down a path he knew was strewn with landmines of frustration and expense? Besides, he had to tell Anderson he was headed back to New York. He needed to uproot the bad idea he'd planted and kill it.

"Well, Bill," he told him at last, "I think my time in the promised land is about over. Time to head back to the Big Rotten Apple and get on with my obscure life. Someday I'm sure I'll find my purpose, and when that happens, I'll give you a call. Thanks for asking me to help with the campaign. It's been a real honor to work with you. You're a good friend, and I wish you the best. And forget the paper—please. It was a bad idea, and I regret bringing it up. Life's too short to be fighting battles all the time. For my sake—for me—don't think about it anymore. Okay?"

"Taylor," Anderson said, looking him in the eye, "I want you to stay and be a part of the *OK Journal*. I'll put up the money and offer guidance, but I need you. You'll be its heart and soul."

Once Anderson made up his mind, everything happened quickly. The project energized him all over again. He hired an advertising manager who encountered an overwhelming positive response. Advertiser after advertiser told him they'd had enough of being dictated to by the *Sun,* and they were ready to sign contracts at once. Anderson was actually optimistic the numbers might work out and that they might even make a little money while doing some good.

The Gilmores thought otherwise. After some of the *Sun's* more or less captive advertisers disclosed the rates the *Journal* was offering, the shit hit the fan. By order of J.H. Gilmore himself, the *Sun* cut its rates fifty percent for anyone signing a long-term contract. The move killed off any chance the *Journal* had to make money. Anderson had to fight just to get the paper's doors open.

Not one issue had been printed, only five people had been hired, the *Journal* didn't have a permanent office or a place to print, and already it was under siege. In hindsight, Anderson knew they should have expected the Gilmores to fight with every bit of clout they could muster. He had no choice but to match the *Sun's* rates. He'd attracted a respectable number of advertisers, but revenue came in far below the *Journal's* estimated overhead. It would lose money much faster than he'd first feared. But a lot of advertisers hated the way they were treated by the *Sun* and volunteered to pay a little more just to help the *Journal* get off the ground.

That gesture was a key to more financial support. Two major banks offered reduced-rate loans based on the number of advertisers signed and the willingness of some to pay more than the *Sun's* rate. The banks had also done it to retaliate for years of abuse by the Gilmores. J.H. sat on the board of the largest bank in town, which enjoyed free publicity in the *Sun* as a result. He had personally written several editorials demanding that ownership structure of all banks in the state should consist only of Oklahoma citizens. The idea was nonsense, and illegal to boot, but it did highlight the fact that several banks were owned by people and groups from other states. J.H. thought he was being clever, but it only earned him powerful enemies.

Anderson didn't like taking on debt, and carefully avoided personally guaranteeing any. That gave him the peace of mind to invest as much as he felt he could afford and not be on the hook. Even at that, he put up a lot. He would have to reduce his losses and make the *Journal* profitable within a few years.

He set a date for the first edition, and his staff moved into their new offices in Midwest City, the town that grew out of Anderson's developments near the air base. Presses and typesetting equipment were installed and tested. Day one of the *OK Journal* was close at hand.

"I hope to hell we know what we're doing," Albright muttered, scanning the newsroom bustling with editors, reporters, and photographers.

"Yeah," Anderson agreed, grimly. "Look, we've attracted some great talent. The mockups look great. Tomorrow we go live, and I think it'll be a big success. The Gilmores are taking a big hit trying to buy off advertisers—and, yeah, it hurts us, but it hurts them, too. Once we're on the street, once we're breaking stories and getting readers, maybe they'll calm down, and we can compete without giving away the store."

"I don't know, Bill," Albright said. "There's a chance the more success we have, the more vicious this will get. We've got to stay focused on what we do best. That begins with good journalism. I'm proud of the team we've put together. They're all committed to making this work."

"As long as the paychecks don't bounce," Bill sighed.

"Well, yeah, there is that."

"Is your column ready?"

"Yep. Calling it 'My View.'" He smirked. "I guess you know absolutely no one gives a damn about my view."

"They will. You've got to hit 'em hard and fast, before they know what's happening. Bring some of that East Coast brass to middle America. We need a little controversy to stir up interest. Just don't get us sued."

"I'll do my best."

The first run of the *Journal* was a complete sellout. They printed a second edition, and that sold out, too. The quality of the printing and the use of color made the *Journal* stand out from the stodgier, grayer *Sun*. Then the hard work began. A daily paper had to be produced.

The newsroom was a new group working together, still far short of a full staff. Even running at capacity, the head count was only about seventy percent of what Anderson needed for a daily paper with the circulation he was shooting for. He set a tight budget.

The first week was not without problems—some logistical,

some technological, and some just plain stupid. In the course of those seven days, the atmosphere went from joyous enthusiasm, to humiliation, to fits of anger. Anderson gathered everyone into the newsroom.

"First," he said, "let me tell you how proud I am of everyone. We've produced a paper every day, and every day we've learned more about what we have to do. I think I started things off a little too tight in terms of budget, so we're going to hire at least a few more people. That should help. Just keep working hard, and don't worry too much about the little problems. We'll work it out." It wasn't a great speech, but they got the idea: relax, do your best, you won't be fired—a small but important message. Everyone calmed down a little, and the mistakes dwindled. The new people took some pressure off, and before long, putting out a daily paper became a routine.

But not for Albright. "I hope *you're* happy," he fumed in Anderson's office. "Looks like about half the letters to the editor are taking shots at my column. Lots of 'he's an idiot,' and 'where the hell did he come from?' And, of course, the succinct 'bullcrap.' Seems I'm not a hit." He'd never thought of himself as thin-skinned, but he'd never been so exposed to public judgment before.

Anderson chuckled. "Negative comments are just comments. Taylor, nothing else in the paper gets as much attention. Besides, you're exaggerating. I saw several positive letters about your column. One lady even said she thought you were a genius."

"Well, I don't know," Albright grumbled. "I should've given this more thought. I'm used to saying whatever I want, and if I don't like the response, I just leave. Now I'm putting my oddball thoughts out there for any moron to make a wise-ass remark about."

"Are they giving you the call-ins?"

"Call-ins? What're they?"

"Some don't write letters. They call the switchboard operator and give their opinions because they can't get through to you or me. The operators keep a list, with notes. I'll have them send you a copy every day. Sports coverage is number one on the list, just so you know. If the sportswriter says anything bad about the Sooners or the Cowboys, the phones ring off the hook. Sports fans almost never write letters to the editor. You should be proud. You're number one for letters and number two for call-ins. You're a star."

Albright knew he needed to work on his under-used sense of humor. Still, a "star" shouldn't have to put up with so much abuse. On the other hand, he was high on the readers' list. It might be better to be known for something besides irritating readers, but at least he was known.

Ray Jacks' problems started badly and got worse quickly. The district attorney was a jackass, going after him like he was a serial killer. Jacks's attorney, David Watts— "the worst lawyer in the whole damned state," according to Louongo—didn't seem very sharp, and Jacks was starting to think he shouldn't have hired someone based solely on a cheap rate. The charges seemed absurd and contrived—embezzlement, grand theft, and tampering with evidence. For the embezzlement, he assumed they claimed he'd taken money from the party, based on documents Patty stole out of his desk. He'd always felt like he *was* the state Democratic Party, and had done more or less what he wanted, although he knew that wasn't going to sound great in court. He wasn't the bookkeeping type, so he had no idea how much they might claim he'd taken. So that was trouble. The other charges had something to do with a typewriter he took from the office to use at home and a set of golf clubs, donated to the party, that he'd given to his cousin for fixing the back porch of his house. The clubs had no value to Ray, so he hadn't given it any thought. The typewriter was missing, presumably because Patty took it. Tampering with evidence? That was most likely about the trash-barrel fire he lit one night after several shots of tequila, into which he'd added a handy stack of old papers off his desk for fuel.

"The best defense against their charge of embezzlement would be that it was reimbursement for expenditures you incurred during your work for the party," Watts told him. "And if you had receipts, we could put together something we could claim was an expense report. But let's see—you stated to the D.A.'s assistant that was part of the 'crap' you burned. Is that correct, Mister Jacks?"

"Look Watts, it's just you and me here. Why do you sound like you're talking to a jury? Plus, you seem annoyed. You'll get paid your hourly rate no matter what happens to me, right? So, what are you annoyed about? It's my ass on the line!"

"Your attitude isn't helping."

His options were to fire the moron or maybe kill him.

20
SUCCESS BRINGS FAILURE

The *OK Journal* was a hit. The public loved getting a different perspective. Taylor Albright's "My View" was the most talked-about column in either paper, even more than national columnists like Drew Pearson. Albright was irreverent, funny, daring, bold, and disgusting—and he drew readers. Most important, he was not one of Gilmore's stooges. He was the voice of a new newspaper.

"My View" took direct shots at the *Sun* and the Gilmores, something unheard of before then. Nobody openly made fun of the established elites like Albright did. He used humor and irony to say things a lot of people thought, but few would dare say.

Anderson liked to think he had a more noble motivation for founding the paper than just beating the Gilmores, but Albright's digs at them felt satisfying nonetheless. Still, the financial problems were there. The paper's growing circulation and the demand for advertising weren't enough to offset the drain caused by the price war with the *Sun.* Subscriptions barely covered ink and paper. The *Journal* was a success in every way but financial. He wondered how long it could survive.

"Morning, Fred," Albright said.

Fred Simpson was considered by everyone at the *Journal* to be the expert on all things journalistic. "Hey, Taylor, good to see you. What daring story do you have for us today?"

"Got a great lead, just a little concerned about the source. It's just *too* good, you know? Need your input."

"Sure, shoot."

Albright laid out what he'd been given by the source, which was about legislation to change most of the state's oil and gas leasing regulations. One clause in the measure was particularity beneficial to oil companies. The source said certain companies were offering Gilmore additional stock if he pushed the bill. If it passed, he stood to make a lot more money, as would the companies' other shareholders.

"Got any documentation?" Simpson asked.

"Not yet. The guy's a lobbyist for the oil companies, and he says he's sick and tired of how these things are being handled. He's promised me something more than just his word. But at this point, nothing."

"You're a long way from having anything you'd want to put in print. Maybe if you could find another independent source to confirm what this guy's saying, you'd have something. But with just one source and no documentation, it's just gossip."

"Yeah, that's what I thought." Albright didn't seem willing to let it go, however. "This source is pure gold, though. I've known him a while, and at this point I trust him. I believe he's telling the truth, it's just—how do I support the story with only one source?"

"The short answer is, you don't. Find another source, or documentation, and you've got something. Otherwise, it's back to embarrassing some senator."

J.H. Gilmore and the *Sun* had been regular topics in Albright's column. He loved to point out errors the paper made and home in on its biases. His second favorite topic was the legislature. He made lots of enemies just by pointing out what they were doing or, in some cases, not doing. So, when the opportunity came along to slam the legislature and Gilmore at the same time, it was too tempting to resist.

Within days he had a second source—an aide to the bill's sponsor in the Senate. He couldn't believe his luck when the man contacted him, and realized his story matched up with the lobbyist's. Still, he insisted on anonymity. Albright felt reluctant to bring it to Simpson, who he knew to be skeptical of unnamed sources.

"Fred, I got a second source. A senate aide. He doesn't want his name used, but he's confirming everything I got from the lobbyist. And the lobbyist is vouching for the aide. Says he's a good guy who wants to see these kinds of backroom deals stopped."

"Well, that's great. You need to run it by Bill and get a legal opinion before you put anything into your column, though. Remember, you are in essence accusing the richest, most powerful man in the state of fraud and theft. Make sure you have your ducks in a row."

"Thanks, Fred." *Screw you, Fred,* is what he thought to himself. Albright knew he had the truth—he could feel it. All this sourcing B.S. was getting on his nerves. He wanted to nail Gilmore.

The column was published the next day. Simpson assumed, because Albright submitted it, that it had been approved by

Anderson and the paper's lawyer. He was wrong.

Albright had been set up. With military precision, they had baited him, then attacked when he bit. Within hours after the story hit the streets, Gilmore's lawyers called. Albright felt panic. It was clear how stupid he'd been. He called every number he had for the lobbyist and the aide, but they didn't seem to exist anymore. The heart and soul of the *Journal* had just been stomped.

Negotiations to forestall the threatened libel suit were frustrating and tedious. The best defense seemed to be simple sloppy journalism, but Albright's history of going after Gilmore made his actions look deliberate. His claim that he'd had two reliable sources was dismissed—where were they? The *Journal* was already struggling financially, and the suit threatened to be the last straw. Defending would cost a bundle and if the paper lost, which seemed likely, it was finished. Then Gilmore's lawyers made a surprising offer. They would settle for a much smaller amount than Anderson feared, if certain conditions were met: Albright would be fired immediately, he would be condemned publicly in the *Journal,* and Anderson would write an editorial admitting the paper's mistake and apologizing to Gilmore and the *Sun.*

"Bill, don't worry about it," Albright said in Anderson's office. "This was my screw-up. One hundred percent me. Nobody else did anything wrong. Even if they weren't demanding I be fired, I was going to resign. I'm sorry I put you in this spot. You need to do whatever you have to do."

Everyone associated with the *Journal* was demoralized. Gilmore and the *Sun* were deliriously pleased. The lobbyist and the aide were gone, and presumably richer.

The common-sense thing for Albright to do would have been to return to the vastness and anonymity of New York. But he felt like he'd fought just one battle, and though he'd lost, the war was still going on. No way in hell he was leaving.

Ray Jacks knew the sources of his grief were both political and personal. The Gilmores hated him because he'd challenged them. He hadn't always won, but to them any challenge was a threat. His fumbling but inexpensive lawyer seemed to think the best defense was simply to stall. Months passed without anything happening, and then there would be a hearing, and Mister Legal Genius would ask for an extension. It worked for a while, but Jacks noticed his counsel's goal seemed to be to rack up hours of legal fees while doing not much at all.

"My recommendation," Watts suggested at last, "is we try to make a deal with the prosecutor."

"A deal? After all this time and the money I've paid you, your best suggestion is to plead guilty?"

"Technically, you probably are guilty."

"Have you ever heard of a guy named Big Frank Martin?"

"No."

"For about half what I've already paid you, he'll eliminate you from my life. I'm considering it."

"Well, threatening a person with violence, including your attorney, is a crime in itself. Ray, I know you think I've messed this up, but that's not true. You don't seem to understand that the evidence against you is solid, and they have several key witnesses who'll testify that you did what you're accused of—although I think we can probably keep your wife from testifying by hinting we might expose her romance with Robbie. Even so, this isn't an easy case."

"I didn't steal any money," Jacks moaned. "Everything I took was a legitimate expense of the party, and I had authority to spend it."

"I believe you. The problem is, there's no documentation to back that up. And they have documentation which appears to have been typed on your typewriter, detailing the money you were stealing."

"Explain to me—why the hell would I do that?"

"I know. It's bizarre. They say you kept the detail because some of this money you were paying to other people was really illegal bribes."

"This is complete bullshit."

The trial was scheduled. Tommy insisted he believed his dad was innocent, but to Jacks he seemed distant. He knew the case was taking a toll on his son, and couldn't do anything about it. And his anger was becoming difficult to control. He wanted to lash out at someone. He felt like a failure.

After several depositions it became clear his wife's willingness to lie was damaging. She not only declared Ray a thief, but also a horrible husband and an unfit father. There was no mention of the jewelry or the car or the money she took, nor did Watts bring up her ongoing affair with Robbie Gilmore.

"I don't get it," Jacks confronted Watts. "Why can't you question her about Robbie?"

"We have no evidence for that except from you. The judge isn't going to give it any weight unless we have someone else who can back it up."

The *Sun* followed every detail of the pre-trial hearings and legal filings, characterizing the case against Jacks as over-whelming. It ran editorials about how such malfeasance had to be prevented in the future, pretending great concern for the Democratic Party while demonizing him. The *Journal* articles carefully insisted on facts and objectivity.

The first day of the trial was rainy and cool. Tommy seemed depressed, so Jacks made arrangements for him to stay with an aunt in Tulsa, even though she was a cold and difficult woman who hated him for reasons she would never spell out, although likely to do with her sister's death. Jacks didn't seem to have much support, but he did find sympathy.

"This," Albright told him, "is for shit, Ray."

"Yeah. It's not good." He wasn't in the mood to talk, but he appreciated Albright showing up. Most of his "friends" had stopped calling.

"I can't believe Bill and the *Journal* aren't running editorials, coming to your defense. He's just been cowed by my fuck-up."

"I can't blame him. We've all suffered for taking on the Gilmores. We thought we were so smart. Now look at us."

"Man, I wish there was something I could do."

The first day of trial was quick and decisive, making it plain Jacks was sunk. The jury wouldn't render a verdict for days, but everyone in the courtroom could see in their eyes that they'd already decided. The judge looked about the same.

The court adjourned at about three, and would start again in the morning. Jacks met with his attorney.

"Ask them for a deal."

"I can ask, Ray, but they may not be interested anymore."

"I know. I screwed up again. Ask."

"Okay."

Jacks was taken to a holding cell in the county jail. He felt the weight of the world on him, so much he could hardly breathe. At around nine he was taken to meet Watts.

"I know you're not going to believe this," Watts said, "but the prosecutor's actually a good guy. He knows the charges are blown way out of proportion. But he's also under a lot of pressure to push hard. It took a lot of talking, but he's offered to drop the theft and tampering charges if you plead guilty to embezzlement. You get a sentence of seven years, but you can apply for parole after five."

"Shit, seven years? It was a bookkeeping mistake. My god!"

"Ray, if you're found guilty on all the charges, it'll be fifteen to twenty, no parole."

Jacks stared at nothing, feeling numb. How could this be happening? He started thinking about Tommy and what a mess this would be for him. The pain was so real and immediate and overwhelming, he began to feel dizzy. He lowered his head into his hands and started to cry.

Watts looked away, reflexively. "I'll tell them you accept," he said, softly.

Jacks nodded.

After Albright left the *Journal,* he started publishing the free, tabloid-style *Banner,* printed on an erratic schedule. Its circulation was in the low hundreds, but it helped him feel like he was still in the game.

It helped that he lived a somewhat judgment-proof life. He'd never owned much, out of personal preference, although he did have an income from a large trust established by his late father. The attorneys assured him the trust couldn't be touched by lawsuits against him, and its revenues could be stopped or placed in retirement funds—also untouchable. *Sue away, you assholes. I have nothing you can get!*

From The Banner, *Issue 11:*

Never have such small-minded plutocrats been able to silence the voice of the people the way the Gilmores and their publishing behemoth have done to Ray Jacks and his populist message. He has been found guilty of stealing from himself, because he didn't keep adequate records with which to demonstrate his non-crime for what it was. Shame on the Gilmores for contriving this fiasco, and on the criminal justice system for allowing it to occur. They have done harm to every honest person in this state. You had a strong democratic voice in Ray Jacks, now a political prisoner because he challenged the elites. Watch your backs, people. They will come after you if you voice any complaint.

From The Banner, *Issue 12:*

Today the Sun ran an editorial bemoaning the demise of the Democratic Party at the hands of Ray Jacks. I know Ray Jacks, and all he did was battle the Gilmores and their quest to destroy the party and the freedom of choice it represents. Jacks went to jail because the Gilmores have immense power, and can influence who is allowed to remain free and who gets locked up in a political prison. Can't happen in the good old USA? Think again, people. It is happening! Right here in Oklahoma—God-fearing, upstanding, freedom-loving Oklahoma. If it can happen here, it can happen anywhere. Time to fight!

Of course, *The Banner* was almost universally ignored. But the power elites and members of the media never missed an issue.

PART III
RELATIONSHIPS

1968. The war, Nixon winning the election, more riots over race—the year wasn't ending on an upbeat note. The president promised law and order, but at what price? The year began with optimism, but for many it was ending with fear.

21
WHAT THE HELL IS HAPPENING

"I have no connections in the police department," Steve Marsh snarled, "and if I did, I wouldn't tell you."

"Why not? I'm a nice guy." Albright smiled. Marsh was not exactly a friend—exactly what he was, Albright wasn't sure. He'd asked if Marsh could give him the name of someone in the police department who might know whether Tony Walters had asked about the Allen Clark suicide investigation before Walters was killed.

"You're a wise-ass who thinks he knows everything, but you don't know shit," Marsh growled.

The two were in Triple's, a bar on Classen Boulevard, not far from Albright's apartment. He'd seen and talked to Marsh there before, and none of their conversations had gone well. This one didn't seem promising either. Knowing who Marsh was didn't give him the right to walk up to him while he sat drinking and watching a football game with friends, but he didn't seem to care.

"I heard you were with Walters the night he was shot," he said. "So I thought maybe you could help me out."

"Not likely." Marsh was getting angrier, but Albright didn't seem to notice. "You need to go away before I put my fist in your damn ugly face." Marsh started off the barstool.

Stylishly clad as always, Max and Nathan walked in at that moment to meet Albright. Instantly, they blocked Marsh's path.

"You'd better tell your dandy boys to back off, or I'll rough up those wonderful suits." Marsh had a silly grin on his face—maybe because he thought he'd said something witty.

Nathan, the quieter of the two, moved so fast no one could follow, grabbing and twisting Marsh's hand, pivoting him toward the bar, and slamming his head onto it. Marsh, out like a light, slid to the floor. Triple's was a quiet neighborhood place. The regulars sat, or stood, stunned into stillness.

Marsh moaned. One of his friends pulled him upright. He didn't look good. The bartender said he'd call an ambulance.

"No," Marsh said quietly, "I'm fine. Let's get out of here." He sounded stronger than he looked.

Before Albright and his sluggers could leave, the police showed up. Even with Marsh gone, they arrested Max and Nathan. Albright tried to intervene, and was told to shut up.

He phoned Louongo, who didn't seem concerned. "Don't worry," the lawyer said. "I'll find out where the cops took them and get them released. If Marsh didn't file a complaint, they can't hold them just because they don't like their looks."

Another day in the Wild West. Albright walked home. The next day he got ready for his early morning jaunt to Denny's, beginning with a trip to the newsstand to get the morning papers. The bus ride to Denny's was predictable and the driver was rude. The passengers were a mixture of morning people, mostly down on their luck and headed somewhere not very important, and a few business people who always looked out of place. Albright followed the same routine every day. He was comfortable in a rut.

And now Tommy came to stand before him right at the time he preferred being left alone to read the morning papers. "They took my lead on a story and wasted it. I need some advice."

"Even though they pay you very little, and do it on contingency, you're still an employee," he said, not looking up. "Employees get screwed. It's life. Get used to it."

Tommy took a seat without waiting for an invitation. "I think there's a big story behind that highway bill, and Mitch Douglas is the main player. It's going to cause problems with my sources if they keep running my stuff in useless stories."

"I read Young's piece. It was very cautious. You're overreacting. How did they know you were working on that, anyway?"

"I told June."

"Now, there's your lesson. Never give a heads-up to an editor. You keep that to yourself until you're ready."

Tommy nodded. He should have thought of it himself. "By the way, what happened with your bodyguards? I saw they were arrested."

"Technically, they're not my bodyguards. There was a little misunderstanding in Triple's between my friends and Steve Marsh. Marsh lost."

"Wow, those guys took down the football hero Steve Marsh?"

"Actually, just one of them did. The smaller one." Albright tried and failed to stifle a grin.

"What was the fight about?"

"Well, first off, it wasn't much of a fight. But I guess it was about me. Marsh and I will never be buddies now," he sighed.

"I asked him if he knew who Walters was in contact with at the police department about the suicide of Allen Clark."

"That TV station manager who killed himself?"

"Yeah. You might know his daughter, Tracy. She's been a television reporter in the city a while. She used to work at the same station her dad managed, but after his death she was fired. She got a job at another station."

"My dad knew her. I really don't remember too much about her—or her dad."

"Someone gave me a tip about Walters. They thought it could've been that Walters was looking into that old case, thinking it was murder, not suicide, and the Gilmores were connected."

"Who gave you the tip?"

Albright gave Tommy a quizzical look. "Tommy, you know I'm not going to tell you. At least not right now."

"Seems strange that Walters would be looking into a case that old. Had you talked to him about it before he was killed?"

"I did. We both thought, based on unverified information, that there might be a connection between Clark's death and the Gilmores. He was going after some leads."

"So you were working with Walters?"

"No, not really. We shared some information, and we talked now and then. But what he was actually doing and what he knew for sure, he never said. I don't know why he was killed, and I for sure don't know who did it, if that's what you're going to ask next. Now and then he'd feed me stuff to put in the *Banner*. He was actually a fan. Matter of fact, most of my juicy little tidbits come from people in the news business. They know a lot of things that they can't get into print or on the air, so they toss 'em my way."

"You really are a gossipmonger."

"Now, Tommy, you need to show more respect for your elders." Albright rattled the paper a little. "Boy," he muttered. "It's like the presidential race is all they care about over there at the capitol."

"Judy? How're you doing?"

"I'm okay."

Even over the phone, Tracy knew otherwise. She could sense Judy still wasn't herself. She'd grown into a beautiful young woman, highly regarded by the senator and his office, skilled beyond her years. But her sadness was visible to anyone who saw past her looks.

"Let's have lunch today. Are you available?"

"Tracy, I'm jammed today. Let's do something next week. I'll call you." She hung up.

Tracy wondered if her avoidance was related to Tony Walters's death. She knew Judy had talked to him a lot, and sometimes met him for drinks. She never thought it was anything romantic, though—they weren't a couple, as anyone could see. But what they were, she didn't know. She suspected, knowing Walters, that he used her to get information out of Bud Evans's office, because that was how he worked. Why Judy would let him do that was the puzzle.

Judy was almost like family to her. They'd shared a lot of pain, much of it from the deaths of their fathers. Judy's had died of a heart attack less than a year ago. But even in her grief, she hadn't seemed as low as now. Tracy was working for her third station in Oklahoma City after being fired from KVY right after her father's death. She knew she could get a better job if she left the Oklahoma City market, but stayed, mostly for Judy. She thought of her like a younger sister, believing she needed someone to trust and depend on.

Although she was attractive and successful, an unmarried professional and only in her twenties, Tracy spent most of her evenings at home alone, watching TV. It wasn't the life she wanted. Why she didn't accept the almost daily invitations she got for dates and dinners was something even she didn't really understand. Everything had come unglued after her father was murdered, although police called it a suicide. Maybe that was what burdened her, what made her so withdrawn and angry with others. She knew in her heart that his death had something to do with the Gilmores. That complicated her connection with Judy.

Judy once had an affair with Robbie Gilmore. She sought Tracy out for consolation, someone to talk to, after he ended it. "I was attracted to him, I think, because of who he was," she confessed. "I knew he was married, but I didn't care. I guess I'm just young and stupid. He was rich and famous, and I fell for him."

The affair began when Robbie visited Judy's college to talk to a journalism class. He'd lavished attention on her. Besides being flattered, she was attracted. A very important man was concerned about her and what she would do after graduation. He asked to see her again the following week—over dinner. She didn't think about how wrong that seemed, or maybe she decided she didn't care.

They had wonderful dinners, always at out-of-the-way restaurants, all expensive and romantic. He made her feel like an adult, in charge and aware of who she was and what she was doing. He talked to her about working at the *Sun* after she graduated. She could be a wonderful help to him, he told her, running one of the biggest organizations in the state. Anyone outside the situation would have heard how absurd that sounded, but not her. He asked her to his hotel room, just for a nightcap. She didn't tell him she didn't drink. She went.

Their affair lasted an intense three weeks. She fell in love, she told Tracy. Her whole life became nothing but Robbie and their time together. When he wasn't with her, she waited on him to call. She knew he wasn't the most attractive man, and he was almost twice her age, but she didn't care. He was her Prince Charming. There had been boyfriends in her past, and she'd even slept with one, but none like him. Her feelings were so intense, it almost frightened her.

Then he told her it was over. It wasn't fair, he said, for her to spend so much time with an older man like him. He mentioned his wife and kids. She later told Tracy how her brain suddenly kicked into gear—she remembered his children were her age. She cried for days, not because the affair was over, but because she felt like something far worse than a mere idiot. Her self-respect collapsed. And she was too humiliated to tell her dad.

Weeks went by. She heard nothing more from Robbie, which was how she wanted it. She began to feel better about herself. At least it was over, and she could find a way to forget it. Then she missed her period. A doctor confirmed she was pregnant. She called Robbie.

He made an appointment to talk to her in an abandoned

office the *Sun* owned. Seeing him again, she couldn't believe she could ever have had sex with him. Everything about him seemed old and ugly. He droned on and on about his position in the community, about being an elder in his church, about how devastated his wife would be, and even had the nerve to say he couldn't believe Judy had been so stupid. If she'd had a gun, she told Tracy, she would have shot the bastard right then and there. She'd never felt such hatred.

He wanted her to have an abortion. Her first reaction was to say no, but she realized all the other options seemed worse. She agreed. He said he knew a place in Shawnee where it could be done, and that he'd pay for everything. She wondered how he knew about such a place, but didn't ask. In a matter of weeks, it was over.

Tracy had her come to stay a while afterward, and helped her get her classes straightened out so she wouldn't fail. She convinced Judy to start talking to her dad again, using the cover story that she'd broken up with a boyfriend. As far as he knew, she'd been upset, but was over it.

Tracy did everything she could, but made one big mistake. Her anger toward Robbie Gilmore, whom she'd always disliked for the way he handled the television station, blossomed into hatred. She'd seen the pain he'd caused up close, and she wanted him to pay. Too angry to think about consequences, she told her father about Robbie and Judy.

She would never forgive herself for what followed. Robbie fired Allen Clark after a confrontation over Judy. Not long after, her father was dead—and she believed Robbie had something to do with it.

22

HI HO, HI HO

Tommy sat in a booth at El Chico, working his way through a large basket of warm tortillas with butter and salsa, waiting for Judy. She'd agreed to meet him for lunch. He'd been sure she'd say no, that she already had plans. But she'd said yes. So, of course, all at once he wasn't sure it was a good idea. And now here she was.

"Tommy! Great to see you. I was so excited when you called. I've been wanting to get together, but I guess you've been super busy, what with your new job and everything. Did I mention this is my favorite place to eat? I just love it."

So far, so good. She looked stunning, and smiled like she meant it about being glad to see him. She was so beautiful and looked so mature, he felt like a child. "Glad you like it. I like it because it seems okay if you eat more than you should." He chuckled, already feeling the heat of inner self-criticism—*You want to sound like you're some kind of pig?*

"I know," she gushed, sliding in across from him. "It's so delicious. Unfortunately, I have to watch what I eat, or I'd weigh a ton. It was great when I was a kid and could eat anything I wanted. Gail, in the office, is on some kind of diet all the time. Seems like all she eats is lettuce. I think I'd rather starve." Judy smiled. It was glorious.

They spent a few minutes looking at the menu. The pause seemed to stall the conversation.

"Tell me how your job's going," she said, jump-starting things again. "I read your column every time it comes out. You're really very good." Once again, she showed a maturity Tommy still needed to work on.

"It's okay, I guess. Still have a lot to learn, so there're days it feels like I'm messing up more than anything. I have a great editor, and she's helped me a lot. My biggest challenge is that I'm supposed to develop stories on my own, and I still don't know a lot of people. And there are some people who won't talk to me because of my dad."

"Well, forget them," she sympathized, earnestly. "Your dad got a raw deal. My dad said it was more like a lynching. He was going to testify, but he never had much to do with the money, so all he could do was vouch for your dad's character. But he wanted to say in court how much your father did and how honest he was. For them to screw him the way they did was just wrong."

She was real. Not a perfect, never-say-a-bad-word type. Hallelujah. She was a normal human being, and she was on his side.

"Thanks. That means a lot." He shrugged. "I've struggled with all that about my dad. Only went to see him in prison for the first time a little while ago. Huge mistake to stay away. As soon as I saw him, I knew we needed each other. He's probably not the best father, but he's mine."

Judy seemed to turn sad. Tommy feared he'd shot off his big mouth too much about having a jailbird for a father. "You okay?"

"Yeah, fine. Just a little sad. My dad died last year. I miss him. You wouldn't have known that, I understand. It's really just fine, now. You need to keep working on that relationship with your dad—it'll mean a lot."

They relaxed after that, talking about how important those relationships can be, especially with no mom around. It seemed to help them to connect. After lunch, he walked her out to her car.

"Thank you so much," she said, smiling. "I want to do this again. Maybe we can make it a regular thing." She gave him a kiss on the cheek and left.

He suddenly felt much more grown-up. He headed back to the press room in the capitol. His task for the day was to attend a hearing on the highway bill. He knew it might be so boring as to be life-threatening. Or, if Douglas was there, it could be nothing like that.

"Let me understand this. You got into a fight in a bar with Albright's bodyguards for no apparent reason—is that about right?" Robbie was unhappy.

"That asshole Albright pissed me off," Marsh replied testily. "I wasn't looking for a fight. I was minding my own business. His queer bodyguards know some kind of judo or something— look at my face. You think I'm happy with two black eyes and a broken nose?" Marsh would have liked nothing better than to bounce Robbie's face off his desk to see how he liked it.

"I don't believe this was anything Steve could have avoided," Rod Baker jumped in. "I don't know if it was a setup, but these are serious people. As soon as Steve gave me a call, I contacted the police, and they went to the bar and arrested the two weirdos from New York. My contact at the department agreed to charge them with felony assault. They could have gotten five years, but that slimeball Louongo shows up and within the hour, they're out. And now they're talking about a misdemeanor, just a fine—maybe even dropping charges. My guy at police headquarters says someone stepped in and overrode what he had in place. He thinks it was the chief himself."

"Those guys don't have any clout," Robbie growled. "Why would the police chief bail them out?"

"Rumor is it has something to do with Frank Martin."

"Big Frank Martin?"

"Yep."

Robbie sighed. "Shit. Why would he be involved with Albright?"

Baker shook his head. "I don't think it's Albright. I think it's the bodyguards."

"Queer bodyguards from New York City with a stockyard gangster behind them? Has everyone gone nuts? What the hell does Albright need bodyguards for, anyway? Rod, do you know?"

Baker looked a little sheepish. "No idea. One thing's for sure, they aren't your usual thugs. What that one guy did to Steve in a matter of seconds was unbelievable. And if they're tied to Big Frank in any way, that'd make 'em untouchable."

"Both of you think real hard before you answer this," Robbie looked at them. "Does this have anything to do with Walters getting himself killed?"

"How the fuck would I know?" Marsh's mood went immediately from foul to dangerous.

"I don't know about any connection with Walters." Baker wasn't about to tell what he knew. It wouldn't be good for anyone in the room.

"Shit. I'm supposed to be running a newspaper, not getting mixed up with cops and gangsters. What a mess. I don't have time to deal with this. We've got major legislation we're pushing, and we've hit some roadblocks. J.H. wants me to get more involved. You guys are going to have to figure out what all this is about with Albright, Big Frank, and whoever else is mixed up in this mess. Just don't get me or the paper involved. In fact, Marsh, it might be best if you went back to the sports desk for a while." Robbie grinned.

Marsh frowned. He and Baker left together.

"I'd like to know where those little pricks live," Marsh snarled. "Can you find that out?"

Baker looked at him. "I know you're pissed, but remember, it was the smaller guy who almost killed you in the blink of an eye. And if they're under Big Frank's protection, you'll want to stay clear."

"A gangster, right here in Oklahoma City. I've been all over this town, and I've never heard of this Big Frank guy. It's like you're scared of him. Are you scared of him, Mister Tough Guy?"

Baker stopped in the middle of the hallway. "You're damned right I'm scared of him. And if you're not, you're just country stupid. This isn't football, Marsh. These guys'll crunch your balls with rusty pliers and smile while they're doin' it. This is serious shit. Don't do *anything* for now. I'll figure out what we can do, if anything. Just lay low and stay out of bars, okay?"

"Yeah. Yeah."

Fred Simpson knew this: he should have been fired, too, when Albright was canned years ago. He'd screwed up just as badly, but Albright took the fall.

Albright told Anderson that he'd claimed to Fred that he had the approvals they needed, and he was completely innocent. After all, Fred had kids, a mortgage, and few prospects if he got fired. Fred hadn't told anyone the truth either, and he still felt sick every time it crossed his mind. He'd let that article go to print because he assumed all the boxes were checked. But they weren't. And he should have made sure. He'd known better, but he let it happen because he trusted Albright. And a good editor never fully trusts his writers.

Fred still loved his job, but the paper was different ever since the Albright incident. Anderson became more involved and more cautious. Fred understood, but it sure took a lot of the fun out of the job.

"June, need you to get hold of Vince and have him get over to the capitol quick as he can. They have a highway bill meeting this afternoon I'd like him to cover. Could be nothing or, if Mitch Douglas is there, it could be something. Also, call Tommy and tell him we want him to start writing two 'My View' columns a week, starting next week."

June raised an eyebrow. "You know; he's fighting to write just one."

"I know, I know," he snapped. "Not my idea. We're cutting one of the syndicated columns—just can't afford it. Bill wants to fill in with Tommy. Either he'll grow with the job or he won't. I can't babysit everybody who works here." Fred stopped. He knew being assistant city editor wasn't a fun job under the best of circumstances, and having a boss in a lousy mood only made it worse. "June, wait. Sorry about that. Help Tommy the best you can. I think he can do it, if he'll just let loose a little. Have him go see Albright. Maybe he can coach him some. Tell him we're really pleased with what he's been doing, and this is a chance for him to step up. Don't mention that stuff about cutting costs, okay?"

"Okay, Fred. Who knows? He might surprise us."

"Two! Are you kidding?" Tommy nearly dropped the capitol press room phone.

"Sorry, Tommy," June said, "I'm not kidding. Look, Fred thinks you're headed in the right direction. He really likes some of the things you've done. This is a chance to have more impact and really be noticed. I know it'll be a challenge, but we're all behind you."

Yeah, way *behind,* he thought. It sounded like a corporate bullshit pep talk. He knew what he'd done hadn't been all that good, and he was struggling to write as much as he did now. It was hard to imagine doing a whole other column. He knew the idea had something to do with money. They were already paying him peanuts, so why not get him to write more?

"It's just that I'm struggling to get enough for one column." He knew he sounded whiny. "Are you sure that's what Fred wants?"

"He even suggested you go see Albright—see if he could coach you some."

"You're not serious—he really said that? I thought Albright was *persona non grata* there."

"He still has friends here. Do the best you can, and let me know if there's anything I can do."

"Okay," he sighed. "Thanks, June."

Were they asking him to steal leads from Albright's *Banner?* Take the off-the-wall items he was sticking out there, clean 'em up some, and run them? Albright would scream bloody murder, and surely Fred wouldn't allow it. Or would he?

If there had been a cot in the press room, Tommy would have taken a nap. When things got too confusing, it was his solution of choice. Oh, well—he figured the next best thing would be the highway bill hearing. Off he went.

The hearing room could accommodate eighteen legislators and about the same number of spectators. Tommy walked in a few minutes early. Inside stood three representatives, a half-dozen staffers, and Vince Young.

"Hey, Vince. Being punished for some reason?"

"Hey, Tommy. How do I know? Got a call from June, said I should be here, per Fred." He looked around, dimly. "Maybe there's another secret meeting where all the action is."

The committee chairman came in. He consulted in whispers with the three legislators, then called one of the staffers over to talk for a bit. They all left except one, who told Tommy and Vince the hearing would be rescheduled.

"What do you think that was about?" Vince didn't seem upset. Reporters were usually put off, asked to leave, or flat-out ignored. "Think I'll go by Mitch Douglas's office, see if he knows," he decided. "Wanna tag along?"

"Sure."

At Douglas's office they found two security guards arguing about something in the hall. The door stood open, through which Tommy and Vince could see the representative in his office, throwing things against the wall.

Vince hit the brakes, but Tommy headed inside. "Representative Douglas? What's all the excitement?"

The man turned on him. "You bastards in the press think you can just go anywhere you want. I've had all I'm going to take of this bullshit." He charged, slamming Tommy into the wall, knocking the wind out of him.

The two guards grabbed Douglas, who was still screaming and ready to fight. All three rolled on the floor while Tommy gasped for breath. Vince leaned around the door frame, an inch at a time. Somehow Douglas grabbed one of the guard's pistols, managed to get away behind a chair, and stood slowly, pointing it at the guards, then Tommy, and then Vince, who ducked back into the hall.

"Mitch, you're making one big mistake," the guard who'd lost his pistol seethed. "My partner still has his weapon, and if you make one wrong move, he'll kill you. Do you understand me?"

Douglas looked like he really didn't care for a moment. Then the more or less normal man he usually was returned. He looked at the gun in his hand and at the guards, at Tommy and at his mostly destroyed office. His face drained of color. With great care, he placed the gun on the floor and sank into the chair.

"What in hell have I done?"

He'd given Tommy just what he needed.

OK Journal

My View—Tommy Jacks

Mitch Douglas, the Republican state representative from Perkins, has no idea what he has done. He said so himself.

Here's the quote he uttered at the critical moment: "What in (heck) have I done?"

Well, Mitch, no one can say for sure. It all happened so fast. But here's as much as we know: whatever you did had little to do with a bill to reroute road construction money. It has to do with the fact that an elected official from a pretty little town near Stillwater has been found out. And there's no way to keep it out of the papers.

The last thing a legislator will put up with is finding himself at the mercy of the public's right to know. When backed into such a corner, some will lash out at newspaper reporters in particular and journalism in general.

Rep. Douglas' attack on journalism left this reporter with a pain in the back or thereabouts. Douglas hasn't spoken to anyone, except maybe the Capitol Police, since the strange incident in his office.

Word on the street is that Douglas's brother, who owns a road construction company headquartered in Perkins, is under investigation by state and federal officials regarding possible misuse of highway funds.

The aftermath of the matter, which Vince Young's story elsewhere in the *Journal* details, was interesting, in the same way that detentions of witnesses to embarrassing incidents in the offices of banana republic dictators can be interesting. Both reporters were wheedled, pleaded with, condescended to, delayed, and plied with every tactic short of the iron maiden to keep us from telling you what Mitch did.

23
FACTS VS. FICTION

Tommy waited in an exam room at the capitol clinic. He'd told everyone he was fine, that he'd only had the wind knocked out of him. Senator Evans and Judy came there once they'd heard, and she'd insisted he either go to a hospital or the clinic. He'd chosen the clinic, and she'd walked there with him, which he liked.

He'd heard of people losing their minds before, but it was a shock to see it happen. He still didn't know what prompted Douglas to fly off the handle. But, no question, he'd flipped out. Tommy couldn't decide whether he felt sorry for Douglas or not. He'd heard how the guy bullied everyone, so maybe he deserved whatever happened to him. Then he recalled the look on Douglas's face once he'd realized what he'd done. He decided he deserved some sympathy, even if he was an asshole.

Vince Young knocked and peeked inside. "Mind if I come in?"

"What's happening out there?"

"Well, they ran me off. Mitch is locked in his office with almost every security officer in the building. The leaders are in a huddle upstairs. If it wasn't for you and me, I think the whole thing'd get swept under the rug. Judy's in the waiting room— looks pretty worried about you." Vince tossed Tommy a silly grin. "They asked me to stick around. I'm not sure they won't toss us in some dungeon and tell everybody *we* pulled a gun on Mitch and the guards. When in doubt, string up the press."

Tommy was beginning to appreciate Vince's sense of humor. "What do you think we should do?"

"We could make a break for it. Maybe take Judy hostage." He seemed to be enjoying himself. "Probably not the best option, though. They'd shoot all three of us." He sobered a little. "I bet in just a while they'll ask us to downplay what we saw, say old Mitch was having a bad day, go on about his family and how hurtful the story would be if we ran it—even if it's nothing but the truth. We'll listen, and then they'll let us go. And we'll go ahead and write up every detail. They already know that, so they're stalling, trying to come up with some kind of cover story. My pick would be that Mitch is on doctor-prescribed medication to help him deal with his stressful job, and that he had a bad reaction to his pills. The guards'll say it wasn't a big deal, and us reporters, being weak, sniveling creatures, are just twisting it all out of proportion."

Tommy snickered. "Or they could suggest the whole thing was brought on by a young, inexperienced reporter who entered Mitch's office without permission and made threatening gestures."

"I like that. I'm sure they'll think of it. '*My god, if it had not been for the brave response of the Capitol Police, who stopped the aggressive actions of the belligerent reporters, we might've had a tragedy today. We appreciate the cooperation of the downright Honorable Mitch Douglas in restoring order.*' How about that?"

They laughed, even if it was as depressing as it was funny. They knew something not that different would happen.

Vince ducked out. The doctor came in and declared Tommy was fit to travel.

"You okay?" Judy asked, in her delicious voice.

"Yeah. No harm. Thanks for waiting. Really, I'm fine." He wanted to scream, *and I love you,* but the time and place didn't seem right.

"I guess I'll get back to work. The security officer said they wanted you to wait here until they could talk to you. I think Vince is in the hall. After this all gets cleared up, give me a call. Maybe we could meet for a drink or something?" She left. Tommy closed his mouth.

Vince's prediction was on the mark. They were asked to delay any news stories until the officers could complete their investigation. They didn't say how long that would take, and it didn't matter because everyone knew they'd file as soon as possible. The mix of pleas and veiled threats lasted about an hour. Vince headed for the *Journal.* Tommy went upstairs to the press room which, although in the capitol building, still felt like a sanctuary.

He was still thinking about what to write when it occurred to him no one had called the city police. And no one asked if he wanted to press charges. Douglas had been the attacker, but all the concern was for him. Another life lesson lay buried in that pile of manure. He started typing.

Vince's article and Tommy's "My View" column appeared in the paper the next morning. He thought his piece was good, but worried his perspective might be off. He decided to seek input from his unofficial guru, at Denny's.

"Congratulations! That was the first column where you actually sounded like you knew what you were talking about."

Tommy wasn't sure if that was meant as a compliment. Could the man possibly be any more irritating? "Thanks—I think."

"Based on this, you can expect some sources like the Capitol Police to dry up, but other doors will open. You declared your independence from the powers that be. That's a very important step if you're going to get people to share dirt with you. I liked your style. Sort of reminded me of someone."

Okay, so I wrote it like you would, your majesty. I'm learning."

"Yep, I think you might be trainable."

"I read those past issues of *The Banner* you gave me. In one you mentioned the Walters murder. You left me hanging the other day with how that could be connected to the Clark suicide. What can you tell me?"

"Not sure. Not trying to be cute. I just don't have anything I can verify, like circumstantial evidence that his death wasn't suicide. There's the state-of-mind issue. Most people, including his daughter, thought he was gearing up to fight the Gilmores. Plus—and this is a big deal—I've been told, although I don't have any documentation for it, that the autopsy suggests he was murdered. I believe that's what Walters found—proof that the cops, or someone in the police administration, declared it suicide, even though they knew it wasn't."

"Then the motive for Walters's killing could be someone trying to cover up the previous cover-up in the Clark murder."

"Could be. I think the logical suspects include someone in the police department who was involved in the cover-up and whoever it was that actually killed Clark. Of course, it could be someone we know nothing about, but I'm convinced they're connected. Solve one and you solve the other."

"What about the Gilmores?"

"What I can guess," he said, "is very different from what I know, which isn't much. I can guess the confrontation that led to Robbie firing Clark also led to him being killed. Does that mean it was Robbie? No, but it could be connected. It's an awfully big coincidence that Robbie and Clark had a blow-up, Robbie fired Clark, and next thing you know, he's dead. We know Clark made himself sick after he was fired, at least according to his daughter. There was something eating at him that he couldn't let go. My guess is that whatever caused the original confrontation was never resolved, and Clark threatened Robbie. But without knowing what that *thing* was, we're kind of lost."

"So, is the prime suspect Robbie Gilmore?"

"Once again, don't know. Your father knew Robbie from when they were younger. I got the impression they went to school together. Maybe they were friends. Based on the person he knew then; he doesn't think Robbie's a killer. He thinks if Robbie was involved, it was more likely that some of his people got out of hand. I'm new to Okieland, so I don't have an opinion on Robbie's character. But remember, there's another connection to the Gilmores. Walters had just been fired by old man Gilmore, and he'd been talking about revenge. Hard to ignore those similarities without thinking the Gilmores are involved. And whether they did it, or suggested it be done, it's still murder."

His father was a friend of Robbie Gilmore? That was news

to Tommy. "I'm going to see my dad this weekend. The last time I saw him he said you were dangerous, and I should stay away from you."

"Your father's a wise man. I think I'd listen to him."

The freakishly tidy bodyguards appeared, unannounced and unheard, making Tommy jump a little when he noticed them.

"My ride's here. We need to talk more about this after you see your dad." Albright left the pile of papers. Maybe as some kind of weird tip.

Tommy ordered breakfast and read the leftovers. Vince's article was perfect. He really appreciated the man's skill. He was starting to see writing not always as some kind of art, but as a way to convey information—factual and concise. As a student, he often used more words than necessary because he thought it sounded good. Now he understood the journalist's challenge was to inform the reader with an impersonal account of the facts and keep yourself out of it. As a columnist, he had more freedom. But he admired the ones who did it right.

Back in the press room, Tommy found a message from June to give her a call.

"Tommy, your column was great. Bill wanted me to call and thank you. You're doing a great job."

Tommy listened, nervous, knowing there had to be a "but" in here somewhere. "Well, thanks, June. Tell Mister Anderson thanks, too."

"I will. On another matter—Chuck, the police beat reporter, told Bill he thinks Frank Martin—not sure if you know about him, but he's the Oklahoma version of a Chicago gangster— was involved in the release of the two guys who got into that fight with Steve Marsh. Anyway, Bill's worried about Albright.

He's afraid maybe Taylor doesn't know what he could be getting involved in with this Martin guy. So, to get to the point, he was wondering if you could look around a bit and see if there's anything going on with Taylor and Martin."

What?! I'm supposed to find out if Taylor Albright is involved in organized crime? Tommy wanted to yell at the phone. "I don't want to be disrespectful, but why doesn't Mister Anderson just call Taylor? Aren't they still friends?"

"Good question." June hesitated. "I think it's just that Bill doesn't want Taylor to know he's concerned."

"So he wants me to snoop around and find out something he's not willing to just call his friend and ask him, right?"

"Look, Tommy, if you don't want to do it, just say so. Nobody'll hold that against you. Bill just thought you were in contact with Taylor anyway, and maybe you could just look into it a little and let him know if there was a reason to be concerned."

Tommy could see the only way out of this was something along the lines of, "screw you." He was about forty years away from retirement age, though, so maybe it wasn't the time to throw his job away. But he didn't have to like it. "Okay. I'll see what I can find out. By the way, the only difference between a Chicago gangster and an Oklahoma gangster is a pair of boots. Talk to you soon."

He went downstairs for coffee, and noticed Bart sitting nearby.

"Hey Bart, how're things?"

"Not sure I'm supposed to talk to you, Tommy."

"Why's that?"

"Not sure about that, either. I was told you attacked someone, and we had to keep an eye on you."

"Well, we can still talk while you keep an eye on me. And if I have the urge to attack somebody, I'll let you know beforehand."

Bart didn't digest sarcastic humor easily. He seemed to be thinking way too hard.

"Just kidding, Bart. I'm not going to attack anyone. And if you can't talk to me, I understand."

"Yeah. But it doesn't seem right, though. You're my friend. It's just that I need this job, and it seems like every day they threaten they'll take it away."

"It's okay. This'll blow over in a few days, and we'll talk then. We're still friends. Take care of yourself." Some overbearing boss was intimidating Bart. Tommy wanted to know who that boss was and find an excuse to bring up the moron's name in his column—and not in a good way.

OK Journal

My View—Tommy Jacks

Our state leaders will give you anything but the troublesome truth.

The Soviet Union came up with two ways to handle that. One was to misinform—to lie, in other words. The other was to dis-inform, to act as if a troublesome truth doesn't exist or never happened. Oklahoma isn't a dictatorship, at least not officially, so it's a bit tougher to mislead people here.

Dis-informing, however, is something our government, and the people who aren't elected but who still work deep inside it, work at. It is a delicate art. Just ignoring a question or issue won't do. The truth has to be cut off at its source. You have to tell the people who know a troublesome truth to clam up, not to talk to us who are paid to let the public know what's going on.

First, it was the murder of Tony Walters, a reporter for another paper. No one with a badge or a title seems to care that he was shot to death, let alone why, so he lies twice buried. Second was Allen Clark, the city TV station manager—another journalist—whose death was ruled a suicide six years ago. That's exactly how long anyone with brains hasn't believed that story, but it gets repeated every time someone tries to dig into it.

And third comes Rep. Mitch Douglas, R-Perkins, and his unhinged behavior. Maybe he was reacting to the sudden collapse of his political and financial duchy up in Payne County. But who knows? The word throughout the capitol is not to talk about it in public, especially not with reporters.

Oh, but they're not covering anything up. Just read their press releases.

24
FAMILY HISTORY

Tommy's second visit to Big Mac went more smoothly. Familiarity with the process helped, tedious and unnerving as it could be. The place was a prison, after all.

"Tommy, it's so great to see you. How are you? How's your new job going?"

He was pleased his dad was in such a good mood, even if he knew it was likely an act. Nobody could feel upbeat locked away. He couldn't begin to imagine. "Everything's great dad. I'm learning more every day."

"When I first saw they'd asked you to take over Albright's old column, I was furious," Jacks said seriously. "I thought they were just going to drag all the old bitterness from my time into your life. But after I read some of them, I decided it might be okay. Plus, I guess Bill needs to play every angle he can to keep the paper afloat."

"Yeah, I wasn't happy about it at first. Seemed like it was just asking people to compare me to Albright. But it's worked out so far. Not real sure about the *Journal*. Seems like most things there are decided based on money. Everyone who works there's just waiting for some bad news about their jobs."

"Well, Bill does the best he can. He's a smart man. If anyone can get a foothold against Gilmore in this market, I'd bet on him. So, what're you writing about next?"

"Oh, this and that." Tommy continued, more carefully, "You know, since I started the columns, I've talked to Albright some. There were a couple of things he said about you that I wanted to ask about."

"Sure."

"One was that you use to be friends with Robbie Gilmore. And you don't think he's a killer."

"Yeah," Jacks said, nodding. "For years and years, he was my best friend. This is family history I should've shared with you a long time ago." He paused as if to gather his thoughts, or maybe his courage. "As you know, your grandparents died before you were born, and it never seemed like the right time. But you need to know their history."

Yes. This was something Tommy wanted to know but never got up the nerve to ask.

"Your grandfather was an extremely wealthy man. In the 1920s, he was one of the most successful wildcat drillers in Oklahoma. He was a gambler by nature, and the oilfields were his game of choice. This was way before there was much science involved in figuring out where to drill. Most of it was experience and a gut feeling. Those wildcat drillers would sometimes be worth a fortune one month and broke the next. My dad was lucky—maybe skilled. He strung together an amazing run of successes like no one had seen before. He was a millionaire when they were really rare.

"When I was born, in 1921, my parents were living in Crown Heights, the most exclusive spot in Oklahoma City, in a big mansion. Our neighbors were the Gilmores. On the wealth scale of the whole state, my father was probably number one, and J.H. number two. He had one son, about a year older than me. That was Robbie. We were playmates and best friends. We went to the same private school. We played the same sports. We were more like brothers than anything, it seemed like we were always together.

He sighed. "Then things went really bad for my dad in 1934. The stock market crash hit him, like it did most people with money. What really hurt him, though, was that investors in wildcat drilling started pulling out. It was too risky. My dad was more gambler than oilman, and I guess he couldn't stop what he was doing, even if he should've. He had a hunch about an oilfield out by Enid. He poured all his cash into a group of wells—every single one a dry hole. Pretty soon, he was flat broke.

"In the summer of '36, two months before my fifteenth birthday, he went out into the gazebo in the back yard, and shot himself in the head."

"That's horrible." Tommy was enraptured and moved.

"Yes, it was. I guess Mom lost her mind. She fell ill, stayed in bed. The doctors couldn't find anything wrong with her, but she'd lost the will to live. And then there were Pop's creditors and their lawyers, all after us. One lawyer who'd been Pop's friend, name of Harlan King, stepped in and helped. After everything was sold—the mansion, too—we moved into a tiny little apartment. Mom got out of bed, finally, but she'd lost all her spark.

"Some of the oilfield assets were sold, and the money came to my mother. I'd graduated from high school by then. She was feeling better, and wanted me to go to school. She bought a small house in Edmond, and I started going to Central State.

She never did get back to her old self. I finished college and got a job through an old contact of my father's at the capitol. I was working as an aide to one of the senators. I'd decided I wanted to be involved in politics, so I got a degree in political science."

"It's so strange I didn't know any of this."

"I'm sorry, Tommy. You know, things got a little out of hand for me after your mother died. If she'd lived, it would've been very different. Anyway, it was then that I met your mother. I needed to hire nurses for Mom, and she applied. I don't want to embarrass you, but there was a spark between us right away. She was the kindest, most caring nurse Mom ever had. They got to be close. And so did your mom and me. I asked her to marry me, and she said yes. We told Mom, and she was real pleased—and I have no idea if my mother had just hung on until I was settled or not, but it seemed like it. Because within a few weeks, she passed away."

"That's sad," Tommy sighed, and thought a moment. "Did you see Robbie after you moved from the mansion?"

"No. I should've mentioned that one thing Robbie and I had in common back in the glory days was that we were snobs. I'd like to say it was just Robbie, but I was as bad as he was. Well, when the money was gone, and especially after Pop committed suicide, the Gilmores just pulled away. They completely ignored my mother and me. All that, and then to have my best friend shun me—well, it was hard. The only time I talked to Robbie after that was at some kind of social thing where there wasn't a lot of choice. I think we both felt awkward. He became a complete stranger."

"Tell me about my mother."

Jacks smiled sadly. "She was the love of my life. She was

everything that mattered to me. I was still bitter, but she made me forget all that and look to the future. We got married and were happy every single day. We worked, and we took time to enjoy each other's company—those were the happiest years of my life. We didn't have much money, but life was almost perfect. And we very much wanted a child, especially your mother. She wanted to be a mom, and stay home and raise kids. And then we found out about you. You were born, and we became a family. Life seemed whole again. We loved it.

"But then she got sick. She was diagnosed with breast cancer. It was hard. Her sister came to live with us, mostly to help with you, but your mother went downhill pretty fast. Everyone was worried, but she was the one who kept telling me and her sister it would be all right. It wasn't long until she was gone. Your aunt hates me to this day. I guess she thought I was supposed to do something to save her. But there was nothing I could do." He looked down, trying to hide the fact that he was crying.

"Dad, I think I need to go out for a little while. Do you think they'll let me? Go out and come back?"

"It's okay, son. I know it's hard. Ask them to let you use the restroom."

Tommy knew his dad had to relive the pain to tell the story. It was hard to listen to, but he appreciated being treated like an adult. One night several years before, after his dad had had way too much to drink, he'd told him that after his wife's death he'd considered suicide. They never mentioned the conversation the next day, and most likely he didn't remember. Knowing his grandfather had killed himself made that night seem even more frightening than it did then.

Tommy returned from the restroom. "I'm sorry for all of the pain you lived with. I love you, dad."

"I love you, too, Tommy." They hugged. The guard gave them the eye, but it was a contact room after all.

They spent several moments sharing the quiet, each absorbed in his thoughts.

"Well," Jacks asked, "what was the other question you had where my name came up?"

Tommy wiped some tears away. "What should I know about Big Frank Martin and Tracy Clark?"

"Well, well. Mister Reporter returns." Ray grinned. "First off, what you should know about Frank Martin is to stay away from him. He's a bad man. And I don't mean sorta kinda evil, I mean *real* evil. People like him can seem normal, but they're not. How did his name come up?"

"Apparently he's got some influence with the police department. When Albright's guards got into it with Marsh and were arrested, he helped get them out."

"Albright's bodyguards are still around?"

"Yeah."

"Wow. I got those guards for Taylor after he was attacked, but that was years ago." He sighed. "I know Martin. He was a contributor to the party, a big one, usually in cash. I shouldn't have taken his money, but I did. Anyway, when I was looking for someone to protect Albright, I asked Big Frank—that's where the bodyguards came from."

"They're Big Frank's men?"

"Not sure I'd say that. He said they were visiting from some other state and could be hired for a short time. They aren't from his usual goon squad. Listen, Tommy, you have to stay as far away as you can from Big Frank Martin. He is dangerous beyond belief."

"What about Tracy Clark? What should I know about her?"

"She's a very good person, someone you can trust. She thinks her father was killed because of his dealings with Robbie. And no, I don't believe Robbie's a killer. I think he's turned out to be a bad person, maybe even evil, and definitely not to be trusted, but he's no killer. I could believe it's possible he somehow caused Allen's death. You should talk to Tracy. She can be a little standoffish, and it might take a while to get her to trust you, but she's been involved firsthand in a lot of the things you're looking into."

Tommy noticed how his dad seemed to liven up at the mention of Tracy. "Do you like her, dad?" He gave him a sly smile.

"What does that mean?"

"Well, you know—do you like her as a friend?"

"This ain't high school. But, matter of fact, I do like her—as a friend." Jacks tried not to smile, unsuccessfully. "Just so you know, Mister Smarty Pants, she came to visit me about a month ago. We had a great time, and I expect she'll be back."

"Ooh. What's this all about?"

The smile became a chuckle. "Kid, I'm still your father, so wipe that grin off of your face."

It was great news. He hoped his father would find someone—hopefully someone the exact opposite of Patty—to have at least a chance at a happier and more stable life. He had another question left, though. "Should I trust Albright?"

"I warned you before that he's dangerous, but I don't mean like Frank Martin. I mean he's a loose cannon. He can go off at any moment. He'd probably describe me as the erratic one, and maybe that's fair. But that man has no fear, and a man with no fear is an extremely dangerous thing. That said, I'd trust him with my life. Plus, I think he might be a genius."

OK Journal

My View—Tommy Jacks

Before we close for the day, let's not forget the customary reminder that Vietnam isn't the only place where people can get killed in service to the American public without anyone in office being concerned enough to act. Two journalists are dead: a television station manager six years ago, and a reporter who covered the capitol just a week ago. The silence hanging over the murder of Tony Walters, shot to death in the capitol parking lot, is deafening. Allen Clark's death, suspiciously ruled a suicide, deserves to be looked into, and seriously this time.

25

A TOMMY DAY

Tommy awoke abruptly, sitting up in bed, shivering, replaying his dream. A monster named Big Dog was chasing him with an axe, and meanwhile he could see himself slowly turning into Albright. He calmed down and started to laugh when he realized the part about turning into Albright was what scared him the most. His "My View" columns had begun to take on an edge like Albright's.

June had passed along Fred's new routine comment, "This better not be crap from the *Banner*," before telling Tommy how they wanted him to change his focus while the legislative session came to an end, and to talk more about U.S. senators and House members. June said Tommy should visit their local offices to get interviews.

"Well, look who's here. Mister Tommy Albright Junior." Albright grinned, but not in a friendly way.

"The only comment I got from Fred was, and I quote, 'This better not be crap from the *Banner*.' They run it as is—no changes. That's a surprise." Tommy slid into the Denny's booth and waved for a cup of coffee.

"It's a daily newspaper," Albright said evenly. "They need content every day. I'd bet you a dollar that Bill's looking for some controversy, too. I know I caused him lots of heartburn in my day, but I sold papers. They want *you* to do that now. Just don't get them sued."

"Yeah, the whole emphasis seems to be on bigger circulation numbers and less cost. I think poor old Douglas is an easy target. There hasn't been anything I said that he'd be able to file suit over."

Tommy wasn't sure what he wanted to discuss with Albright. He knew there were lots of things he hadn't been completely candid about, but maybe that was for the best. His dad seemed to trust him, so maybe it was time to stop suspecting him of being deliberately misleading. Tommy wanted to know what Albright knew, or at least he thought he did. But he needed to be careful.

"Saw my dad. He says 'hi.' He also said he thinks you might be a genius."

"Was that *evil* genius?"

"Oh yeah, I guess *that* was what he said. No, he just said 'genius.' He said you're dangerous because you have no fear. Is that true?"

"You share many annoying qualities with your dad."

"I take that as a compliment." It was obvious Albright wasn't going to answer the question, so Tommy joined him reading the papers for a moment until something else began to bother him too much not to ask. "One more thing. Dad said those bodyguards were hired a long time ago. So, if they're still around, you must be paying them yourself, right?"

"Okay." Albright folded his paper and slapped it on the table. "I've told you many times, they're *not bodyguards*—they used to be. Now when I see them, it's because we've become friends. Nobody's paying them. Maybe you think I have to pay people to associate with me, but there are some discerning folks who seem to enjoy my company."

"Was it Big Frank Martin who got them out of jail?"

Albright looked confused. "Not as far as I know. I thought it was Louongo. What is it you think you know?"

"Not sure I know anything. I've been told Gilmore's got a man named Rod Baker who was pushing to have your buddies locked up for what they did to Marsh. He had things all arranged with the police, when suddenly someone nixed the idea, and now they're treating Max and Nathan with kid gloves. Someone suggested the only person who would have that kind of clout was Martin."

"Well, if that's what happened, it's news to me." Albright looked unhappy. "Got to run, today is a *Banner* day. Maybe I'll include some tidbits about the new investigative reporter at the *Journal*. What do you think?"

"Threat noted. I'll be careful what I say."

Tommy headed for the capitol press room, hoping it was open even if the legislature wasn't in session. It had become his retreat of choice—he didn't like spending time at the *Journal* headquarters with so many bosses around. Right away, though, he saw more activity than normal. He stopped an aide to find out what was going on.

"Governor's office just announced they're firing the head of the highway department," the aide said, in a hurry. "And the attorney general announced that bribery charges are being brought against two people in the department. I think there's going to be a news conference in an hour or two."

Talk about timing. He headed to the press room, where once again he found many more people than usual, with phones ringing and a general clamor.

"Tommy Jacks?"

"Yeah."

"Call for you."

"Hello."

"Its June. Guess you heard about the news conference?"

"Yeah. Just heard. Anything I should know?"

"Not sure. Vince is headed that way, so you might want to meet up with him. Most of us think it's about Mitch Douglas and his brother, but no details yet. This is a big deal for Butler and the Gilmores. Everybody involved has to be appointees of the governor, so it'll be hard for him to claim he wasn't involved. Plus, the Gilmores have been pushing the new highway bill, and they've had a lot of influence in the highway department. And bribery is always good copy. Give me a call once it's over. Good luck."

He felt energized. This was real journalism. It wasn't a surprise that Mitch Douglas was somehow involved. No doubt his conniption the other day was because of something he knew, something related to what was about to happen.

The press room was getting crowded with people Tommy had never seen there before.

"Hey, Tommy."

"Vince. Where'd all of these people come from?"

"Word spread pretty quick. The last thing Butler did like this was about two years ago. He doesn't like press conferences. You've got the wire services, folks from small papers close by—even saw a couple from Tulsa. And over there's a guy I know who writes freelance. We love corruption."

The governor's conference room quickly packed full of reporters. The TV people, with their large crews and bulky cameras, toiled to make everything work, dominating the space. They could broadcast the news as it happened, which seemed to make them feel they were the most important people at any such gathering. Their coverage was almost always superficial, and often impertinently silly, but they could get immediate attention, so the people in charge always looked toward their cameras.

The governor's press aide appeared at the lectern and tapped a microphone. "May I have your attention? The governor will be making a short statement. Following him, the attorney general will also make a statement. Neither will take questions."

Tommy heard low-grade groaning, almost like boos. No questions meant they could have just given out a press release—why drag people down here from all over just to hear a prepared statement?

But everyone followed the script, however absurd. Butler read his statement, which announced who was being fired and explained how disappointed he was that the men in question hadn't properly carried out their duties. The attorney general read an even shorter statement naming two people employed in the Highway Department who would be indicted on charges of accepting bribes, fraud, and making false statements to investigating officers. Both men turned to exit the room, chased by shouted questions.

"Do these crimes involve Representative Douglas or his brother?"

"Who's running the highway department?"

"Bribes from whom?"

"When will you tell us more?"

They were gone. Everyone, other than the TV people, felt cheated. This was a no news conference. It was a press release without the paper. The grumbling spread into the hall as everyone shuffled out.

"Tommy?"

He looked up to see a very attractive TV reporter, and registered that she was Tracy Clark. "Hello."

"Didn't mean to ambush you. Just wanted to say 'Hi.' I'm Tracy Clark. I know your dad."

"Yes, hello. I-I knew who you were. I mean, I know who you are. Hmm. Well, you know what I mean."

Tracy laughed, apparently entertained. "It was a long time ago, but on election night for Butler's first term I saw you at the watch party for Anderson. You've grown into a very handsome young man."

Tommy blushed. "Thanks."

"Now I'm embarrassing you. I didn't mean to. Your dad's a great guy who got a raw deal. I think one reason it happened was that he was trying to help me, so I owe him a lot. If there's anything I can do for you, please give me a call, okay?" She handed Tommy one of her cards.

"Sure. I will." He was still having trouble saying anything that made sense.

Tracy reached out to shake his hand. His mind still fuzzy for reasons even he didn't understand, he stepped forward and hugged her. She hugged him back.

"Sorry." He blushed. "That was rude of me."

"I thought it was very nice. Take care of yourself." She left with her crew.

What the hell was he thinking? She was beautiful, quite a

bit older, and seemed very kind. Maybe he was still, in some ways, a little boy who wanted a mother. He felt close to tears, but kept them from showing. Maybe he needed therapy or something. It all seemed beyond his understanding.

He found Vince in the press room, much less packed now that the news conference that wasn't had ended. "Did you expect that?"

"Hell, no. Even for Butler that was bizarre. My guess is they scheduled the news conference, and then something else happened—something they had to stonewall. But it's bizarre, and not very smart. The general public doesn't really care, but putting on a show like that'll have every journalist alive trying to find out what the hell they're hiding. Might as well wave a red flag and scream, 'Something crazy's going on, but we won't tell ya what!' Makes no sense."

"I know Butler's just an empty suit, but what about the other guy?"

"He's a Gilmore man, too, sort of, as long as they don't ask him to bend his ethics. He's very religious, probably more preacher than prosecutor, so he doesn't forgive transgressions easily. Depending on what we're talking about, he can get pretty hard-ass, especially if it's got anything to do with sex."

"Sex? I think this is mostly about money." Tommy grinned.

"Yep, follow the money and we'll find the guilty party. Talked to June. She said you didn't need to call since nothing happened. See ya."

"Yeah, see ya." Tommy felt a little deflated. Plus, he needed a little time to think about why he'd hugged Tracy Clark so impulsively. Sometime before, he'd discovered a vacant office next door to the press room and, thinking that it wouldn't hurt to have a place to take a quick nap, he'd hidden a sleeping bag in its closet. It could even be locked from the inside. He unrolled his sleeping bag and tried to dream his problems away.

Tommy had always known he was a little unusual, even odd. His occasional need for a nap was one of his oddities. Sometimes you just have to be who you are. After a brief one, he felt better, and decided to find Judy.

"Hey, Tommy. Were you at that news conference today?" Gail gave him a "wasn't that weird?" kind of smile.

"Yep, it was strange. No questions, quick statement, and good-bye."

"Senator Evans has been in meetings all day. I don't know what's going on, but something big must be happening."

Tommy appreciated the info. "Is Judy working today?" He could see she wasn't at her desk.

"Yeah. She had to run some errands, but I expect her back any minute."

He asked to leave a note on her desk, and headed to Risso's.

He chatted with Lopez about the non-news conference and a few other current events before he went into the bar. His note to Judy had said he'd be at Risso's for a little while if she had time for a drink. He put back a few gin and tonics while waiting—unusual for him. He needed something to eat, and ordered a small pizza, always a favorite. Eventually he decided it was long past time for her to be there. He got himself together to go home.

"Tommy, are you leaving?" There she was.

"No. Well, yes. I thought you weren't coming." He wanted to hug her, too. Maybe it was just his day to hug people. He didn't.

"I'm sorry. I was leaving, and someone stopped me and, well, it just held me up. I was hoping you hadn't left."

They went to a booth in the back, ordered another gin and tonic for him and a wine for her. He asked if she liked pizza, which she did, so he ordered another and they drank, ate, and laughed. He relaxed.

"I read your column," she said. "Boy, you're really getting good. It felt like reading one of those guys from Washington or New York."

"Oh, come on, don't B.S. me." It was especially great to hear her say it, though. "Maybe it was as good as some of the Washington guys, but New York? I don't think I'll be that good until maybe next week." That was good for a laugh.

She paused. "It's been a long time since I laughed. Thanks." She looked sad, again.

He was ever aware of her sorrow, but didn't know how to ask her about it. "How about another drink?"

"Why don't we go to your place? Is that okay? We can have a drink there, can't we?"

"Huh." He felt a little ambushed. "Not sure I have much there to drink, and it's a little messy. Well, it might look *very* messy to someone who isn't used to my messes. You know, really, my place is a hole in the wall and might not be suitable for a lady."

Judy leaned over and gave him a kiss on the mouth. "I'll fit right in."

OK Journal

My View—Tommy Jacks

This is what comes of being thrown against a wall.

Gov. Rick Butler, for the first time that anyone can remember, called a press conference. Sort of. Well, not really. In fact, not at all.

It's not a press conference when the press is called there just to stand, listen, take notes, and shut up. Look it up in the dictionary, where it says a conference is a "meeting for discussion."

Butler had a script, and he likes scripts. Besides, his subject for the day carried extra meaning he wasn't about to get into. That extra meaning was standing in the room with him—two report-ers who saw a state representative spin off the axle. One of us—that would be me—had been thrown against a wall by that state repre-sentative.

That representative, Repub-lican Mitch Douglas of Perkins, had made a career of covering up for his brother in the road and highway construction business and the people who were siphon-ing state money toward him.

The few sources who will talk say the Douglas brothers were the reason why Butler had to "release" five public servants—in-cluding Hobart Mitchell, chair-man of the state highway department—from their duties because they didn't "carry out their obligations properly." Two, besides Mitchell, face charges, Attorney General Robert Blasingame said. Neither Butler nor Blasingame mentioned the Douglases, but of course they wouldn't.

So that's one more for the pile of unsolved, unspoken, and unsung at your state capitol. Amazing how these things accumulate. Tony Walters, whose name will not be left out of this column until someone summons up the guts to investigate his death, was shot in the parking lot of the capitol, where he worked as a journalist—a lot like your columnist. Allen Clark, the television station manager, is dead; his demise suspiciously ruled a suicide. But, according to sources who must be protected and who are known to be credible, it's because he dared to raise a hand against the powers that be in this state.

But the next time a politician—of either party, for whatever reason—bloviates about how the press is out to mislead and sensationalize in order to make a few measly extra bucks, go ahead and listen. Just don't try to ask questions. They don't like them. ❧

26

AUTHORITY FIGURES

Tommy heard the door shut, and smiled. He knew he was in love. In a perfect world they would've spent the day together, maybe in bed. But it wasn't perfect. Judy had told him the night before she'd have to leave early in the morning to get to her apartment and prep for a day of work. That was less of a priority for him. Apparently, she was the responsible one. Also, it was a universally acknowledged unfairness that women took longer to get ready for their days. Unfair or not, Tommy went back to sleep. Then the doorbell rang. He ignored it—probably a salesman trolling for housewives. It rang again. And again. Tommy sat up, yawned, and frowned.

"Are you Tommy Jacks?" An unhappy-looking state trooper stood outside.

"Yeah."

"Need to talk." The trooper pushed inside, being big enough to do so without worrying about anyone trying to stop him.

Tommy stepped backward, intimidated. "What's this about?"

"We're investigating the incident in Representative Douglas's office. I understand from Douglas that you attacked him for no apparent reason. Why'd you do that, Mister Jacks?"

Tommy gaped, stunned a moment. This had to be a joke.

Vince and I, we even laughed about it—did Mitch Douglas actually accuse me? The shock receded, pushed out by a building fury. "Who's accusing me of that? You? I didn't see you there. Who said you could come busting into my house?"

"Well," the big cop snarled, "looks like you're the wise-ass Mitch Douglas said you are. Look, kid, I'm a captain with the state police, and my authority is that I'll arrest your ass if you don't cooperate."

Right, said the angriest part of Tommy's brain, *we'll see about that. I've got Louongo.* "Go to hell!" *Okay,* the meeker part put in, *this may not turn out well.*

The cop stood still. He seemed aware his next move would likely determine how things would go.

"I'll be back, asshole, with a warrant for your arrest," he steamed. "You can bet your sweet ass on that. Douglas told me you got a grudge against him because of what he did to your dad, but I wasn't expecting you to be *this* stupid. You've made a big mistake." He backed out, slamming the door.

So much for a perfect morning. *What he did to my dad?* Tommy had to call Louongo—no answer. He called Albright—no answer for both numbers. It was a little late to catch Albright at Denny's. He headed to Louongo's office.

"Did you get the guy's name?"

"Name tag said, 'Jackson.' He said he was a captain."

"Go out in the waiting room. I'll make some calls."

Tommy knew, by logical and legal standards, the whole thing was absurd, but he couldn't help feeling nervous. He wasn't used to encounters with the police beyond the odd

traffic ticket. But this was just stupid. There were witnesses—
Young and the Capitol Police. If Douglas charged him, it was
for no reason but to hassle him. So why?

Louongo came out. "Big fuck-up on their part," he said.
"This Jackson prick is a buddy of Douglas's—apparently he
only became a state trooper because Douglas insisted. The guy
I talked to, a Captain Swan, said the guy's an idiot and they've
been trying to get rid of him ever since. There are no charges
against you. There's no investigation, either—nothing. Swan's
more worried you might sue them than anything else." He
raised his eyebrows. "And if you want to sue them, you just let
me know. I'm your man."

Tommy exhaled, letting his rattled mind absorb what Louongo said. Problem was, it made him angry all over again. He'd
known about patronage—even when he was young, he'd heard
his dad talk about it. He'd figured it was usually harmless, but
it also led to corruption like he'd just tangled with. He took a
deep breath. "Thanks. By the way, he said something weird. He
said Douglas told him I had a grudge against him because of
what he did to my father. Do you know what that means?"

Louongo frowned. "No. I mean, Douglas is a Republican, so
he and your dad likely didn't care for one another. But I don't
know what he might have done to Ray. And you owe me the
onerous fee of one whole dollar, just to keep our relationship
up to snuff with all the legal bullshit and ensure that you've got
legally binding confidentiality. Tell you what—buy me a coffee
and a sandwich sometime, stay out of trouble, and we'll call it
square."

Stay out of trouble? Not likely. This was his country, his
state, his hometown, and the bad guys weren't going to win.

He headed straight to the press room, found an unoccupied typewriter, and snapped out his next "My View."

> *This reporter has just come into contact with the political police here in Oklahoma, in the person of a state trooper named Capt. Jackson. (He wasn't in a mood for a relationship on a first-name basis.) In an act best described as thuggery, Jackson made a failed attempt at intimidation on behalf of Mitch Douglas, representative from Payne County.*
>
> *Jackson threatened arrest on false and absurd charges, all based on nothing but Douglas's word. A call to his supervisor revealed an unflattering portrait of Capt. Jackson, along with a polite request that a certain reporter not seek legal redress for the incident. To quote from the source, "they (the State Police) have been trying to get rid of Jackson for months." Welcome to the wonderfully politically corrupt Third World, Oklahomans.*

Tommy sat back and re-read it. He wasn't sure about the quote, because it was Louongo's, but if June didn't ask, then maybe it could slide. He had other parts of the column ready, and called the *Journal* to ask for someone to take dictation. After he hung up, it crossed his mind that Jackson carried a gun, which meant maybe he should talk to Albright about keeping Max and Nathan handy.

He thought about going to see Judy, but worried that it might seem pushy. He walked into the main building, aware of how familiar he'd become with the capitol, a big difference from his first days getting all turned around. He knew he still had a lot to learn, but he felt fairly smug and a little victorious.

"Hey, where you headed?"

"Hey, Bart. Nowhere particular. What's goin' on in your world?"

"Same old stuff. Just heard in the break room, state police arrested Mitch Douglas. That guy was the biggest jerk in the building. Hope whatever they got on him sticks."

"Hey, guess that means you can talk to me again." Tommy grinned at the former door troll.

"Yeah, maybe. Gotta run, see ya later." Bart seemed happier.

Pushy or not, Tommy wanted to see Judy, maybe just to see her. He headed that way.

Albright took a late afternoon cab to a restaurant downtown called the Hub. Max and Nathan were no longer welcome at Triple's, and had suggested a new meeting place. It was a surprise, though, that they'd called for the meeting. He was almost always the one who set up meetings. Other times they simply showed up when he needed them.

The Hub sat near First National Bank, a thirty-three-story, art deco-style building at the core of the Oklahoma City skyline. The sophistication of its architecture seemed a little out of place on the plains of Oklahoma, although the comparably handsome Skirvin Hotel stood not far away. Albright was always intrigued by the contrasts within this young city in the middle of the country—part cowtown, part modern urban center.

He found them in an oversized corner booth, facing the front door, of course. "Nice place. Fancy. How's the food?"

As usual, Max spoke for both. "It's fine. Menu seems to focus on steak and potatoes, but the quality is excellent."

"You know," Albright remarked, "I'm starting to miss New York, What about you guys?"

"Well," Max said, nodding, "that's one reason why we wanted to talk to you. Due to various circumstances, we feel it's prudent for us to return there. But," he added, lowering his voice, "before we leave, we have some things we need to tell you. Taylor, this needs to be very clear: Frank Martin is as bad a guy as anyone we've seen, and believe me, we have seen some pretty nasty people. Sometimes we New York City guys think all the toughest thugs live back East, but not so. He'd be bad news, very bad news, anywhere. Fuck with him, and you're dead, very unpleasantly."

Albright frowned. "Am I right if I guess that you guys have information that somehow ties him to these murders?"

"Yes," Max admitted, "but not in the way you might think. Frank, and we mean him or his goons, didn't kill Clark or Walters. He does know a lot about them, though. To be clear, Taylor, he's working his own game. That's why this is so dangerous." Max glanced at Nathan, who nodded. Their seriousness seemed to settle like darkness on the booth.

But Albright needed to know more. "Okay, but you kinda lost me. 'His own game?' What's that mean?"

"It means he knows a lot about what happened and why, and he's using that knowledge to get what he wants."

Albright still felt puzzled. "Like what?" Big Frank was already an untouchable power. "What could he possibly want out of it that he doesn't already have?"

"We think he wants respect and power. And not the kind you get from being a gangster."

Albright chuckled, still confused. "Well, shit, what does that mean—he wants to be mayor?"

"Bingo."

Albright gaped, numbed by surprise. "He wants to be the mayor?"

"Or something like that. Basically, he wants a bigger hand—the biggest hand—in politics, maybe behind the scenes. He wants to be the boss of politicians here in Oklahoma. He's one of the most ruthless men we've ever met, but we think he even sees what he has now as a kind of political operation. I know, it seems absurd, but that's the way he looks at it. And now Big Frank wants to go from crime boss to political boss."

"That's crazy."

"Yep. Look, the two murders are connected, and we know Robbie Gilmore's connected to them, too. We believe Big Frank knows all the connections, and he's using that knowledge to leverage his way into Gilmore's turf. And before you ask for details, we don't have any. Big Frank likes us, and he's talked to us, but you know he won't give up details. We just know he thinks he can put the squeeze on Robbie, force his way inside. We also think the old man J.H. is going to be killed."

"That's crazy," Albright whispered again. "Look—maybe he was just shittin' you, pullin' your leg or something?"

Max shrugged. "It's possible, but there's more. There are at least two people in the Gilmore organization who are working for Frank—Rod Baker, an ex-cop and head of the paper's security, and Pudge Peters, a not-too-bright muscle guy. Baker, we think, is in it willingly. Peters isn't, but we're pretty sure Big Frank has something on him, so he doesn't have a choice. The point is that Big Frank has been setting this up for months, and he's ready to put the pressure on Robbie." Max glanced at

Nathan, who tilted his head meaningfully, "we've seen things like this before. Our experience tells us Big Frank has overstepped what he can control, and this is about to get ugly. So, we'll go back to the calm of Manhattan before it does."

Albright let that soak in. He nodded gravely. "When do you think you'll be leaving?"

"Tonight."

"Tonight?"

"Yeah. We think a little distance between us and Big Frank Martin seems like a good idea. We brought you a parting gift." Max smiled. "It comes with a warning label. We worry about you, Taylor. We think you don't really recognize risks too well. So, fair warning, this gift is risky. If you use it in the wrong way, bad things could happen."

"So, what the hell is it?"

Max handed Albright a brown paper package. "It's tape recordings. They're of Big Frank making his plans, once or twice with us, mostly with Baker and Peters. There's also some talk about crimes he or his goons might have committed. But here's the thing. You know a lot of people, like Louongo, think Martin also has some kind of pull at the police department. Based on what we've seen and heard, we think he has information about the chief and is blackmailing him. That means if you get in trouble, you can't rely on the cops. You're a friend, and we feel bad about leaving. Honestly, we think you should leave right away, too."

"Wow. Tape recordings, corrupt police chief. This may be out of my league."

"You think?" Max breathed. "Taylor, pack your bags and head out with us tonight."

"I'm thinking about it." But what Albright was actually thinking about was the fact that he was a philosopher more than anything else. His weapon of choice was words. He didn't want to go to war against a man described by dangerous men as a dangerous man. Still, he wondered if he could just walk away. He'd entered this real-life adventure on a lark, and its outcome hadn't seemed important at the time. But somehow it *had* become important, and he felt a responsibility to it. The logical thing to do was to run, now. But he couldn't, even if he couldn't pin down why.

"Don't try to be a hero," Nathan said quietly, speaking for the first time. "Most of those guys end up dead."

Albright shook his head. "I can't leave. I'm not a hero, and I don't want to be one. But I know I've got to stay and see what I can do to help. It's a mess, but I'm part of it. I know, I'm making a mistake. But I can't leave it to someone else."

"Well," Max said, "I guess we understand. Remember, you can change your mind. And if it becomes a shooting war, give us a call and we'll come back for you. But if you've decided to stay, we have one more parting gift. Be careful and don't hurt yourself." Max slid over another package.

Albright was damned sure he didn't want a gun, but he didn't want to be an easy target, either. He took it.

"A couple more things, then." Max spoke quietly and seriously. "If Big Frank knew about these tapes, he would kill to get them back. But he doesn't. We got them because he's an audiophile. He owns all sorts of reel-to-reel decks, mostly for classical music. These tapes were made on some of that equipment. Frank's a drinker, so he puts on music, drinks gin and rambles on, talking about whatever's on his soused mind. After a while, he passes out. We made a few changes to some of his equipment to get these recordings. So, to listen to them, you have to get a special kind of deck. Here's the address of a store on Main Street that has them. And understand," he added, gravely, "after you listen to the tapes you *must* destroy them, and the tape deck. The tapes burn easily. Take the deck apart, piece by piece, and don't drop any two pieces in the same trash can. Tell no one about them. The only people who know about these tapes are sitting at this table—it has to stay that way."

27
MURDER BY ANY OTHER NAME

Albright spent days listening to the tapes, taking notes, playing some parts over and over. As he expected, they revealed Clark *was* murdered, just like everyone but the police believed, and his murder was connected to a conflict with Robbie Gilmore. But they didn't say what the conflict was about.

The whole picture, Albright could tell, centered on Rod Baker. Apparently, Baker figured Robbie would be pleased if he roughed Clark up a little as a way to persuade him not to mess with the Gilmores. Baker didn't ask first, though. He planned it on his own, and recruited Pudge Peters to help. The idea, Baker told Martin on the tapes, was to kidnap Clark, take him out into the country, rough him up a bit, scare the hell out of him, and leave. They would wear masks so he couldn't identify them. They figured he'd never bother Robbie again.

But nothing went right. Clark was a fighter. He socked both of them when they tried to push him into their car. Peters took a cut above his eye, and his mask was ripped. That pissed him off, so he slugged Clark much too hard, knocking him out. They drove him out to an old vacant farm near Guthrie and dragged him, still unconscious, into a bare field. They meant to wait for him to come to so they could scare him some more, maybe hit him a few times, and then leave after warning him to stay away from Gilmore. But he wasn't coming to right away, so Baker went back to the car to get some rope to tie his hands.

That was when Clark woke up, grabbed a rock, charged Peters and tried to brain him. They fell in a heap, with Peters in a panic. He pushed Clark away, pulled out his gun and it fired, although he didn't mean it to. The bullet went through Clark's skull, killing him at once.

Baker knew Robbie would throw them to the wolves in an instant, so he turned to Big Frank. He'd known for years he had something on the police brass, probably the chief. If he could get the cops to say it was suicide, everything would be okay. It helped that Clark had turned his head so the bullet entered at his temple. They wiped the gun, which couldn't be traced, and left it.

The tapes proved Clark was killed unintentionally by Pudge Peters and Rod Baker, and that his death, which justified at least a charge of manslaughter, was covered up with help from Frank Martin and the police. But the testimony on the tapes wouldn't convict anyone of anything, even if he dared to divulge their existence, which he'd been warned not to do. The recordings themselves were inadmissible as evidence, and neither Max nor Nathan would testify about them. Any half-decent defense lawyer would say they might be nothing more than actors saying what they were told to say. In fact, if he even told anyone about them, much less tried to use them in court, Max and Nathan would become loose ends, and Big Frank would have them killed.

And the crazy part was that Robbie, whatever problem he might have had with Clark, was innocent.

The only thing he could do was to honor the deal with Max

and Nathan and destroy the tapes. It seemed very much like a religious ceremony to light his fireplace and place them, one at a time, into the flames. They puffed and hissed—and damn near exploded, they were so flammable. Soon all evidence was gone.

In the mood for a late lunch, he headed to Triple's, appreciating the pleasant walk to the tree-lined Classen Boulevard.

"Well, look who's here," came Steve Marsh's voice, "the famous ex-newspaper asshole. Where're your babysitters, Albright?" He was in a foul mood, and drunk. There went Albright's pleasant afternoon.

"They're around when I need them." Albright said, trying to push past the looming hulk.

Marsh moved to block his path, his face purple with alcohol and rage. "Yeah, right. I bet those assholes left town with their tails between their legs. Now it's just you and me, wiseass."

"Include me in this, will you?" Tommy, who'd been in the back talking to Tracy Clark, noticed when Albright came in, and saw Marsh trying to intimidate him. He walked over to where they were standing.

"Tommy, stay out of this. I'm fine." Albright looked almost as angry with Tommy as with Marsh.

"Sorry, no can do. I need copy for my column, and this drunken asshole is Steve Marsh, famous football player and sportswriter for our biggest competitor. It's the perfect story. A second drunken brawl in just a week. What in the world has become of our national champion quarterback? Does he have a drinking problem? Is it serious?"

Marsh wavered, snarling and confused. He knew he didn't want to be in this moron's column. And another fight at a bar, especially involving these people, meant Robbie would fire him. He stood still and fumed, trying to think. "Fuck you!" he finally growled. He pushed past Albright, headed for the door.

"I'm going back to Denny's," Albright said. "The waitresses there would never allow this kind of behavior." He smiled, but he was still trembling.

"I'm here with Tracy Clark, the TV reporter. Why don't you join us?" Tommy was a little unnerved, too.

"Nah, I'm okay. I'll just get something to go and head back to my apartment."

"Come on and meet her, then you can go."

Albright followed Tommy back to the booth and introduced himself, immediately aware of a sense of melancholy around her. Even if he'd been invited, he felt like he'd interrupted something.

"We have a mutual friend, Mister Albright. Tommy's dad." Tracy looked at Tommy with a warm smile.

"Call me Taylor. Yes, Ray mentioned he'd talked to you. Seems I recall you from the watch party for Anderson, four years ago." He remembered her as having been more glamorous then. Today her manner and style were more subdued— still very attractive, but going to less effort to keep up appearances.

"Yeah, I was there. Sorry you lost."

"The odds never were in our favor. My apologies for interrupting your evening with that stupid encounter. Marsh and I seem to have a running feud, although I'm not real sure why." Albright felt a discomfort, a sense that perhaps she didn't want him there.

She shrugged. "I know him. Steve and I even dated a while.

I've never seen him drink so much, though, or act like that." Her eyes went from Tommy to Albright, as if looking for understanding.

"I only talked to him once,"Tommy said, also seeming ill at ease. "The night Walters was killed. Seemed like an okay guy then."

Albright tried to change the subject. "Well, how is the TV business?"

"It's tough," Tracy said. "Everything changes so fast, and everybody's so young. I feel ancient sometimes. My new boss is about Tommy's age and thinks he knows everything." She winked at Tommy.

"Yeah, I remember when I was the young know-it-all who everybody hated," Albright quipped. "Oh, the good old days."

Tracy laughed, but Tommy rolled his eyes. "Okay, enough nostalgia for the long-lost glory days." After all, he was the young know-it-all at the table. "I think it's important for you two to talk. I've talked to Tracy about some things that have come up regarding your conversations with Walters. Maybe we should put together what we know and see where it leads."

Tracy nodded. "I hope Tommy didn't say anything you didn't want out in the open, but as you can imagine, I'm still interested in learning how my father died. I can't change anything, but it's important to me to know what happened."

"I understand. I can tell you I'm sure he didn't commit suicide. I mean I'm one-hundred percent sure. I did talk to Walters, but much of what I know is based on information I just came across. Walters was investigating your father's death for his own reasons, and he'd focused on a cover-up in the police department. He knew it wasn't suicide, but I don't think he knew much else. He did suspect that it was tied to Robbie Gilmore. But then, he hated the Gilmores and might've believed anything bad about them."

"Well, of course I knew my father's death wasn't a suicide. He wasn't defeated. He was going after Robbie."

"Do you know what their confrontation was about?"

"Maybe. It's very personal and it's about someone else. I don't think I have the right to speak about it, but it's something that was very troubling to my father, and to Robbie."

"Sounds like you do know what they argued about."

"Yes, I probably do. I can't tell you, for my own reasons, but—yes, I think I know." Tracy covered her face, looking like she might cry—or scream.

Albright looked down, and Tommy followed his example, both waiting for calm. Tommy laid a hand on her arm.

"In my mind," Albright said after moments of silence, "it's obvious that Walters was killed because he was digging into your dad's death. Based only on my gut, I don't think it was the same killer." He was being cautious, trying not to slip up and say anything that came from the tapes.

"You know something, don't you?" Tommy jumped in.

"No," he said, calmly, "I don't. What little I can surmise is still based on very weak evidence. But I think I can say without a doubt, at least there's no doubt in my addled brain, that what drove all of this was the conflict between her dad and Robbie Gilmore."

"I think so, too," Tracy said, keeping her voice low. "My problem is that it only makes sense if Robbie killed both people, or at least had them killed. And whatever else you want to say about him, that doesn't seem to fit who he is. Tommy's dad told me he can't believe Robbie would kill anyone. So, even if I think both crimes go back to the confrontation and my dad's firing, I still have no idea who could have done it."

Albright stayed quiet, understanding he would have to be the catalyst to get some action going. The pot had to be stirred so that the right people would make some kind of mistake, allowing the truth to come out. How to do that, he didn't know.

"I've written columns about Walters's murder and I've gotten feedback from the readers," Tommy spoke as though thinking aloud. "They want to know what happened. I need to push harder. I need to write about your father's murder, the police cover-up, and how Walters was investigating it."

"Hold on," Albright whispered, urgently. "You need to be careful. For one, you have editors, your bosses, who aren't interested in accusing anyone of murder in their paper, and for damn sure don't want to say the police department was party to the cover-up of a murder of a leading citizen. They'll shut you down. I know, I've been there. There's a line you can't cross, unless you have absolute proof, and even then, the correct thing to do is to take the proof to the authorities, not hype it up in a column. Tommy, you could stir things up, but it might be the wrong cauldron that starts to boil." He glowered pointedly at Tommy.

"I'm going to do exactly what you would do if you still had the megaphone," Tommy said. "I'll be cautious, but I won't stay silent."

OK Journal

My View—Tommy Jacks

The popular impression of journalists is that every day we run out to dig for fresh leads, snap them up, and deposit them on newspaper pages or radio desks or TV screens.

But in reality, reporters gather information, too, usually in bits and pieces, here and there. Sometimes those pieces come together to make a story. Pieces of the biggest stories can be few, far apart, and difficult to find.

Allen Clark was the manager of an Oklahoma City television station. He died six years ago. There are still pieces missing from his story, but there are now enough of them that you can say you read it here first: Clark was murdered. We don't have the whole picture of his death, so we can't say who's to blame, or even whether it was intentional, but we can say that the suicide story is a lie. In fact, it's a cover-up. There aren't enough pieces to nail down who's responsible for the cover-up, either, but there are enough that the person or people who are should be getting very nervous just about now.

There aren't enough pieces to point the finger at whoever shot down *Sun* political reporter Tony Walters in the capitol parking lot, either. Who pulled the trigger is still a mystery. But there are enough pieces to show us a trail that seems to point toward one of the centers of power and influence in this state.

This isn't about a crusade to catch bad guys. It's about a system so rotten that the lives of honest folks don't matter. But there's hope. The empire of evil may crumble before our eyes, piece by piece. When that last piece falls into place, there will be a reckoning, big and heavy enough to shake us all.

28

UNSURE ALL DAY

Tracy suffered through a sleepless night, tossed between the fact that she couldn't do anything about her father's death, and the constant, haunting feeling that she caused it. Every day it was harder to push back the guilt. She would crumble in the middle of the day for no apparent reason. She'd yell at a co-worker over something petty, and people at the station started to avoid her. She was headed for a full-blown breakdown soon if something didn't change.

Talking to Albright and Tommy made her feel less alone. But it was still up to her to somehow resolve the horrors of what she'd done. She knew the first step was to talk to Judy. She needed her permission to tell someone about why her father and Robbie Gilmore argued. She'd been sympathetic, but it was time for Judy to take responsibility, too.

"No way in hell!" Judy burst out, her hands in tight fists. She was exactly as angry as Tracy feared. "I'm sorry about your dad, I really am. But you should've never told him. That's your fault, not mine. So, no—you can't tell anyone about that, ever!"

"Judy," she said, trying to reason, "this is going to be a curse on both of us unless we admit what we know. Robbie is responsible, and he needs to be held to account."

"You don't know that," Judy snarled. "You just *want* it to be him. Maybe your dad did commit suicide—how the hell do you know? Maybe he was shot by somebody because of something that had nothing to do with me or Robbie—you can't prove anything."

"I know in my heart he didn't commit suicide." Tracy said, holding herself in check. "But apart from that, Taylor Albright told me he's one hundred percent sure it was murder."

"Taylor Albright's a washed-up old gossip who'll say anything to get his job back. He's just lying to you. Or maybe he's hot for you, or something."

That did it for Tracy. She stood up.

"Judy, you've been impossible to be around for a while. Now, every time I talk about anything related to my dad, you blow up. Robbie Gilmore's had affairs with hundreds of women—you're nothing special. And every day women get abortions, too, for the same reasons you did. You need to grow up and face facts. You chose to have that relationship with Robbie. You're not innocent in this—you said that to me yourself."

"Get the hell out of here. Leave now, before I hurt you." Judy seethed, her face distorted by rage.

Tracy had never seen her like this, but she was past caring. "I'll go. But any obligation I had to stay quiet is gone. I'll do what I think is right. Got that?"

Judy lunged, knocking Tracy onto the sofa. They tumbled to the floor. "I'll kill you, you bitch!" Judy shrieked. Tracy broke free and staggered to the other side of the room, still ready to fight. Judy crumpled to the floor and sobbed wildly.

Tracy knelt and stroked her hair. "It'll be all right, sweetheart. Just calm down. It'll be all right." It was all she could think to say. She cried too, worried about them both.

Tracy held Judy until she went to sleep, and covered her with a blanket. A few hours later, Judy woke up, acting like things were back to normal. Tracy fixed some soup. They didn't discuss what happened.

Tommy had written what he thought was a good column. He'd included the rumor that Walters was investigating Allen Clark's death, suspecting it might not be suicide. He felt good for having done what he said he'd do in a way that no one at the paper could object to. To Fred and Bill, the column, as written, read like good investigative work on Walters's unsolved murder.

He was at his apartment drinking coffee, having one of those days when it was hard to get started. He wasn't sure how to move the story forward, and it troubled his thoughts. The phone rang. Even if more people had his number by now, that ring always startled him.

"Hello." He expected it to be June, wanting to know why he wasn't at work yet.

It was Judy. "I need to see you."

"When and where?"

"Is now at your apartment okay?"

"Absolutely. I'll see you in a bit?"

"Yes." She hung up.

He was excited she was on her way, but he could tell by her voice something was wrong. Judy was the most exciting person he'd ever been with, and their lovemaking was a new experience for him. There was no question, at least for him, that he was in love, and he knew she liked him. Still, it somehow felt forced, like she was holding back. He knew she was troubled, chalking it up to her father's death. He wished he could make her really happy and help her deal with that inner sadness.

"I want you to stop writing about Allen Clark and Tony Walters." The first words out of her mouth. She looked like she had just gotten out of bed—her hair wasn't fixed, no makeup. And she looked frayed, distracted.

"I don't understand. Why?"

"Tracy and I had a huge fight," she said, sniffling. "I can't believe some of the things I said to her. It's just too much, all this talk about her father's suicide. It doesn't change anything, and it just keeps her upset. She's obsessed. Now she's saying Taylor Albright agrees with her. Why the hell is she talking to Taylor Albright?"

"Well," Tommy admitted, "that may be my fault. She and I met at Triple's because she wanted to ask me what I knew about Walters's murder. Taylor showed up, so I introduced them."

Judy glared at him. "I can't believe you were out with Tracy."

"I just told you—it wasn't a date," Tommy explained, defensively. Things were getting weird, but he hesitated to blame her for it. "She talked to my dad about her father's death, and my dad asked me to tell her what I'd found when I visited him. I don't see how that's wrong."

"You can't see why that's wrong," she snarled. "That's just great. My best friend and my boyfriend meet behind my back at a bar, and you can't see why that's wrong."

"You're making it sound like something it wasn't." Tommy

was starting to get angry. She didn't make sense, or listen to him. She seemed out of control.

"I don't want you seeing Tracy," she said, shaking a finger at him. "And I don't want you writing about Allen Clark's death. And you're completely off base saying there's a connection between Tony Walters's death and Clark's. There isn't. Just leave it alone."

Tommy was stunned. How in the world would she know whether there was any connection? "Judy, what the hell's going on? You can't tell me what not to write. I'm a reporter, that's what I do—I write. This is an important story, involving important, powerful people, and I've got to go after it. Tracy thinks I should. So, if this isn't about hurting her, what's it about?"

"Just drop it, or we're through!" She ran out, got in her car, and left; driving way too fast.

Tommy left the door open. He dropped onto his worn-out sofa. He definitely heard her say the word "boyfriend," at least—he liked that part. But he didn't like how the rest left him feeling.

Albright had only visited Ray a couple of times since he'd been locked up. He knew that was lousy, but the whole experience was so damned depressing. Ray Jacks maybe should have gone to prison for serial drunkenness, or for being a horrible husband and father, or maybe even for the crime of being a world-champion stretcher of truth. But embezzlement? It was just stupid.

With help from Louongo, he managed to piece together

how the injustice was done, and how every participant was connected to the Gilmores. It became clear Jacks had been played for a sucker by an unholy cast of characters, brought together just to get him out of the Gilmores' hair. David Watts was Number One. Jacks's attorney was paid off, under the table, by Gilmore. Albright had proof. The judge on the case had been Albert Morrison, a known lowlife who preferred whisky bars to legal ones. Just before he passed sentence, a substantial sum was deposited into his personal account. Louongo hadn't been able to get proof of the source of the money, but it made for strong circumstantial evidence. Then there was a small print shop owner, named Fred Corker, hired by someone to forge documents planted in Jacks's office by another conspirator, quite likely Patty. Louongo had a signed confession from the printer. Albright never asked how he'd come by it.

"The famous Mister Albright. I'd have bet a million bucks you'd be in New York by now. What happened?" Jacks chuckled.

"Not sure I have an answer for that, Ray. Somehow, I got stuck here and couldn't get unstuck. Good to see you. You know, I see Tommy quite a bit. He's a great kid." Albright hated these kinds of conversations. They reminded him of family gatherings, which he'd spent much of his life avoiding.

"Yeah. Kind of surprising, considering his father."

"Okay, Ray. We're not small-talk types. Let's get to it." Ray smiled. "I hadn't discussed this with you because there was no point if we couldn't get enough solid evidence. That 'we' part includes Louongo, who, despite my misgivings, has shown some real talent in espionage and general shiftiness. We've pulled together documentary evidence that will likely support your release. The biggest piece is ineffective representation by your attorney. He was being paid by Gilmore."

"You're shittin' me! Righteous David Watts, a crook. What's the world coming to? How much?"

"We figure over ten thousand dollars."

"Well, no wonder the bastard was willing to work so cheap. Wow!"

"Yeah. All that advice to take the deal was based on what they wanted to happen. Our assessment is that a lot of the evidence they had against you would've actually looked pretty weak in court—lotta smoke, not so much fire. But you were being advised by a sellout, so you never got the advice you should have, which was to fight it tooth and nail."

"Sonofabitch. Screwed myself. Should've hired Louongo."

"Yep. And there's more. All those documents they wanted to use against you were forged. The amount of money you sup-posedly embezzled was made up, figuring you had no way to contradict them. The agreement you had with the Democratic Party, actually, would have given you complete control, so even if you'd taken the money, it was legal. You were elected chair-man, and the old chairman had worked out your authority agreement for you, but apparently after he died, it just sat in his files. No one else had a copy, so no one knew what it said."

"This is humiliating. I'm not sure I've ever read it myself. So, I'm in jail because I'm a dumb fuck, is that it?"

Albright shrugged, beyond taking pleasure in black humor. "Well, close. Another key piece is the judge. We think we'll get conclusive proof of a bribe, but the evidence right now is circumstantial. Just before you were sentenced, he made a big deposit in his personal account."

Jacks drummed his fingers on the table. "What can I do?"

"First, don't be too hard on yourself. The Gilmores spent a hell of a lot of money and had a big support team, including Patty, all to convince you to plead guilty. At the time, I was just as convinced as you that their deal was the best you could get, and that if you'd fought it, things would've gotten worse. And Ray, if you'd fought, the jury might still have found you guilty, what with your own lawyer being their inside man and the judge on the payroll. So, I know it feels like you screwed up, but I don't know if that's true."

"Yeah," Jacks sighed. "Seemed like the thing to do at the time."

"For now, you can present this evidence to a court and almost certainly get a new trial, or you can negotiate with the DA's office to see if you can get the sentence reduced. Regarding that second option, Louongo has approached someone he knows who's a prosecutor, and showed him what we have. That guy says he thinks they'd offer a deal to release you in a matter of months."

"Well, I sure don't want a new trial. I just want out. Why would it take that long?"

"He said they'd be careful to keep it quiet to avoid backlash from our friends at the *Sun*. I'm convinced this whole thing was dreamed up by the Gilmores, but there's no direct link to them anywhere. The court might pursue charges against Watts, the judge, and the printer. If they then point the finger at the Gilmores as part of a plea deal, then a prosecutor might go after them—maybe. But what's most likely is the lawyer will be disbarred, the judge will resign for health reasons, and the printer will pay a fine. Sometimes there's not a lot of justice in the justice system."

"So, I get a year knocked off my sentence, and the Gilmores get off scot-free."

"Yup, that's probably the size of it. How valuable is that year of freedom?"

"Beyond anything I could imagine."

OK Journal

My View—Tommy Jacks

"Politics," Senate President Pro Tempore Bud Evans, R-Oklahoma City, once said on the chamber floor, "is about people."

Those people have lives and names. Some are bigger than others—that's politics, too. There's no level playing field—otherwise, it isn't politics.

Back to names. The former chairman of the state Democratic Party during the time the publisher of this newspaper you hold ran unsuccessfully for election as governor is named Ray Jacks. I'm his son. And you likely know where my father is now, and why he was sent there.

Even if he's not around right now, my father's name opens doors. And it closes some. People I need to talk to in this business don't treat me like every other reporter. They treat me even worse, because of that name.

I suppose others—like you, maybe—figure I have a dog in this fight we call state politics. OK, I do. Don't we all? Some dogs are big, some small. I guess mine is kind of medium-sized, which I think helps my perspective. I use it to try to see things both ways.

I know why my dad went to prison, which doesn't mean I accept the official reasons as the truth. This playing field isn't level. Some names are bigger than others.

And some names need to get bigger. One is Tony Walters; the name of the dead reporter whose body grows cold while the killer's trail grows even colder in the chill of official indifference. The other is Allen Clark, whose death is dismissed as a suicide by the only people on Earth with enough chutzpah to even imagine such a transparent lie. Sources say Walters was looking into Clark's death.

I am here in their names, too. I write this while a stack of letters from readers sits just to the right of my typewriter, urging me and the *Journal* to keep telling the truth about them. ❧

29
THE WINDS OF CHANGE

Robbie Gilmore punched the intercom button. "Yes?"

"Mister Gilmore, it's an emergency. Your father has fallen. We called the ambulance." Just like that, his world changed.

Robbie bolted through the hallway, heart pounding, into J.H.'s broad office, where his alarm grew. People—lots of them—ran here and there, all in a panic. Two guards and a secretary were bent over his father, who lay on the floor.

"Move away!" he barked. He knelt. J.H. looked unconscious. "Did anyone see him fall? Did he hit anything?"

Only the secretary answered, "No, sir. He was alone. I came into his office to bring him his coffee, and I found him there."

Ambulance attendants burst through the door, pushing a gurney. "Sorry, sir, we'll need you to step back."

Robbie stood, took one more look at his father, and turned away.

Within minutes they had J.H. in an oxygen mask, checked his vitals, given him two shots of something, and hung an intravenous drip over him. They spoke with the hospital by two-way radio, saying they'd be bringing in a heart attack victim, male, in his nineties, in critical condition.

Robbie stood, silent and stunned. A heart attack at his father's age was always serious. He thought he'd seen J.H. respond just a little, but was not sure.

One of the attendants appeared in front of him. "Are you a relative?"

"Yes, I'm his son."

"Well, he's alive. I'd say he had a very serious heart attack. Doesn't seem to be hurt from the fall, but at this point that's not our real concern. He's still unconscious, but his breathing's near normal. We'll take him to Saint Anthony's, where they have a cardiac surgeon waiting. A massive heart attack at your father's age is about as serious as it gets. But those people at Saint Anthony's are pretty good. So, let's hope for the best."

"Thank you."

J.H. was wheeled out. Robbie didn't move.

"Mister Gilmore?" It was J.H.'s secretary, who'd materialized at his shoulder. "Your car's ready in the front. Is there anything we can do?"

He snapped out of it. "Yes. My car. Thank you. No, I'm not sure what anyone can do. Just, uh, go on with what you were doing. Everything will be fine." He headed back to his office and told his secretary to call his wife and his father's personal doctor to tell them he would meet them at Saint Anthony's.

He arrived at the hospital just after the ambulance backed into the emergency entrance, where what seemed like an army of medical personnel waited. J.H. was wheeled into them and gone. Robbie could feel the emotions welling up inside. He wanted to go someplace and hide.

"Are you Mister Gilmore?" The man who asked appeared to be a doctor.

"Yes, how is he?"

"We won't know anything for sure until we get some test results back. He's still not conscious, which isn't good. Has your father had heart attacks before?"

"I don't think so. Doctor Stevens is on his way. He can tell you more than I can."

"All right. He's been taken to intensive care, and for now, no one will be allowed in there until we know he's stabilized. I'm Doctor Mewhorter, and I'll let you know how he's doing as soon as we find out."

The waiting room was empty. Robbie found a seat in the back. He realized he was shaking. His father had been the center of his world for so long it was impossible to imagine life any other way. Soon his wife and kids joined him, followed by friends of his father's, most whispering and wondering.

Reporters found their way to the hospital, too. Their presence immediately changed the atmosphere from quiet family uncertainty to shouted questions and glaring lights. The hospital staff ushered the family into a private waiting room, leaving the throng of newspaper and TV people to discuss among themselves what was happening. Robbie understood the irony of being irritated with the intrusion. About half the people in the other room who'd made him so angry had some kind of connection to the Gilmores' businesses. He could, if he wanted, go out and fire a bunch of the pests, and thin the herd by a goodly chunk. But they only did what he paid them to do, even if up to now he'd expected them only to do it to others—not to him or his family. The hypocrisy was clear. But right now, he didn't care.

After two long days, J.H. regained consciousness and was moved to a private room. The doctors said he'd most likely be bedridden for months. The heart attack had done severe damage, and his condition remained critical. It deprived his brain of oxygen, they said, and they were still assessing it. Robbie went in to see his father, but J.H didn't show any reaction. He stayed long enough to reassure himself that his father was still alive, although he could see in J.H.'s eyes that some vital part of the man had died. He left, with no intention of coming back.

Weeks followed wherein not much changed at the *Sun*. Robbie was in charge now, but for the most part everyone waited, wondering what might happen. At last, with efficient swiftness, he initiated the paperwork to have himself installed as president of the company. He made it clear the business was now entirely under his command.

One of the first things he did was to fire Rod Baker and Larry "Pudge" Peters. It had been J.H., and his paranoia, that had led to a staff heavy with security and men who were little better than goons. That wasn't what Robbie wanted.

Baker wasn't happy about it. "You'll regret this, you pompous asshole!" The new security people had to forcibly remove him. Peters just shrugged and left. Robbie had an uncomfortable feeling he hadn't heard the last of Baker.

In another clean-up move, Robbie held a meeting with Steve Marsh.

"Steve, you're a good sportswriter, and people like you here. I got you involved in some things I regret. That's my fault, not yours. I want you to concentrate on covering sports. There won't be any more of this clandestine stuff. But I want to make this clear," he said, firmly. "If I hear of any bar fights or public drunkenness, you'll be fired."

Marsh nodded all along, uttering a series of "Yes sirs."

Robbie moved one of his own people into the managing

editor position and reshuffled others, building a layer of people loyal to him. The changes had a ripple effect—some people were pleased, some clearly weren't. He felt a new sense of power.

"Fired you, huh? Well, maybe you needed to be fired. What the fuck you want me to do about it?" Big Frank Martin had a direct way of communicating.

"Look, I've helped you a bunch," Baker pleaded. "Can't you make Robbie change his mind?"

"Rod, you're an idiot. Old J.H. is as good as dead. Robbie's in charge now. Don't you get it? All that secret cop shit was the old man's doing. Robbie's through with it, and my influence with him is zero. And look, asshole, I got my own problems. I don't want you making any trouble, got it? You and that weak-minded buddy of yours need to get out of town—now."

"Man, that's not right. I've been giving you inside crap for years. I need your help. You can't just tell me to leave."

"I kept you and your moron pal from going to prison after you shitheads screwed up and killed that TV guy. I owe you exactly nothing. You leave or I'll stomp you. Hard."

"Well, fuck you. Sure, I'm leaving town. Just great—let me take the fall for everybody. I'm out of here. Fuck you." Baker left.

Martin watched him go, figuring he might have to do something about Baker sometime, maybe. Right now, he had a bigger problem. His long-term relationship with Police Chief Underwood had taken a bad turn. The chief had operated for years under the impression that Martin was somehow connected to J.H. Gilmore. Martin had fueled that impression with tidbits about Gilmore and his operation, all of them inside information from Baker. That, and the substantial amount of cash passed to the chief to support his lavish lifestyle, had been the basis of their entanglement. Martin was always surprised the chief could flaunt his ill-gotten wealth so openly without anybody questioning it. Once Robbie took over the *Sun* and the other Gilmore assets, Underwood became concerned that Big Frank would lose the edge J.H. gave him. Big Frank assured him it wouldn't make a difference, that he'd still get his "salary." But he could tell the chief was getting nervous, especially since that little twerp, Tommy Jacks, was writing about Clark's death. The chief could see far too many people had information about that mess. He'd been a good ally over the years, Big Frank thought, but he could become a dangerous enemy if he got scared.

It seemed best to go whichever way the winds were blowing. Big Frank was an evil and dishonest man, but candid with himself. When you see a storm headed your way, he always thought, it's best to head to the cellar. He'd spent the last few days making plans for that contingency, destroying records, cutting ties, moving large amounts of cash to remote places, and hiring new legal counsel in Dallas. The new lawyers were creating a maze of companies and ownership structures that would be a challenge to penetrate. He hated attorneys, but when you need them, what are you going to do?

He thought he might need to spend time at his new villa in Trinidad. First, he would tie up a few loose ends, so he could relax and not worry about surprises.

The bodies of Rod Baker and Larry Peters were found on a remote farm south of Guthrie. Police noted an odd coincidence.
About six years earlier, the body of former KVY executive Allen Clark was discovered there.

After the media learned Baker and Peters once worked in
security at the *Oklahoma Sun,* they cautiously approached Robbie Gilmore for a statement. His office issued one in writing.

"We are very sad to hear about the untimely deaths of two
former members of the *Sun* family. These employees were recently discharged as part of our administrative restructuring
and reduction in security staffing. We offer our condolences
to their loved ones. We urge the police to pursue with all their
resources the people who committed this horrid crime. We at
the *Sun* continue to be very concerned about the increase in
crime in our city, and call on all Oklahoma City residents to
hold the police department and Police Chief Underwood ac-
countable."

OK Journal

My View—Tommy Jacks

The last thing anyone with any stake in Oklahoma power politics expects is real, significant change. But it looks like change might be in the air.

As you have read elsewhere in your *Journal*, the publisher and president of our competitor, J.H. Gilmore, suffered a severe heart attack. We extend our respect and sympathy to him and his family. Whatever else you might say about J.H. Gilmore, no one can deny that Oklahoma wouldn't look like it does now without him.

His son, Robbie, has taken control of the enterprise that spreads from the heart of the state to all its corners. The word from observers with sources inside the colonnaded building off Main Street is that our competitor's newsroom is starting to concentrate more on putting out a quality product.

Let's hope so. We mean that. It isn't easy to compete with a good, crackerjack opponent, but it's harder on everyone if the stronger competitor wastes time on trying to control people and votes rather than reporting the news as it really is.

But there's more to the story, it seems, and that "more" may lead to questions about Robbie Gilmore's dedication to good, honest, public-minded journalism.

Two men, each of whom once worked as security personnel for the competing paper, were found dead not long after the change of leadership that led to their dismissal.

The story becomes a strange one after that, because their bodies were found in the same spot where the remains of Allen Clark, former manager of television station KVY, were discovered six years ago. 🦋

30

EVIL WEB

Tommy dropped by Evans's office to see whether Judy was in. She wasn't, and hadn't been for days. Gail said her friend Tracy had called her in sick, yet again.

"This makes more than a week, Tommy," Gail said, her concern clear. "The session's about over, and we've got a ton of work to do. It's a madhouse around here. Senator Evans made a comment this morning at the staff meeting about her not being there, and that's not good. You might want to give her some kind of warning."

He sighed. "Yeah. I'll give her a call. My guess is she has the flu or something, but you're right. She should let everyone know what's going on."

In truth, he had no idea what was going on with Judy. He'd called many times, but never got to talk to her. After sitting through a mind-numbing conference committee meeting, he thought he might run by her apartment. He didn't want her to lose her job. She'd said she loved it.

No one answered the door at Judy's apartment. He headed back toward the capitol, spotted a pay phone, and pulled over to call Tracy.

"Hello."

"Tracy, it's Tommy. Do you know where Judy is?"

"She's okay. Where are you?"

"Around 23rd and Penn. What's going on?"

"Meet me at the Classen Grill in thirty minutes, okay?"

"Okay."

Tommy took a booth in the back and ordered some french fries and a Coke—a perfect late lunch.

"That's not a very good meal."

"Thanks, mom." Tommy smiled, realizing how important Tracy had become to him.

She slid in on the other side of the booth. Despite the light exchange, she looked worried. "She's at my place," she explained. "I'm worried she's having some kind of mental breakdown. She's physically okay, but she won't be going back to work for a while. She just isn't emotionally stable enough to be around people."

"Mental breakdown? What's going on?"

"Tommy, you had to know she was under a lot of stress," she said. "She put on a beautiful front, but you had to see the sadness."

"Yeah," he admitted. "What I saw was someone who always seemed worried about something. Was it her dad, or something at work?"

"She needs your help. I know you're a good person, and I know you love Judy. She needs you to be strong and to help her, and help me. What I'm about to tell you may hurt you, but I think you can handle it, and help Judy through it."

"I'll do whatever she needs."

"First I'm going to tell you what has her so upset. She may hate me for this, she might even consider it a break in our friendship that can't be mended. She may also hate you for knowing." Tracy told Tommy of Judy's affair with Robbie Gilmore and the abortion. He listened intently with no visible emotion. She told him that she'd told her father about Judy and Robbie, and how Allen Clark challenged Robbie and was fired, and that she believed it led to his death.

"My god," he muttered after she finished. "I don't know, Tracy. Maybe I'm not strong enough for this. I just don't know." He slowly rose and headed to the restroom.

Tommy was in his early twenties, but about half the time he thought of himself as a kid. Sure, he was technically an adult, but he knew he was still a puppy. What Tracy had told him was beyond anything he could process. He realized he'd pretended to be grown up, especially with Judy. It didn't change the fact that he loved her. But it wasn't easy to get past, either. He wasn't a prude. But what she'd done was not something he could easily forget—an affair with a married man twice her age, and an abortion. It wasn't right.

He stood in the washroom, caught up in a violent mixture of feelings. He wasn't sure what he could do or wanted to do. He knew he had to go back out and deal with Tracy, first of all. She was asking for his help—not just for Judy, but for herself, too. He wanted to help Judy, and knew he couldn't do it alone.

"I have to think about all this," he told her. "I'm sorry, Tracy. Maybe I'm not the person you think I am. I just need a little time to come to grips with it."

"It's okay." She seemed sympathetic. "I understand. This is a shock. People are complicated. It'd be great if everyone we knew was perfect, or simple, but they're not, even you and me. But you have to decide for yourself."

Tommy felt like shit. He could see disappointment in her

face. She'd hoped he'd step up, but he'd reacted with hesitation, and maybe judgment. "Tracy, I will help you and Judy. Just give me a little space to think this through, okay?"

"Of course. Take the time you need. I'm going back to my place—nothing has to be decided this very minute. Give me a call."

She got up and left. He felt like he'd lost his girlfriend and his friend in one fell swoop, and all he had to do to keep them was to lie. He headed back to the capitol. It was close, and maybe he could take a nap. He really needed to recover a little, and he needed solitude to think.

Due to the session ending, the parking lot tunnel at the capitol was almost empty. It was odd not to see people rushing back and forth.

"Hey, Tommy. I was just writing you a note."

Albright caught him by surprise. He'd never known him to come to the press room before, and he wasn't sure he wanted to talk to him now. He really needed that nap to clear his head.

"Got some news for you." Albright seemed unusually upbeat.

"What kind of news?"

"Looks like your father is going to get out of prison early. Matter of fact, could be in just a few months."

"Really?" That woke him up. "That's great. Is it because of good behavior or something?" Tommy's mind spun. How would life change? It'd been a long time since he'd had a dad around.

"No. It's because your father shouldn't have been in prison in the first place." Albright told Tommy how his father was framed, and how he and Louongo dug up proof of what happened. To Tommy, it revealed more than that.

"So *that's* why you were seeing Louongo," he said, grinning. "You know, I had some pretty wild theories about why you kept going to his office." He had to laugh. "I'm going to have to apologize to Louongo for all the stuff I was thinking."

Albright's eyes widened. "What about me?"

"What about you?" he joshed. "Okay, I'm sorry I thought you were up to no good. So, is anything going to happen to Robbie?"

Albright shook his head. "I doubt it. Blasingame has no appetite for going after Robbie over something like this. He can't even prove Robbie was involved. Besides, our goal was never to put Robbie behind bars. It was to get your dad out."

"Robbie seems to get away with a lot."

"Yeah," Albright looked down. "The benefit of being rich and powerful. Little guys get boulders dropped on them from on high. People like Robbie get awards." Albright noticed a quick, sour frown. "Something bothering you Tommy?"

"Nah, everything's great." He didn't sound like he meant it.

Albright didn't buy it, but left it alone. "Well, guess I'll be going. Just wanted to drop by and give you the news. Keep that under your hat for a while. Blasingame's going to push for the release as soon as possible, but on the QT. They don't want to stir the pot at the *Sun*."

Tommy thought of something else. "Speaking of the *Sun*, did you see where Rod Baker and some other guy who used to work there were killed? Their bodies were dumped in the same field where Clark was found."

"I did. Morbid coincidence. I think that Baker guy is the goon who attacked me outside campaign headquarters four years ago. I bet he had a ton of enemies. But in the same corn-field? That's just bizarre."

"There's got to be a connection. Tracy's convinced it was Robbie who had her father killed, and these guys worked for Robbie." Tommy seemed more upbeat discussing the murders than any other current events.

Albright shook his head. "If you're saying, same field, so it must be the same person, namely Robbie, I can't agree. Matter of fact, I'd say that *because* it's the same field, it couldn't be Robbie. If he ordered Clark's murder, would he have had the thugs killed and left in the same place? I don't think so. He'd more likely have them shipped someplace far away."

"Yeah, that'd be stupid. Robbie's lots of things, but not stupid."

Albright left. Tommy went next door and found his sleeping bag. He needed to think.

He awoke from his nap with a clearer understanding of what to do. He went back to the press room and called Tracy. No answer. He found the telephone directory, or what was left of it, to see if he could find where she lived. Sure enough—T. Clark, with an address.

He knew now, with absolute conviction, that he would help her and Judy. He'd been hurt by what she'd told him, and felt rejected by Judy. But those reactions had been about him and his fragile ego. He had to admit, at least to himself, how stupid and insensitive his reaction to Tracy had been. He loved Judy, and was ready to do anything to help her get better. He had to find them and tell her how he felt.

31
WHAT HAPPENED

Tracy returned to her apartment. She knew Tommy had every right to pause rather than jump in to help Judy. She couldn't help being a little disappointed in the young man she'd grown so fond of, but reminded herself he *was* young, and what she'd told him today had to be difficult to bear. Like all young men, he wanted his love pure.

"Where have you been?" Judy demanded, looking disheveled and angry.

"There were some things I had to do." Tracy had a pounding headache. She headed to the bathroom for aspirin, Judy right behind her.

"You shouldn't leave me alone. You don't know what I might do."

"What do you mean?"

"I might kill myself—you don't know."

"Don't talk like that just because I have to go out," Tracy shot back. "Please don't threaten me."

"Oh, so my killing myself would threaten *you*," Judy taunted. "It's all about you, isn't it? The big TV star, having to take care of crazy Judy. Well, you don't have to take care of me at all. I only stayed here because you asked. But now I'm leaving." She turned on her heels.

Tracy chased after her. "Please, Judy, don't leave. You need help, and I'm trying to figure it out. You need to stay here until we can find a good place for you to be."

"You really do think I'm crazy, don't you?" Her voice climbed. "Funny thing is; you don't know anything. You think all I worry about is that stupid bastard Robbie and my affair with the creep. Or maybe you think the abortion put me over the edge. You don't know anything."

"Please stop yelling. Let me get you some tea or something."

"I don't want any damn tea. I just want to be left alone. Like I was before. I can take care of myself." She settled on the couch, arms wrapped around her knees, staring off. "My life was going to be great. Even after that nightmare with Robbie, it still was. You know how I got that job with Bud Evans? I called Robbie. Told him I needed a job, and he'd better help me. Just like that, I was hired. I needed money for clothes, I called Robbie. The envelope came by special messenger. You think I was blackmailing him? You bet your sweet ass I was, and he paid. And it would have gotten better and better. I was going to be somebody in the capitol, all thanks to Robbie. Then that loathsome, ugly, smelly moron started hounding me. Practically every day he'd ask me about Robbie and your dad. Every day, some new stupid angle about me and Robbie. Walters was driving me crazy."

Tracy was shocked. So that was why Judy and Walters met over drinks. "What do you mean?"

Judy grit her teeth. "He hounded me. I couldn't get away. He'd gotten the name of my roommate at college. She knew about my dinners and romantic weekends with Robbie because I told her everything. She wasn't even a friend, but I just wanted to tell someone I was having an affair with the rich and famous Robbie Gilmore. She told Walters all about it. He was creepy—he'd find me in the capitol and get too close, even touch me, and say if I didn't do what he wanted, he'd make sure everything got out. He was slimy—he wanted me to sign something saying what I'd done with Robbie, and I told him no. Told him if he didn't go away and leave me alone, I'd tell Robbie. He just laughed. He said Robbie was the one who was going to suffer, that he was going to expose him."

"Judy, why didn't you tell someone what was going on?"

"What for—so they could pity me? If I told anyone, everything would get out, and everyone would know about Robbie and what I'd done. Your father died because of *me*—look how you suffered. I hated Robbie, but I wanted to be somebody, and he could make it happen. But Walters found me out, and I didn't know what to do. Somehow, I had to shut him up. One time he was actually pawing at me, telling me I only had a few hours to make up my mind or everything was going to be published in that rag *The Banner*. I asked him to give me a little time. Later that night I called him and asked him to meet me. I knew I might be in danger, what with the way he'd been looking at me, so I was ready. I got there first. He started in on me about how he was tired of waiting for me to give him the evidence he needed and then he said, 'Guess what my latest contact told me today?'" She imitated Walters's husky voice. "'You were pregnant. How about that, Judy? So, you had a bastard child by the unholy Gilmore. Where's the kid now, in some kind of institution?'" She frowned bitterly. "Then he laughed at me. I pulled out my dad's gun, and I shot him."

Tracy held her head like it might explode. "My god! You

killed him? My god!" Never had the possibility crossed her mind. Beautiful, gracious Judy had killed Tony Walters.

"Yes, I killed him. I wasn't going to. I brought the gun because he scared me. I'd made up my mind I was going to contact Robbie and give him all I knew about Walters, and let him handle it. If the news got out about the affair or a child, so be it. I was ready to deal with it. But the way he said it—the way he laughed. He had to be out of my life. I just reacted."

Tracy was stunned. This wasn't something she could help Judy resolve. A man was dead. "You've got to tell the police. I'm sure this isn't murder, it's—maybe it's some kind of self-defense, or something. It wasn't murder—it was a fit of rage."

"Call the cops? Oh, that's great advice," Judy raged. "You just want to be rid of me now that you know everything. You should know, Tracy dear, I still have my dad's gun. So you're not going to tell anyone anything, understand?"

The look on Judy's face frightened her. "Judy," she said, trying to sound calmer, "listen to what you're saying. I'm your friend, and you're threatening me. Is that what you want to do?"

Judy's face softened a little, but her words didn't. "You stay away from me. You can't tell me what to do." She grabbed her purse and ran outside. Tracy hesitated before following, wondering for a moment whether Judy might be waiting for her to come out. Then she saw her car speed away. Now what?

There was only one person with enough power and money to keep this from turning into a tragedy. Tracy called the *Sun* and asked to speak to Robbie Gilmore. The receptionist told her the paper was closed for the day, and Mister Gilmore wasn't available.

"Listen very carefully. The paper may be closed, but he hasn't left for the day. My name is Tracy Clark. You call up to his office and tell him or his secretary that I'm on the phone and need to talk to him about Judy Jackson. Let him know it's an emergency and it's very important that he talk to me before I go talk on television, got that? Now, do it!" The receptionist put her on hold.

"Miss Clark, Robbie Gilmore. What can I do for you?"

"You need to see me, right now. This is about Judy Jackson. I know all about your affair with her, but this is about Judy having a mental breakdown. I need your help to save her life. I don't mean you any harm, not now or in the future. I just want to keep Judy from doing something that might hurt her."

"Where do we meet?"

Tracy was surprised. He sounded calm and concerned. "How about the capitol? I'm not far from there. The parking lot next to the east tunnel."

"Kind of a remote spot, Miss Clark," he said. "I didn't kill your father, and I didn't have him killed, so just in case you're thinking of shooting me, I guess I'm not interested in meeting with you in a dark parking lot."

He sounded reasonable, which frustrated her. "I told you, I have no intention of doing you any harm. This isn't about me, and it isn't about my dad, it's about Judy. She's not in a good state. Maybe you can help."

There was a long pause. Tracy expected him to say something about making an appointment to meet tomorrow at his office, or just hang up, but he said, "Okay, I'll be there in about thirty minutes."

Tracy headed to the capitol, thinking it might be where Judy had gone because she'd felt safe there most of her life, playing in the halls as a kid when her father was working, and as an adult spending hours there at a job she loved. Tracy pulled into the parking lot and looked around, but didn't see Judy's car. She waited.

A set of lights appeared—a large, black car. Not Judy's. Tracy got out and walked toward the tunnel entrance. A tall man appeared, walking toward her.

"Miss Clark?"

"Thank you. I know it's unexpected, but I think Judy might try to kill herself. She's upset about a lot of things, including her affair with you. I need to tell you something you don't know, but you have to promise you won't use it to hurt her."

"I've been a lousy human being, Miss Clark. I put Judy through a lot of pain. If I can help, I will do whatever it takes."

"She killed Tony Walters."

Gilmore stood still, his expression evolving from disbelief to sorrow. "I can't believe that. Judy killed Walters? No, that's impossible."

"He was blackmailing her, using your affair. He thought there was a child involved—he didn't know about the abortion. He'd threatened to make it all public if she didn't sign documents telling everything about it, and saying the child was yours. She shot him in a fit of rage."

"Jesus."

"She hasn't been able to live with what she did. She needs to get help. She needs lawyers to defend her—if it wasn't self-defense, it was manslaughter, at worst. She needs—"

"I don't need a goddamn thing from either one of you," Judy's voice interrupted. "Tracy Clark, you are an evil, wicked person. Why have you dragged my ex-lover out here for this touching little charade of caring about Judy? I told you, I can take care of myself."

She stood in the tunnel, hard to see—but her gun wasn't. Tracy and Robbie were under the lights—easy targets.

"Judy," Robbie said. "I'm sorry you aren't feeling well. If you'll let me, I can get you into a good place where you can rest and get better. No concern about money—you'll just get the help you need."

"Nice speech, Robbie. Does the gun make you more eloquent? I never had any doubt I was going to get a lot of your money. While we're all here, why don't you tell Tracy why you had her father killed?" Judy tilted the gun up slightly, a small, menacing move.

"I've already told Tracy I had nothing to do with that," Robbie said calmly. "I fired him because he made me angry, I'll admit. But I had nothing to do with his death."

"Isn't that wonderful?" Judy demanded, her voice tight. "Everybody's innocent except me. I suppose that wasn't really you screwing me all those years ago, right Robbie?"

"I'm sorry Judy. I made a horrible mistake. I should have known better. You were so young, and it was all my fault. I should be punished."

Judy pointed the gun at him. "Well, maybe I can take care of that for you."

"Judy what are you doing?" Tommy had come up behind them. "Put the gun down."

"Tommy," Judy breathed, all the starch seeming to go out of her. "Oh, Tommy, what are you doing here? You need to get out of here. I'm bad, Tommy. Please, just—just go away." She cried, still pointing the gun at Gilmore.

"Judy," he called to her, "I realized today how much I love you. Tracy told me everything. At first I was hurt, and I guess I reacted badly. But I took a little break to clear my head—you know how I love my secret naps—and I realized I do truly love you, and I want to help you get better. You mean everything to me. We will work though this together."

"Oh, Tommy." She began to turn to look at him.

"Police! Nobody move!"

Judy blinked, sudden terror in her eyes. Instinctively, she turned toward the shout from behind her, the gun still in her outstretched hand. The police reacted, firing from inside the tunnel. She was thrown back by the bullets, ripping her body apart before their eyes.

"Everyone, hands on your heads, now!" an officer barked.

Tommy wasn't listening. He fell to his knees, wailing, "Oh my god, no! Oh please, god, no!"

Robbie and Tracy raised their hands to their heads, looking stunned.

Judy was dead.

32

GOOD DAYS ARE COMING

Police arrived by the carload—Oklahoma City police, state police, cops everywhere. The Capitol Police who shot Judy were escorted away. A coroner's wagon was joined by a converted bus from the city police, set up as a command center. Judy's body was outlined in chalk, covered with a sheet, picked up and taken away.

Tommy and Tracy spent hours in the tunnel office of Capitol Police. Robbie Gilmore was identified and taken somewhere else that was probably nicer. Tommy said very little, mostly staring into the middle distance, sometimes crying quietly. Tracy sat alone, having no words for him, her own grief crushing her.

They were questioned by three different people, given statements to sign, and let go. With only each other around, they embraced for several minutes, saying little. Neither had the words.

The state police released an initial report, concluding the Capitol Police had acted appropriately under the circumstances.

Tommy spent the next several days doing little other than sleeping. His phone rang often, but he didn't answer. He knew, though, that if he didn't write something soon, he'd be fired.

After a couple of days, he walked to the 7-Eleven on the corner and bought both papers. He read Vince Young's article. Just reading Judy's name in the paper put him back in bed for most of the day, but eventually, because a friend showed up and pushed him to, he managed to call the paper.

"Hello, June."

"Tommy, my god—at last. Are you okay? We've been so worried."

"Yeah. I'm okay. Getting better, anyway. Look, I know I should've called earlier, but I just couldn't. But if you guys could give me just a few more days, I'll start writing my column again—if you want me to."

"Of course we do. Bill said, as soon as I could talk to you, to tell you to take as long as you need. He said he was praying for you and—and Judy." He heard a little catch in her voice.

"Thanks. Tell Mister Anderson thanks, too. Just a couple more days and I'll get a new column to you." He hung up.

"What did I tell you?" Albright sat on Tommy's ratty old sofa, looking not much out of place.

"Yeah, they're good people. Thanks for coming by and pushing me to call." Tommy was still so broken, it hurt Albright to look at him.

"I wish there was something I could say to make it better. But it's going to take time. You've got lots of things to do, though. You're going to be a voice for your generation for a long time. Great things are in your future."

"My god, an optimistic Taylor Albright. What's the world coming to?"

"Still a wise-ass kid, though." Albright smiled.

Tommy started writing again, but never about Judy or what led to her death. He stayed focused on political matters, of which there were many, and tossed in gossipy stuff about Chief Underwood. It didn't take him long to get back into the groove.

He called Tracy to asked if it was okay for him to come by. She agreed.

"I've never felt so bad in my entire life," he confessed. "And I didn't treat you the way I should've. I'm sorry."

She hugged him, like a mom would. "We've both lost someone very dear to us. It is going take a long time to deal with that."

"Tracy," he muttered, hanging on to her, "please don't laugh when I tell you this. I never really had a mother. You're kind of like one to me, I think." He blushed immediately, wondering if she'd be offended. *Augh!* he thought. *That was childish, stupid.* He felt her shoulders convulse, but couldn't tell whether that meant she was sobbing or laughing. He risked a look.

She smiled. "Tommy, if you'd let me be like a mom to you— nothing could make me happier." She ran her fingers through his hair—again, like a mother.

They talked for hours, even a little about Judy. Together they began to get better.

Tommy started working more out of the *Journal* newsroom, partly because someone moved into the vacant office next to the capitol press room and partly because the session was over. He turned the change into an opportunity to get to know Bill Anderson better, and began to feel more like a part of a team.

Today he was headed to McAlester and the state penitentiary. His father was being released. He felt excited, but worried about whether they could adapt to being father and son again. He still felt like a child in many ways, even if he'd been on his own for a while.

The plan was to move Ray into Tommy's awful apartment for a few weeks while he looked for a place of his own. Even the prospect of that brief stint made Tommy nervous.

It was a glorious Oklahoma autumn day—not a cloud in the sky. The anticipation on the drive turned to melancholy and uncertainty when he parked under the gray gloom of the prison. Would his father really be let out?

The minutes felt like hours, but at last his father came walking through the release gate. Tommy had never seen him smile so broadly. He could see in his face that his dad wanted to jump into the air. Tommy got out to embrace him.

"Great to see ya, kid," Ray said. "Thanks for coming to get me."

"You must be pretty happy to get out of there."

"You can't imagine. If I could sing, I would." His father grinned so widely it seemed it might hurt.

Tommy began to notice differences between his dad before prison and the man who now sat in his car. This quiet, thoughtful man was definitely still his father, but changed. He seemed more interested in Tommy than in himself. He'd assured Tommy that during his short stay in the apartment he wouldn't butt into Tommy's life. Prison had changed him in some good ways, it seemed.

"Listen dad, um—there's something I've got to tell you. I've found a new mom." He grinned. "I think you're going to like her."

Ray Jacks regarded his son with a quizzical, intrigued expression. "Well, hmm. That sounds good. It's good to have a mom. Right?"

ABOUT THE AUTHORS

Ted Clifton has written mystery novels which feature the settings of New Mexico and Oklahoma, places where Ted spent considerable time. One of his books, *The Bootlegger's Legacy*, won the IBPA Benjamin Franklin award and the CIPA EVVY award. Today Ted and his wife reside in Denver, Colorado, after many years living in the New Mexico desert.

Once a month, Ted sends his readers a newsletter with a little of everything in it: southwest US culture, be it art, recipes, or local sights; his thoughts on writing and reading; book recommendations; updates on his current writing projects; and from time-to-time a short story.

To sign up, visit TedClifton.com and either wait for the pop-up window, or scroll to the bottom of the page. Everybody who signs up receives a mystery gift, with Ted's compliments. You can also learn more about Ted and his latest books by visiting TedClifton.com or emailing him at ask@tedclifton.com.

Stanley Nelson lives in Oklahoma, and works for what is presently the only book publisher staffed and operated by a Native American tribe. His background includes several years in newspapers as an editor and columnist. He edits and supplies text for several of the publisher's titles, and authored *Toli: Chickasaw Stickball Then and Now*, winner of an IBPA 2017 Gold Medal for Regional Non-Fiction.

BOOKS BY TED CLIFTON

Available from popular booksellers.

MURDER SO STRANGE

Muckraker Mystery #2

In an exclusive residential neighborhood, a U.S. Senator's wife has died. Tommy Jacks and his fellow journalists don't believe the police chief's story blaming it on natural causes. It has the smell of a crime. So begins a new journey set in the 1960s involving numerous dead bodies, high-tension political intrigue, police corruption, the drug underworld and unsavory hidden pasts. Tommy has a lot to write about in his My View political column.

Only in his second year as a political columnist, he finds new romance and emotional healing among a chaotic mixture of characters, from his new mother and his recently out-of-jail father to his acerbic journalistic mentor and antagonist and a foul-mouthed lawyer of questionable ethics, all wrapped inside the saga of two competing daily newspapers still at war.

Lurking in the shadows is the powerful and corrupt police chief, who seems to think it might be best if Mister Jacks, even so young, was dead.

Murder So Strange continues the 1960s saga of Tommy Jacks: Muckraker.

MURDER SO FINAL

Muckraker Mystery #3

Tommy Jacks, reporter, encounters new love and old threats while covering one of the most brutal U.S. Senate races in history. With a massive oil fire threatening the city of Tulsa, three candidates face off: a ruthless oil baron, an idealist college professor, and a reverend running under the God Party. When the race suddenly turns deadly, the winner may be the last man standing.

The final book in the Muckraker trilogy, Murder So Final brings to a close the stories of Louongo, Albright, Robbie Gilmore, Tracy and Ray Jacks, and Tommy himself.

DOG GONE LIES

Pacheco & Chino Mysteries #1

Sheriff Ray Pacheco returns from his introduction in The Bootlegger's Legacy to start a new chapter as a private investigator, along with his partners: Tyee Chino, often-drunk Apache fishing guide, and Big Jack, bait shop owner and philosopher.

The trio are pulled into a mystery immediately when an abandoned show dog appears at Ray's cabin and the dog's owner is reported missing. Ray and his team pursue leads that bring them into confrontations with the local sheriff, the mayor, and the FBI, while in the meantime two bodies are found—neither of which is the missing woman.

SKY HIGH STAKES

Pacheco & Chino Mysteries #2

Tired of spending his days fishing, Ray Pacheco takes on his second assignment with his partner Tyee Chino when the state Attorney General asks them to find out just what the hell is going on in Ruidoso, New Mexico. With the town's sheriff in the hospital with a mysterious illness, acting sheriff Martin Marino is running rough-shod over everyone around him.

What seems like a simple assignment becomes more complicated when Marino is found dead, shot at close range while sitting in his patrol car on Main Street. The suspects include most of the town, from Dick Franklin, manager of Ruidoso Downs racetrack, to bar owner Tito Annoya, to members of the local law enforcement.

At the same time, Ray has an uneasy feeling that the AG is withholding critical details about what exactly is going on in Ruidoso—and why the state was so slow to respond.

It all comes to a surprising conclusion with the involvement of a Spanish princess, a drug lord gone mad, and a few other lowlifes . . . and leaves Ray wondering if maybe fishing wasn't so boring after all.

FOUR CORNERS WAR

Pacheco & Chino Mysteries #3

Rejoin Ray Pacheco and Tyee Chino in their latest adventure unraveling a maze of misdeeds involving wealth, power, political corruption and Navajo warriors.

Farmington, New Mexico, located in the Four Corners area

where four states meet, is about to experience a level of crime and mayhem never seen before. The local sheriff has abandoned his post and taken old military equipment, including a tank, off to Colorado to prepare for the beginning of the end. Left behind is the body of his wife, who was having an affair with the richest man in town.

Money, sex and all known sins come into play in a small-town drama that will take Pacheco and Chino into a conflict that will involve many of the good citizens of Farmington and the nearby Navajo Nation.

SANTA FE MOJO

Vincent Malone Book 1

Vincent Malone was once a hot-shot Dallas attorney, but booze and bad judgement brought that and his marriage to an abrupt end. Battling gout and barely paying the bills as a legal investigator, Malone's unreliability costs him his last client.

Heading south with no idea of what the future may hold, Malone takes a know-nothing job as a shuttle driver for a B&B in Santa Fe, where he meets the clients of a big-time LA sports agent. Gathered to celebrate their success, things go sour quickly when missing millions, sexual entanglements, and personal histories lead to murder.

Malone finds himself in the middle of a major murder case with the lead detective giving him the evil eye. Malone teams up with an aging gun-slinger attorney to find the real killer and clear an innocent man.

BLUE FLOWER RED THORNS

Vincent Malone Book 2

Vincent Malone, hot-shot attorney turned shuttle driver, finds himself in the middle of another murder case.

The international contemporary art scene has come to Santa Fe, New Mexico, and brought plenty of ego, feuds, and sexual entanglements along with it. Vincent's employer, the Blue Door inn, is hosting a big artist for her U.S. debut and nothing is going smoothly. The artist and gallery owner are threatening each other, and before long there is one dead body and plenty of suspects.

Malone dusts off his private investigator skills to solve this tangled mystery with an unusual cast of characters, plenty of false leads, and a surprise ending following many twists and turns.

FICTION NO MORE

Vincent Malone Book 3

A mystery author staying at the Blue Door Inn claims she is being followed. Vincent Malone volunteers to find out what is going on, and things quickly get complicated.

The author's first book is about a murder that took place forty years in the past, but the details are suspiciously specific. The victim's adult son would like to know how the author came by this information. Soon, a bullying sheriff and a wayward priest are involved, along with a priceless—and stolen—collection of Pueblo Indian artifacts.

When the situation turns deadly, Malone must find out

who committed the murder, and why. Past misdeeds long buried will come to light, and fiction will be separated from fact, as Malone pursues the truth.

THE BOOTLEGGER'S LEGACY

Prequel to the Pacheco & Chino mystery series.
When an old-time bootlegger dies and leaves his son Mike a cryptic letter hinting at millions in hidden cash, Mike and his friend Joe embark on a journey that takes them through three states and 50 years of history. What they find goes beyond money and transforms them both.

This is an action-packed adventure story that partially takes place in the early 1950s. It all starts with a key, embossed with the letters CB, and a cryptic reference to Deep Deuce, a neighborhood once filled with hot jazz and gangs of bootleggers. Out of those threads is woven a tapestry of history, romance, drama, and mystery; connecting two generations and two families in the adventure of a lifetime.

Winner of the IBPA Benjamin Frankling Digital Awards (2016 Silver Honoree).

> "The Bootlegger's Legacy takes the reader on a wild ride through Oklahoma's bootlegging history. It makes for a wonderful escape into a fascinating, dangerous, and strange world filled with characters your mother warned you about. Most readers will only ever interact with these types in make believe, but while the ride lasts it's a rollicking good time."
>
> —*Self-Publishing Review, 4 Stars*

"Although the mystery elements in this novel are certainly engaging enough to keep readers turning pages, it's Clifton's superb character development that makes this story a transformative journey of self-discovery. The noteworthy narrative also includes vivid backdrops, brisk pacing, and a meticulously researched, historically accurate account of the Prohibition era in Oklahoma and Texas. A tale with an authentic, immersive setting, inhabited by well-developed, endearing characters."

—*Kirkus Reviews*